My Legacy of Secret Souls

by

Bette A. Pasquarello

My Legacy of Secret Souls

by

Bette A. Pasquarello

RoseDog❧Books
PITTSBURGH, PENNSYLVANIA 15222

ISBN: 978-0-8059-8610-5

Printed in the United States of America

First Printing

For more information or to order additional books, please contact:
RoseDog Books
701 Smithfield Street
Third Floor
Pittsburgh, Pennsylvania 15222
U.S.A.
1-800-834-1803
www.rosedogbookstore.com

Dedication

I would like to dedicate, <u>The Secrets of My Soul</u>, and my sequel, <u>My Legacy of Secret Souls</u>, to my mom and dad, Betty and George, who told me I could do anything I put my mind to. I was blessed with wonderful, loving parents; and

To my brother, and my best friend, Alfie, who always amazed me with his strength. His laughter kept me sane and his unconditional love gave me faith. Alfie taught me a mind will always control a body in any situation.

In memory to my childhood friend, Barbara, who had the purest soul of anyone I ever knew.

Acknowledgments

I have read many books zeroing in especially on what is written about the authors. I envy their education, life achievements, and obvious intelligence. So, came the time for me to write something about myself…wow, that was one of the hardest pieces to put on paper. In my pondering, I realized that no matter what education or degrees you have, no education could ever prepare a person for real life. No matter what, throughout life, never lose sight of who you are; and, sometimes the hardest thing and the right thing are the same.

I had no initials to put after my name, a high school graduate, but I have life experiences to beat the band. My greatest achievements, of which I feel I graduated <u>Summa cum Laude</u>, are my children. Honestly, there should be some initials to follow "Mother" but alas, nothing to date. To me it was the hardest job of my life, raising three wonderful children in today's world—children I feel have compassion, loyalty, kindness, and love in their hearts.

Tracy, my oldest and wise beyond her years, has done a fabulous job raising my two older grandsons. Budd, at seventeen years old, is super intelligent and excels at everything he tries;

and Dominic, at ten years old, is a sweet 'old soul' and a devout sports enthusiast who aspires to be the next pro 'anything' athlete. Tracy does this wonderful feat as she works three jobs, and she always has a joke or a smile for anyone—and God forbid she find an animal wounded on the road. All traffic must come to a standstill as she rescues yet another creature to deposit at an animal hospital. I smile when I just think of her.

Krista, my second daughter, has just given me a beautiful grandson, Nicholas, with beautiful blond curls and bright blue eyes. Krista is my brilliant scholar... however she lacks in the common street sense of Tracy. Together they make a winning team. Krista, extremely strong willed, has always been determined and motivated and has reached every goal so far. Loving and forgiving, she keeps all my many family traditions alive—traditions I thought had long been forgotten.

Bobby, my son, is the youngest. My daughters say he is 'the favorite,' but he has grown into a man who knows the value of a woman, and how to appreciate them. He is kind and polite and realizes that the world revolves much more easily when you treat women as equals. I have seen him mature with life experiences and, luckily, learn from every tiny mistake.

To my family, who have supported me no matter what. To my cousin, Bob, who always believed in me; and to Wally, I miss his sense of humor every day. My brother Al, who was my heart and knew my soul; my sister-in-law, Miriam, for her constant love and support; my niece, Mimi, who is so much like me it is scary; and to all the family I have loved and lost. To Rich, who gave me the gift of his love, adopted me as his sister, and watches over me every day from above.

To my husband, Bob, who taught me how to hang on by the fingernails at times. It was always memorable. I thank God every day for my lessons. Growing up together is nothing compared to growing old together.

In addition, certainly not last, my friends, who have kept me strong and sane. I have been most fortunate in that there have been too many to name—it would require a new book. You all know who you are: Geri, Dee, Marion, Pat, Warren, Anne, Ruthann, Beverly, Elisabeth, Mary, Carol, Dick, Barbara, John, Bea and Fran, to name a few.

I, raised by wonderful and adoring parents, who I miss every day, know how hard life can be, and I thank God every day He has given me the strength to handle whatever comes my way. Think of what you would want in your life...the answers are right there in your dreams.

Chapter One

I sat quietly, surrounded by beautiful lemon and orange trees, and a breeze blew across my face. I closed my eyes. If I could stay this way, maybe my life would find some peace. What was it Vito had just asked me? Was I ready to open this Pandora's box? My mind was swimming. Before Luigi died, he told everyone that everything I wanted to know about my family, my name, my life was in this box. I almost expected a wizard to appear and tap on the damn thing. Maybe if I just clicked my heels together three times I would not be in Sicily anymore. There's no place like home. There's no place like home. Well, that didn't work!

I shivered as a cold chill whipped up around me. I gently handed the box to Vito and said, "No! I do not think I am ready right now. For all I know, this could be the second Pandora's box. What the hell will I unleash?" Mano seemed puzzled, and I had to smile. Vito definitely was the more intelligent of these two.

Vito laughed, "Missy, tell Mano what a Pandora's box is."

I smiled. "Mano, if I remember my Greek mythology correctly, Epimetheus (Greek for hindsight) was responsible for giving a positive trait to all animals; however, when it came to man's turn, there was nothing left. I can certainly believe that! Therefore, Prometheus (Greek meaning foresight), supposedly the more intelligent brother, stole fire and gave it to man. This would make man superior!"

Mano interrupted, "I always knew that, but go ahead."

I smiled at this huge man who now reminded me of a schoolboy listening intently to his teacher. "Anyway, Zeus, getting his horns in a twist, created a woman named Pandora as a poisoned gift for man to seduce 'hindsight'."

Mano interrupted again by laughing, "See, Vito, I told you about women!"

I responded, "Be nice and listen! Pandora had a box...." Just then, Mano snickered. "Mano, excuse me, a second box, which was her dowry and was never to be opened. As long as this box remained closed, life was a paradise. Similar to a virgin, from a man's standpoint, who gets all sour after losing that virginity? But, Mano, did she listen? No! One day she opened the box to release every misfortune of humankind, closing it in time to save only hope. After many tragic times, hope eventually was released. But, if it is indeed still in this unopened box from Luigi, it has a hell of a lot of catching up to do with me!"

Mano questioned Vito, "Did you know this stuff? I must have been out of school that day and with Pandora! Some of those boxes gave me a lot of misfortune, I'll tell you!"

Just then Vito yelled, "We have a lady here, state zitto!"

I said quickly, "Mano, if I open this box, I might grow a nose like Grandmother, inherit a black cape like my spirit friend, and receive a lighted sword like a Jedi to fight freaking evil! It would be my luck that Darth Vader was my father too, and I will have to go to the dark side. Hell, come to think if it, I have been on the dark side all my life."

Vito looked at me and said, "No joking your way out of this!"

I answered quickly, "Who the hell is joking?" I just continued, "Or better yet, Yoda. Maybe that is where Claudio got those pointed ears!"

Vito and Mano laughed and Vito handed the box back, saying, "It is your decision. No one here will force you to do anything right now. After all, Luigi had this for a long time; it can wait a little longer."

In my soul, I knew there was something in the box someone might use against me. This was my one chance to obtain a piece of information about myself that no one else could see and use. Right here and now I was not going to allow that to happen. I joked with Vito, "See! There's a lock on the box. Even Luigi was afraid! Is there a note or key from Luigi for me? Does anyone know?"

Vito answered, "Let me go find Dom or Pietro. Maybe they know something."

As Vito left Mano and I, Isabella came looking for me. "Well, girlfriend, how you holding up? Come with me and let's hide and drink!"

I smiled broadly. "You don't have to ask me twice. Mano, tell Vito I will be back after about ten martinis! Lead the way, my friend!"

I very gently picked up the box and Isabella laughed. "You look like there might be a bomb in there!"

I answered smiling, "I am afraid! If I shake this, maybe a big, mean, green, ugly male genie will appear and ask me to grant him three wishes! I can't be taking chances now!" We left laughing.

Isabella and I walked for twenty minutes to the other end of their mansion and found a quiet room. She had already asked her cook to bring hors d'oeuvres, large Italian olives, and plenty of martinis. It seemed so peaceful in that room with the sun shining through the windows. I hoped neither Dom, nor any of the men, would find us for days.

After Isabella's maid, Caterina, left, Isabella removed her shoes, lounged back on the chaise, and said, "Let's talk! What are you going to do with Luigi's gift? You know me, Elisabetta; I tell it like it is! If I were you, I'd wait until I was in a dark closet with a flashlight and the door bolted." I had to laugh at this remark. Isabella and I were so much alike with both of us having to deal with the big D!

"Isabella, that is my sentiment exactly. I have to open this alone. The idea of a dark closet might just work for me! I'll toast to that." We clicked our glasses. It was time now to get serious, so I asked, "Isabella, have you looked at the box closely? Was there anything else left for me by Luigi? I knew Luigi trusted you and Vito; however, Vito has nothing. So, girlfriend, spit it out!" We had already finished one martini each, and Isabella poured us another. Before she sat down again, Isabella picked up her dress and fumbled around at the waist.

I laughed. "What the hell are you doing?"

Isabella then pulled out a small black pouch, fixed her wrinkled dress, and flopped back on the chaise. "That was too much work! Maybe I'll wear this to bed and tire old D before he can reach anything important!" I laughed at how much Isabella had become just like Gina over the years with the comebacks. The very first time I met Isabella she seemed reserved. Not any more—thanks to my friends and me! Isabella just held the pouch for a moment, "You were right, honey; my Luigi gave me this a few months back. I hid it where no one ever goes! I was to give it to you, alone, after he died. I swear I never looked inside, and not one soul knew I had it. You have to believe me!"

I knew better! "Isabella, of course I believe you. I wish you had looked so I could stop wondering. It has to be for the box. I don't think I want to look right now. Let's just drink a toast to our Luigi, but first I have to hide it. However, for me, no one will see it even if I scotch taped it to my naked butt." I took a pin from my medals inside my bra and pinned the pouch next to my heart. "Tomorrow's another day, Scarlet." We clicked our glasses. "To Luigi, one of the good guys!"

Isabella continued, "I want to thank you for the reality check alongside Dommy's head. He has been a different person since the fiasco. I am proud of you. I know my Dom, and no man would have gotten away with that. It was about time!"

I thought for a second and replied, "It broke my heart what he did to my son. Nevertheless, my gut tells me I should not let down my guard. However, the speech Dommy just gave me in the study brought tears to my eyes. I never knew Dom had a heart!"

Isabella choked slightly on her martini and replied, "If you honestly believe that, you are in desperate need of an enema. I would appreciate you not telling him that!" Isabella pushed the tray of hors d'oeuvres towards me, poured both of us another drink, and asked, "When do you leave for the States?"

I had lost track of time and was not sure of the date. "I think it's the end of the week. I have to look at my ticket. I will be glad to get back. Maria will need me with the baby coming soon. I just pray there are no problems; she has been through enough! I want to have a baby shower for her in a month."

Isabella seemed sad when she replied, "I am envious of you! I always have been. Please don't leave without my gift for the new little one, okay?"

We talked about families, Luigi, and generally just enjoyed each other's company until the knock on the door. I laughed, "I thought you told me we could hide."

Isabella, feeling no pain by this time, yelled, "Go away or I swear I'll shoot!"

There was a short pause, and then we heard Caterina, "Permesso, Mrs. Isabella, everyone is looking for you and Elisabetta. What should I tell them?"

I looked at Isabella, and she knew my answer. "Per favore, Caterina, tell them you did not find us. We will be back to the dining room later. Grazie!" Isabella then poured two more drinks, started swaying, and sang, badly, "What are you doing the rest of your life…."

I smiled. "Keep your day job, Isabella, please! I really don't know. But, as I just told Dominic today, it is my decision, my choice, and I hope he took me seriously. My life is so screwed up after that incident two years ago in Rome. It has left me void of any feelings inside for anyone. Can you understand that?"

Isabella got serious with me and said, "Stick to your guns! Whatever those rules are apparently work for you, so do not change course now. If I can help in any way, you know you can always call. After what we have been through, I hope I am still on your trust list. Now, let us go join the cafonis {uncouth people} before they send out Mano!"

We walked about twenty steps and ran smack into Dominic yelling, "Where the hell you two been? I was worried. You just up and disappear like that?"

Isabella gave him a peck on the cheek and answered, "I got lost!"

Dominic, in his never-sense-of-humor attitude said, "You live here, for Christ sake!"

Isabella put her arm in mine and we walked away as she giggled, "Damn! I have to find another hiding place!"

Chapter Two

As we entered the dining room, it was my turn! Vito yelled, "Missy, don't do that to me again. Mano told me you would be right back. You have to be more careful. You are not in the States now and things run differently here in Sicily. But, from the looks of the two of you, it was fun, right? And, Missy, I couldn't get any more about the box. Dom and Pietro don't know."

I kissed Vito on the cheek and the four of us joined the many people still there for Luigi's memorial.

As Isabella and I approached the food table, a very old man in a motorized wheelchair, with two young large men following closely behind, came up to me. He softly asked if he could speak to me privately. I looked at Vito and he just nodded that it was okay. "Of course. My name is Elisabetta." I put my hand out to shake.

"Io conosco {I know}, my dear. My name is Don Lazzaro," he said in his very broken English as he shakily kissed my hand. As we were moving to a quiet spot of the dining room, I kept thinking to myself, When Jesus raised Lazarus from the dead, he really meant it. Of course, that was the martinis talking, but this man had to be at least one hundred years old.

I waited until he settled, waved the two men away, and I sat on a chair next to him. "E un piacere cococserti {it's a pleasure to meet you}. Don Lazzaro, were you a friend or family of Luigi's?" I asked.

In his old wisdom, he responded, "My dear, both! This is Sicily. But, I know he think you familgia Luigi. Tu sei speciale {you are special}, so many men protect you—Dominic, Vito, Mano, and Luigi. Well, no Luigi now, Dio, Dio." Don Lazzaro blessed himself and I almost wanted to help him get his hand up to his forehead. God, maybe he was older than one hundred years. It is hard to tell age in Italy.

"What can I do for you, sir?" I asked sweetly.

Don Lazzaro cleared his throat and said, "My son, Vittore! Two years ago, I lose him. He second son lose to this life and world."

I tried not to act scared, but the sweat was running down my back. "I am so sorry for your losses, Don Lazzaro; I just cannot imagine losing my children." I was trying to be cool but could feel my face turn beet red. What did this man know or suspect? Vito seemed to think it was okay to talk with him. I looked around the room to find someone, anyone, to rescue me from this conversation. I finally saw Pietro, Vito, Mano, and Dominic watching me from the veranda doors.

Don continued, "Luigi a friend, a brother; but Vittore, too avido {greedy}, wanted tutto adesso {everything now}. He never wait." He sat for a moment in silence and then took my hand. I promise Luigi speak you if he die." I was in shock. I had no idea if this man knew anything about Vittore or who would have killed him. I remained silent for Don to continue. "Luigi say you sure to know who you now, inside", he pointed to my heart, "before open box. No can of worms change. Luigi love you. Say for me say you 'no pass to anyone.' Non lo so perche {I do not know why}. What you find only for you, no you children. Time now no stronzate {bullshit}! Enough!"

I sat silently for a second and said, "Thank you so much, Don Lazzaro, for your time and message. I just wished I could have been here before Luigi died. I appreciate your time."

I got up slowly and kissed him on both cheeks. Don Lazzaro pulled me closer and whispered, "I am old man, listen. Get out! No place for beautiful like you. Man today no understand honor."

I whispered back, "I promise." As the two men approached the Don, I walked toward the bar for another martini.

Isabella met me halfway to the bar and locked arms with me. "You hold me up, please!"

I had to ask, "Isabella, why didn't any of the men save me from that! I was petrified when he told me he was Vittore's father!"

Isabella whispered, "They know better than interrupt Don Lazzaro. He is the Boss around here, even if he is older than dirt. Luigi was his second in command, even after Rome. Their friendship never wavered because of Vittore. Vittore was half a wise guy on his best day. Don is a good man. Whatever he said to you, remember and listen, okay?"

I had to ask. "Who were the two men with him? Bodyguards?"

Isabella glanced back and said, "Yes. The bigger one is Joey Thumbs. I understand he can break a man's Adams apple with one thumb. The other is Frankie Tomatoes…maybe he just likes to eat tomatoes, I don't know," Isabella snickered.

We reached the bar the same time as the men. Of course, Dommy was the first to speak, "You okay? You have any trouble with the Don? Is there something you need to talk to us about?"

I just nonchalantly said, "Don Lazzaro asked me for a date!"

We all talked and reminisced about Luigi. I had to leave for my casa tomorrow to pack for my flight home to the States. Dominic decided that Vito would accompany me and Lorenzo would take me to the airport. No one asked about the box!

That night, alone on my bed, I laid the box between my legs

and held the small pouch to my heart. My mind was reliving the last few days in Sicily and all the days I had remembered with Luigi. I wished I could go back to that horrible meeting in Rome. Maybe I would have done something differently. A real no-no in my book of rules, I was second-guessing myself. It took a lot of willpower not to open the box, but I knew, whatever it was, I definitely was not ready.

Just then, there was a soft tapping on my bedroom door. I put on my robe and asked, "Chi e" {who is it}?

Isabella replied, "Your drinking pal, and I come bearing olives!"

I opened the door quickly and pulled her inside. "You are a nut case, you know that, right?" I laughed.

Isabella lay the tray of glasses, a shaker of mixed martinis, and olives on my dresser. "Elisabetta, I am just going to miss you so much when you leave. All I will have is the big D and he is not much fun! Besides, it gives you and me more quiet time together!" I hugged Isabella as she poured our drinks.

When we settled on the bed, Isabella said, "Everything seems peaceful right now, honey, but don't you get a sense of security. I think you and I should come up with a plan to have old Don Lazzaro stuffed. When he finally does go to that big tomato garden in the sky, there is going to be hell to pay around here. Then we both might need a place to hide! Seriously! You got a glimpse of what is coming up, those goons with the Don today. That type of mentality, stupid, you know?"

This surprised me; I felt whatever happened in Sicily would have nothing to do with me. "Isabella, tell me why should we be afraid; I don't even live here!"

Isabella whispered, "Honey, I am married into this mess. You work in this mess! There is a big difference. I can get out of it when Dom dies or I kill him, whatever comes first. You, on the other hand, can't, and it frightens me!"

I responded, "You! It seems like every time there is a meeting someone dies of natural or unnatural causes any more. It frightens me to death!"

The only other thing Isabella told me that stuck in my mind before she left was, "Save your loved ones. Don't do work here in Sicily with these new cafonis! It isn't the same as the old days. If you get your loved ones out now, there would be no reason to use any of them against you! If you have to get away from your family to do it, then do it! The less they know, the better and safer they are, okay? It would be better to break all ties than have your heart broken over losing any one of them. You understand?"

It was the Bible story I remembered hearing as a child, how a mother gave up her baby to another rather than have him cut in half! I knew exactly what Isabella meant. "Isabella," I responded, "I wonder if I have enough guts to change this way of life. If I did, how could I accomplish that without retaliation from both my families? Believe me; I have no romantic ideas about the family!"

Isabella said, "Just walk away. Anything to save your family."

I wanted to take these words back as soon as I said them. "Isabella, you don't have children and grandchildren. How can you really understand?" I never meant to cut her so deeply. It never was my intension. I always knew Isabella missed having children in her life. I had to apologize as I hugged her. "Honey, I am so sorry. I did not mean to hurt you! It is just going to be hard to walk away from the family I always dreamed of from a young girl. The children I always prayed for and, now, my beautiful grandchildren.

Chapter Three

The next morning we all met for *colazione* {breakfast}. This is where everyone was happy, always! When they were eating, everything was right with the world. I looked around the table and remembered how many men had died. I wished Guido were still around. Then I thought, *How the hell did I get here? My life has flown by me. I was always so busy I had no time to enjoy my life fully. I was anxious to get back home to some normalcy, if that is what you called **that** life there too!*

My thoughts were interrupted by Vito. "You okay, Missy? You are deep in thought. Everything is going to be fine, you'll see."

I leaned in and whispered, "It will be fine if you promise never to die!"

Just then, Pietro came up behind my chair and asked to talk to me. "Vito, let me borrow Elisabetta here for a few moments. I promise I won't keep her long." Vito and Dommy both seemed annoyed.

I smiled at Pietro, "I was wondering when we would be able to talk. It has been crazy around here since I arrived."

Pietro and I walked outside to the veranda, and he started, "Everything straightened out with you and Dominic, I hope." Pietro shook his head and took a deep sigh, "Dominic can be pazzo {crazy} a lot of the times. Are we still following the rules there, Elisabetta? I hope you are, honey. The one thing I wanted to be sure of is you and I, along with Vito, of course, am working together and not through Dominic. Am I correct?"

I answered quickly, "Yes. Pietro, I think it best since the wounds are still fresh from the problems with Dommy. It is best for right now. If anything changes, I will definitely speak to you about it, okay? However, there seems to be problems brewing here in Sicily. I might want to reconsider. You understand?"

Pietro surely did and replied as he hugged my shoulders, "Smart girl. I am proud of you. I know you can handle yourself now. But I never really had any doubts these past few years. Everything will be fine, and you can do whatever you want. I am more reasonable than Dominic!"

I thought to myself, as we walked back inside, *But maybe not as protective. We will see!*

The goodbyes, especially to Isabella, were tough. However, the ride back to my casa was happy with Vito and Lorenzo. We stopped along the way to take in the breathtaking scenery. It felt as if Vito did not want to say goodbye. At one stop we were sitting having coffee when Vito spoke up, "Missy, your remark this morning at colazione made me do a lot of thinking. Guido and Dom might have been the ones in that meeting with you, Moe, and Pops many years ago, but I would never allow anything to happen to you. Just like your promises to your mother, I also take them seriously. I promised Guido. Even though there is a sense of honor with the familgia, I am very worried about the future. I am old now, and what happens when I am no longer around to watch over you? I have no idea 'bout the information in that damn box, nor do I care. You are important to me. Just know that if you need help in anything, any decisions, whatever, I will be there for you. Okay? I am thinking I might just return to the States and stay closer to you. I feel it's possible you will need me!"

From the driver's seat came another voice. "Missy," said Lorenzo, "listen to Vito. Please, honey, things are going to get a little nasty. The punk wise guys today have no friends. Everyone is an acquaintance."

Vito immediately spoke up, "Lorenzo, let's not put the jackass before the cart here and scare Missy to death. Just keep your belt on, please!" I laughed thinking about the episode with Lorenzo and the dogs.

I was silent for a few seconds and said, "Vito, am I in trouble? Does this have to do with Don Lazzaro when he dies?"

Vito grabbed my hand and replied, "Honey, there are only a few of the old 'trusted and honorable' men left. Yes, it could be a problem." I remembered my little secret conversation with the Don to 'get out of it;' however, I said nothing to Vito about that. I had to admit I was thrilled that Vito would be spending more time in the States.

Chapter Four

Before I knew it, the day came for the trip back home. My one regret, I did not have another chance to see Sergio. And, as I expected, the softy Vito came along for the ride with Lorenzo. Those goodbyes at the airport were as emotional as with Isabella. Vito promised to be back in the States within the month. "Until then, Missy," Vito said, "no work! That is an order. Just rest and enjoy the family. You have a new bambino arriving and this *familgia* in Italy will just have to step aside for a while. *Capisci* {Understood}?" I more than agreed. I boarded my flight carrying my box from Luigi with the black pouch still attached inside my bra!

My flight was smooth. I thanked God again. I spent the time making plans for Maria's baby shower. In talking with Maria these past weeks, I was happy to know that Penny was getting many things together already. Penny had always loved my children. She was Maria's babysitter and my friend always, and she thought of Maria like a daughter. It certainly would make it easier for me. I had a lot to deal with when I returned with Roberto. He was becoming more miserable as time went on, and I knew it was my fault. I had hoped the birth of our new grandchild would bring him back to reality.

With Roberto, everything had a price tag attached. He put such importance on things that did not matter and ignored what did in life! I had many decisions to make, and Vito's advice to forget about the other life sounded wonderful to me.

I was only in town about two days when Sergio called. He was upset I had left Italy without seeing him. I reminded him again that the big D did not allow it. I told Sergio, "Just keep your work going and make money over there. Take care of your family!" Sergio was not happy with that and said he would talk to Mr. Dominic and quit. I assured Sergio it was not that easy to do. Sergio would now have to deal with Pietro. After that, when I saw it was Sergio calling, I would not answer.

In April Penny and I, with help from Sheri, Gypsie, and Gina, had the shower. Maria received everything she needed for the baby. She and Davido bought a new house and moved in just a week before the arrival of my new grandson, Niccolo Davido, in June. Another bright spot in this life of mine, and I thanked God for giving me such blessings as these beautiful children and grandchildren. They gave me a sense of normalcy.

Lizzie married the father of Anastashia, a good family man named Dale, and I could not have been happier for her. My brother Claudio was smiling, I was sure.

The baptism of Niccolo Davido in late summer made my heart so full with happiness. I watched Claudio and Sheri stand as godparents for Maria's new baby and I cried. My three children and grandsons were the reason I got up some mornings.

I had little time to spend with Sir Dad, but as usual, his face lit up when I entered his home. At ninety-six years old, he looked better than I felt inside at that moment. God bless him, he was still the same, and no one could get him out of the house he loved so much. The people I hired for his meals and nursing were doing a wonderful job. As I hugged him, Sir Dad just cried. "Wish the hell I could go with you next time. It is so lonely when you are not here."

That was another rotten thing about this 'life' of mine; I

could not be with him in these last years of life. Sir Dad was a good man, a good father to me all these years, and both of us missed Momma terribly. "Just stay well for me, please," I pleaded. I did not tell him I would have to leave again in September. "Dad," I asked, "I need to tell you about something that was left to me by an old friend of my dad's. Is it okay?"

Dad answered, "Why wouldn't it be? You can tell me anything."

I sat down and explained about the box and that I had not opened it.

"Does it really matter what is inside, honey?" queried Sir Dad. "It will not change who you are. I knew your parents and they would be very proud of you. Everything else is just horseshit. Life is all about what you have inside you, not what name you go by. It's the soul that matters, the heart."

I said, "Dad, that's the problem. My soul is twisted out of shape as it is. I don't know if I want to know anything more!"

Dad simply said, "There is a solution, I think. Don't open the damn thing! Who cares what it holds? It is just a box! Everyone knows who and what you are: a wonderful, caring, and loving person." I thanked Sir Dad and left.

What was that Pops always said about being ready for the other shoe to fall? Sir Dad was the only person, except for Gina, I had told about the box. Ironic, I thought, after all these years, I should confide to the father of Ron. Why Ron ever popped into my head amazed me, but I guessed because Ron's parents took my side after our divorce. My constant thoughts of divorcing Roberto had to be the reason. Who knows? My head hurt! I knew I had a lot of work to do before the trip to Italy for the annual September meeting. This time I would have liked to stay here with the new bello nipote, Nicky. I also knew I had to make a decision about Roberto. He would be one of the people I needed to save, as Isabella put it, from the cafonis!

Chapter Five

There was one thing I wanted to do before getting back into the 'job.' Cassie had finally graduated from college, at her age. I told her and Melissa we would take a trip to the casino and have fun before I left again. That was my gift to Cassie, and I was looking forward to it. I had not been away with them for quite a while and I always had a great time. We had jokingly called our trips, 'A.A.A.' because they were 'Always An Adventure.' More crap happened to us during our trips; we just had to laugh about them. But, to me they were more than just trips. They were 'normal' and not connected to my other life.

Dominic had arranged a room for us along with a free pass to the casino's high rollers lounge. Of course, that was the first thing we hit after checking in. What a great time we had for almost three hours; that is, until I saw Dominic, through the mirror behind the bar, as he entered. He took one look at us at the bar and left immediately. I thought, What is he doing here. Dom knew I would be here, for God's sake. He has to be up to something. I was sure. I never mentioned anything to my friends.

We stayed at least another two hours, meeting a couple from

Canada, and I could not remember ever laughing as much as I did that night. We helped Melissa to the room that night, or maybe it was the other way around. I was tipsy too, leaving Cassie as the only sane one that night.

When we retired, I knew I had overdone it. Seeing Dominic there did not help either! My irritable bowel was kicking ass, literally. The next morning I tried to call Vito. He had moved back to his place in the States, as he promised, around the end of May. Unfortunately, I received no answer. Vito would know why Dominic was here, I hoped!

Melissa, Cassie, and I left for breakfast. We relaxed for at least two hours and decided to pack up and check out. We were going to hit the boardwalk. As we were leaving, Melissa's drinking caught up with her from the night before and she had to use the casino bathroom. Cassie and I went upstairs. Knowing how my irritable bowel had always been, I needed to be alone and not somewhere where the smoke alarms would draw a crowd.

When we reached the room, however, our keys would not work. My bowel was screaming at this point. Cassie ran for the house cleaners, who told her to go downstairs. I was so upset I entered the room where the house cleaner was to plead to her humanity and allow me to use the bathroom in our room. I knew she had the passkey. She started screaming at me, "Get out of here. This room has been sanitized!" I looked around to see if I had dirt, dust, or other mess coming off my body, but arguing with her was futile. Now I could not move an inch, and Cassie ran downstairs to the desk.

As I tried to wait, the pains were getting worse. On top of everything else, I had on white pants. Well, if your memory were as old as mine, you would remember the way Groucho Marx used to walk hunched over, holding his cigar. Well, that was me making it to the elevator to the casino floor. I walked that way to the bathroom and hoped Melissa was still there. I was now sick to my stomach and had my ass cheeks clenched so tight a fart could not escape.

I entered the stall and proceeded to unzip my pants only to

have it not move! One of those damn plastic zippers that only work when they are off your body! You know the kind! No matter what I did, it would not budge. I had no choice as my irritable bowel problems started to seep through the tightly clasped cheeks. I ripped the pants, only slightly to break the zipper, or so I thought. I tore the pants all the way down to the embroidery along the bottom. I was sure the helper in the bathroom would be calling the SWAT team for the odor and noise. A problem for later, I thought.

After twenty minutes, I felt safe enough to stand up. Now the problem was, how could I get out of that bathroom, without underwear, in white pants ripped all the way down one leg? I called, "Melissa, are you in here?" No answer. I had to think! What the hell was I going to do? My pants would button at the waist, but my whole leg was showing. I had no underwear because I had thrown them in the trashcan. I remembered the ever faithful, always worn, medals in my bra. I had two pins. I pinned one halfway up the leg, the other halfway on the zipper, and pulled my shirt as low as I could. I carried my handbag on that side of me and left the bathroom. I caught myself hiding behind machines, generally trying to walk sideways, so no one would see through the white pants to my bare ass.

I made it down the escalator to where Cassie was standing at the counter. I came alongside her and she knew something had to be wrong. The woman behind the counter told us we needed a credit card. I did not have one and was embarrassed. The woman started to give us a hard time. Somewhere along the line, Dom's comp room did not show up on the computer. Cassie started to argue because the woman was becoming belligerent. Eventually Cassie gave the woman a card, telling her exactly where to swipe it! The woman left to talk to someone in the back.

Cassie then looked at me and asked, "What's the matter?"

I nonchalantly said, "My pants are ripped off my body, I shit myself, and I have no underwear on, just to name a few things wrong. If I take this handbag from my side, people will be blinded instantly." The bitch laughed so hard, if I'd had a free hand, I would have choked her. It was funny though. I just hoped I didn't run into Dominic.

The woman returned after more than fifteen minutes and apologized profusely. I just wanted to get to the room, and quickly. God knows where Melissa was or how she was doing. She had to be better than I was at that moment. However, Melissa was waiting outside our room for us. I changed into the pants I had on the night before and everything was right again with the world on our normal A.A.A. (always an adventure) trips.

As we were walking the boardwalk and laughing over the escapades, my cell phone rang. "Missy," said Vito. "Sorry, honey, it took me a while to get back to you. Is everything okay? What's the problem?"

I was happy to hear his voice and excused myself to talk. "Vito, I am fine. Thanks for calling me back. I am at the casino and saw Dominic, of all people. Why the hell is he here? Do you know?"

Vito hesitated too long before answering, "No." I did not like that hesitation. Vito then responded, "Maybe Dom is worried about the September meeting or your work?"

I was annoyed and answered quickly, "Have I ever not finished my work to the end?"

Vito seemed concerned. "Missy, I'll check it out. Just enjoy yourself. The meeting comes fast enough. Let me know your travel dates. I am probably going to be on the same flight." I was very happy to hear that.

"Vito," I asked, "can I ask you a simple question?"

Vito seemed surprised, "Of course, Missy. What?"

I had to ask. "Is this meeting going to be okay? No one will die again, will they?"

Vito laughed. "Don't tell me that spirit friend is visiting you again."

I joked, "I left him at the craps table. Amazing how he can make people take their chips and run! Call me later, okay?"

Even though I was only away a weekend, I missed the baby. I was glad to return from the casino trip. I never found out why Dominic was there, but somehow Vito would get back to me, I was sure.

Chapter Six

Before leaving for Italy, I finished last minute paperwork and could spend more time with the baby. I loved it! There was so much going on in my head about Roberto. The children were feeling it as well. He was constantly worrying about money. I told him I would have an extra big box and send it all with him. So what if we left the children the house with a loan on it? It would not make any difference to us after the fact. Why Roberto could not enjoy his hard work and money now was a puzzle to me.

It was a very hard decision, but I was determined to keep all my family safe even if it meant being alone. I would talk to Vito about protection for them. Not knowing what would happen down the line frightened me, not for myself but for my family. As far as I knew, only one person had been raised from the dead, and Roberto certainly was not that holy!

I tried repeatedly to get Roberto to understand. I wanted him healthy, happy, and safe. This brought me to the decision I had been chasing of resubmitting the support papers. I originally had been upset, knowing Dominic would have something to do with ending it another way! He did not like loose ends and absolutely forbade the divorce, since Roberto 'knew too much.' However, Dominic would behave now since I was working with Pietro. After Dom's speech at Luigi's funeral, I felt this was the perfect time to act before I got into this deeper in Sicily. I had to admit to myself that I did love Roberto and this was for his own good.

It had been over five months since Luigi died. So, a few days before my departure, I filed for support from Roberto. I never realized it had been two years since the divorce papers. I would not find out until later, in Italy, that the Courts contacted Roberto and gave him twenty days to respond or the divorce would become final. I honestly thought the paperwork was for support; however, the two years were up and the divorce would be final automatically if not contested.

I went to see Sir Dad. I told him of the upcoming trip and what was going on in my life. I needed some of his wisdom. After telling Dad everything, he responded, "Honey, you have always been a wonderful daughter to Momma and me, but you always want to fix something or someone. You never let the kids find an answer or find their own way. You always tell me you were born to be a caretaker. I think you lost your family so young and wanted a family so badly, you felt responsible for everyone. It was as if you paid people to be around you. That is how you got into financial problems."

Dad continued. "Now, you know I always liked Roberto. He has been my son-in-law a long time. But Momma would tell you if she were here, I was never a good husband. I don't know what all happened between you two just as no one knows behind any closed doors. The one thing I am sure of is you only deserve the best and you should not settle. Change sometimes is not good! On the other hand, it is time to move on if Roberto does not treat you like an equal partner or does not listen to your needs or wants. Then change can be good."

Dad took a deep breath and said, "Whatever happens, you are my daughter and know you have always been loved as such."

Dad leaned down to where I was sitting at his feet and kissed me on the forehead.

I felt tears fill my eyes. "Dad, please stay well until I get back. I will start paying for these sessions to figure out my brain, okay?"

Dad just patted the top of my head and said, "Hurry back. You be safe!"

Chapter Seven

After the meeting with the lawyer, the days flew by and my trip was upon me before I knew what hit me. I had never opened the box or the black pouch. I questioned if I should before the trip. I was damned if I did and damned if I didn't. So I kept busy! However, about two days before my trip, I became even more persuaded.

I received a call from Angelica in Italy saying, "I received the strangest call from Bruno the other day. He asked if I knew if you and Roberto were still married. I told him it was not my business and certainly not his. He should ask you himself when you arrive. Was that okay?"

I knew instantly that it had to be information for Dominic! Now what the hell was Dominic up to? Maybe he thought I had not seen him at the casino. I hoped Vito had information for me on our trip. I was in for a bumpy ride all the way this time. Where the hell was my spirit friend? Did he finally go to the light with Luigi? That was the last time I saw him, almost six months ago.

Gypsie was good enough to take me to the airport because I did not tell her I was meeting Vito. I had hoped she and Vito would talk a little before I had to go to the gate. Unfortunately, it did not work out that way. Gypsie had to leave me at the curb, the new rules of security for the airport. I was disappointed for Vito and Gypsie but thrilled over the fact I would feel safer on the plane. Little did I know at that time!

Gypsie pleaded, "Please be safe and careful. I do not want to worry like a few years ago. How long have you been doing this crap for," she whispered, "you know?"

I tried to make light of the separation by looking at my watch and saying, "Let's see, what time is it now? Since about half-past eighteen years old. Watch over Gracie for me, please. And keep Gina out of trouble if that is at all possible. I'll be back before you know. Love you." I then went inside to find Vito.

I was surprised there were so few people. However, I could not find Vito. I waited about ten minutes and then decided to check in and get to the gate. I always hated to rush and preferred to be at the gate hours before. I felt relaxed then when boarding.

I stopped at a stand to buy a magazine and a bottle of water. As I was paying, a nice-looking man accidentally hit the back of my knees with his computer bag, almost knocking my legs out from under me. He apologized as he grabbed my arm to keep me from falling. "I'm so sorry," he pleaded. "I am always in a hurry. Someday I am going to hurt someone badly, or myself. You okay?"

I never liked talking to strange men at the airport, so I just nodded, "I'm fine. It's okay, honest," and walked back to the gate area. I looked around for Vito, still not seeing him. I was beginning to worry. Vito had said he would be on this flight.

I sat for almost forty-five minutes when I saw the jitney pull up with Vito. I do not know why I did not go over to him—intuition maybe. However, when he departed the jitney, Vito walked behind the telephones. I could not see him from the seating area. I looked down at my magazine for a few minutes and looked around nonchalantly. As Vito caught my eye, he frowned and shook his head 'no' as if there was a big problem. I have been around these men too long not to know there was trouble and I had better keep my distance from Vito. I thought, Damn, what now!

Just then the man who literally ran into me at the magazine stand approached me, asking, "How's the knees? I want to apologize again."

I merely looked up and said, "I said it was okay, honest. There is no problem," and went back to looking at the magazine, hoping he would go away. No such luck; he took the seat next to me.

"My name is Mike, and yours?" he asked as he put his hand out for me to shake.

I did not extend my hand but said, "Elisabetta." I replied as I turned my back slightly to him. Maybe he would get the hint I did not want to talk.

He was a pushy bastard, "We got off on the wrong foot, or leg, as it were. Don't you just hate these long flights?"

I sighed to show I was annoyed and answered, "Not really!" We sat there in silence until boarding. As I have 'preferred status' with the airline, I board earlier. I was happy to get away from 'Mike.' I still ignored Vito. In fact, I never looked in his direction again.

Chapter Eight

On board, I stored my computer overhead and proceeded to settle in for the long ride. An elderly woman came to sit beside me and I was happy it was not a man. She asked if I would give her a hand with her overhead luggage. I was glad to accommodate her and then excused myself to go to the bathroom before the plane filled up completely.

It was only a matter of five minutes before I returned to my seat. The elderly woman was gone and I figured she was also in the restroom. I was busy setting up my other carryon beneath the seat in front of me, taking out my eyeglasses, tissues, hand wipes, earphones, socks, and things I use while traveling.

When I settled back with my blanket and pillow on my lap, I was shocked to see Mike arranging his overhead luggage. "You must be in the wrong seat, Mike. There is a woman sitting there," I said.

"You are not going to believe this! I was on a standby ticket and they must have bumped her to envoy class. Must be fate or something," he smiled. I thought. Fate my ass.

As Mike settled next to me, my mind was racing through all

kinds of scenarios. Why this seat next to me; and is that why Vito was ignoring me? Where the hell was Vito in this huge plane? Was this man with the familgia or against it? Crap, literally, I had to excuse myself again for the bathroom. At the same time, I remembered exactly how I positioned my bag under the seat.

As Mike got up to allow me to leave, I made note of his height, weight, coloring, and the fact that he had not taken off his jacket. Strange, that is usually the first thing people do before sitting.

As I walked back to the restroom, I was glad it took quite a while as people were still settling into their seats. I looked around for Vito, finally seeing him about five rows behind me. Vito always had to buy two seats if not going first class because of his size. Well, I wanted to be sitting alone but not have an ass as big as Vito's!

Trying not to be obvious, I whispered to Vito, "What is going on? Do you know this guy?" Vito leaned over and handed me a folded note, which I immediately put into my pocket. I turned to see that Mike was not looking back and felt relief.

I finally made it to the bathroom as the pilot was asking everyone to return to their seats for take-off. I looked sympathetically at the flight attendant who said, "Okay, hurry. It will be another five minutes or so before we taxi."

I locked the door and opened the note quickly. It said, "Missy, be careful. Watch your words. Know him through contacts. He is FBI. You don't know me in Rome. Just go with Lorenzo." Okay! I now had less than five minutes to handle the bowel problem that suddenly erupted! I flushed the note down the toilet, washed my hands, ran cold water on my wrists, and left to be seated. As I passed Vito, I just tapped on the back of his seat.

Mike looked back as I approached my seat and stood up. Ironically, I thought to myself, Well, FBI could be 'Firmly Built Individual'. I smiled and buckled up for this yet-another-test from someone. Haven't I been through enough tests already?

Mike started, "I'd like to only know two things, if you don't mind."

I was very skeptical and thought. Not already. This is an eight hour flight; but I replied, "Sure, what?"

Mike smiled, "First, do you get airsick; and, second, do you mind if I remove my shoes?"

I breathed a sigh of relief and said, "No to both. But thanks for asking."

As soon as we took off, I proceeded to unwrap the earphones so I might not have to talk. However, my luck, the flight attendant announced that there was a slight problem with the video system and it would reboot in a short time. I mumbled, "Great," quietly. Stupid! Stupid! It gave Mike a chance to talk again.

"It's amazing how packed this flight is considering the problems in the world. I thought for sure a stand-by flight would be easy. I was lucky they bump people to envoy. You go to Italy often? Have family there?" he asked.

I answered, "Not often, but I have family and friends there. I am trying to be a writer. I just sent my first book to a publisher and plan to start the second while in Italy."

Mike continued, "I noticed you are married. Are you going to meet him?"

Now I was annoyed. "You seem to be very curious for someone who tried to knock me down at the terminal," I joked. "My husband's work prevents him from taking many vacations. This is more like a working one for me to start the second book!"

Mike said, "I can relate to the job taking over your life, my job certainly does. I work for the government and travel a lot!"

I could feel my whole body tense up. I was desperately trying to relax so not every emotion showed on my face. My dad's words, strangely enough, came to my mind, 'Honey, you can do anything.'

I said, "Mike, that sounds interesting." Just then the movie screen in front started and I quietly thanked God.

Fortunately the next few hours were quiet between Mike and me as I continued to watch a movie. He seemed to be busy using his computer. I tempted to see what exactly he was checking and hoped not to see any familiar names or faces. When the flight attendants brought our dinners, I hoped Mike would just eat and leave me alone. However, no such luck!

"Well, Elisabetta, I don't believe I ever really met an author before. I wish you much luck with your book. Is it fiction, auto-biography, text, what kind?" Mike asked.

"It actually is a fictional novel. I always loved to write and thought, what the hell; I am retired, so why not keep the mind busy? And, as for you, Mike, for what part of the government do you work?"

Mike leaned in a little closer as if it was a big secret and answered, "I work for the FBI."

I nonchalantly answered, "That's great. I worked with a woman at a university and both her husband and she got jobs with the CIA. I was very happy for them. I believe they live somewhere in Virginia."

If Mike thought he was going to impress me, he was mistaken. I was brazen enough to ask, "Mike, is this business or pleasure for you; or, am I not allowed to ask?"

Mike answered quickly, "It's mostly for business, but I am sure looking forward to seeing a little of Italy."

I thought a second and asked, "Are you staying in Rome? It's a shame to come this far and not see some of the sights."

Mike was freely responding, but I felt he was trying to hide something from me. "Yes, unfortunately, my business only will take me to Rome and back in a few days. It's a shame, huh?" he asked.

I tried to laugh and said, "Get back at them and make the FBI pay you in Euro. That would fix them! I think I am going to get some sleep, Mike. The flight does go by pretty quickly that way." I pulled up the blanket and pretended to sleep. I could never sleep on these trips, but I would rather pretend than talk any more to Mike.

I lay there with my eyes closed, thinking, Is this my luck or what! A plane this big and an FBI agent had miraculously gotten a stand-by seat next to me. I don't think so! This could not be a coincidence. Luckily, Lorenzo was a bona fide limo driver and maybe this Mike would just lose me in the crowd at customs. One could only hope. Then I wondered who would be picking Mike up at the airport. What would Mike do this time in the terminal, tackle me to the ground?

My guard was so up I could feel the hairs on my neck standing. What was I saying about luck? The lights went on and it was time to eat again. Give Mike a chance to pump me some more?

Mike, however, surprised me when he stretched, "Hey, it is nice waking up next to you. You sleep very quietly."

I had to smile. "Mike, do I have an FBI agent flirting with me? Isn't there some kind of rule against that?"

His answer was unexpected, "I never follow the rules. I am sort of a renegade FBI agent."

Mike did not have a clue I was raised solely with rules. I innocently answered, "Well, that's scary in today's world!" After we ate, Mike went back to his computer and I looked into that magazine for the twentieth time.

Chapter Nine

I was relieved when we arrived in Rome. That was the most intense ride I had ever taken. The flight itself was smooth, but sitting beside Mike was intense. I hoped it would be the last time I had to see him. "Mike," I extended my hand, "it was great talking to you, and good luck with your work. I hope you have time for some of the sights."

Mike shook my hand and said, "It certainly was my pleasure, and good luck with the books, both of them. Hopefully our paths will cross again, who knows."

I thought to myself, Just so it isn't in some kind of line-up. I quickly gathered my computer and carryon and walked away.

Because of his size, I knew Vito always waited until everyone was off. I just hoped Lorenzo was on time. It amazed me, though, how cool I was with that whole situation. Was my identity as a person becoming what I do and not who I am? I did not like myself as that type of person. Crap, Elisabetta, I thought, don't start trying to self-analyze yourself. I don't live in black and white and it would be scary!

Somewhere along the way, I did lose Mike. I went through

customs without a problem. At the baggage claim, Mike was nowhere in sight. I struggled with my huge suitcases and proceeded to look for Lorenzo. Good, my luck was changing. Lorenzo was exactly where he always was. He smiled widely when he saw me but acted professional as always, as if he was nothing more than a limo driver. As I started to walk away with him, I said quietly, "We are to go ahead without Vito. I'll talk to you in the car."

As usual, getting to the car at the Rome airport was a nightmare. Fortunately Lorenzo was not that far away. He loaded my suitcases, slid into the driver's seat, and finally spoke. "Elisabetta, what is going on? Did they stop Vito at customs? Was he on the flight?"

I told Lorenzo, "You are not going to believe this crap. There was an FBI agent sitting next to me. Some problem or another had to be going on. Vito warned me to go with you alone. I have no idea where Vito is now. Maybe he will call your cell phone."

Lorenzo's response, "Valfanculo! FBI! Oh, Elisabetta, scusa! Why? What is the FBI doing in Italia? What did this FBI say to you? You okay? You think he was following you or Vito?"

Now, I was scared. I never gave it a thought that he would actually be following me and not Vito!

"Lorenzo, let's just wait to hear from Vito. Maybe you could wait at my casa in case Vito needs you to take him to Sicily," I said.

When we reached my house, Lorenzo needed to stretch and relax anyway and was happy to wait around for Vito. We did not have to wait long when Lorenzo's cell phone rang. Lorenzo quickly answered, "Pronto! V, Dove sei stato fino adesso {where have you been till now}?" Then all I heard from Lorenzo was grunts and "Si, si, si."

When he hung up, Lorenzo was not happy. "Elisabetta, everything is okay with Vito, but I have to go to airport near here and pick him up in an hour. Okay if I just wash a little before I go?"

Lorenzo was not getting off that easy with me. "Of course, but you cannot let me hang like this, Lorenzo. Tell me about the FBI Mike."

Lorenzo seemed a little nervous and merely replied, "Honey, let's wait for Vito. He is better explaining things than me. My education didn't go so far and I don't wanna make a mistake. It's okay, capito {understand}! Onesto {Honest}! It is okay!"

I had no choice. I had to wait for Vito. I gave Lorenzo towels, soap, and a Jack Daniels on the rocks. Thank God for those six ice cube trays I brought from America when I moved in. They were big suckers, too!

When Lorenzo left, I started to unpack and settle in. It was so good to be back at this home again. I do love it here! I had everything around me from home, pictures of my family and friends, one thing from everyone I loved was here, and it felt welcoming.

Hours passed by when the outside gate-phone buzzed in the house. "Ciao, Missy. Unlock the gate," said Vito. I buzzed him in, opened my door, and went directly to the ice cubes. I did not know if Vito needed a drink, but I certainly did. Besides, Vito was not getting out of here without telling me what happened!

I was in the kitchen when he and Lorenzo entered. "Permesso, Missy."

I yelled from the kitchen, "Of course," and continued to put out cheese, grapes, prosciutto, and olive pizza that Angelica bought before my arrival. As I entered the dining room, I gave Vito a short hug and lay the food on the table. I then went to the liquor cabinet. "What do you want, Vito? A Jack for you, Lorenzo?" Lorenzo nodded yes and Vito pulled out a chair and replied, "Vino, and leave the bottle."

When I finally sat at the table with them, I asked Vito, "Well?"

Vito drank down his glass of vino immediately and poured another. "I stopped in customs and talked to a few amici. They tell me that all government agents register when they enter any country. This FBI was here for problems with 'hackers,' whatever the hell that is!"

I had to smile at Vito's obvious lack of knowledge for computers. I explained, "Hackers are people who get into computers of other people and steal their identities. However, if they were international, I would assume the government is concerned over terrorists' activities."

I laughed as I remembered the airport, "Vito, I had to laugh at you trying to hide behind a telephone booth! It was like trying to hide a fire in the middle of an empty room."

Lorenzo laughed, "V, and you tell me I'm big!"

Vito leaned over and punched Lorenzo's arm, "Ma tu cervello piccolo, {but your brain small}." Vito continued, "I knew this culo from other times. Missy, what did you feel? Think this was just niente {nothing}?"

I had to be honest and go with my gut. "Vito, after talking to this Mike, by the end of the trip, I did believe it was just that, niente. You know me, my gut usually is right. He wasn't exactly truthful, but I don't think it had anything to do with you and me!"

Vito finally relaxed, "Bene!"

Vito and Lorenzo stayed for almost three hours before leaving. I asked, "Vito, when is the meeting, and will you and Lorenzo be back to pick me up?"

Vito surprised me again by saying, "I am not going until you go. I don't know when the meeting will be but I will let you know pronto! Missy, no worries this time! But are you ready for it?"

I had to laugh. "The last time you asked if was ready for it, I got that box from Luigi of God knows what! I have not looked inside yet. And besides, why didn't I get your word on any worries?" It bothered me that Vito did not give me that.

When they finally left, I walked to the nearby store for food, water, and other necessities. I wanted to really settle in and relax. My mind and body was tired. I thoroughly was enjoying the peace and quiet, right up until the phone call from Roberto. He had returned home to receive papers of the finalization of the divorce.

I was shocked! I had not realized two years had passed and it would become final unless he opposed. I thought he would only receive the support papers for some money. This was a big miscommunication on my lawyer's part. Roberto was devastated, "Elisabetta, I am contesting this. I don't want a divorce!"

What bothered me the most is that I felt indifferent, a worse feeling. Had I become that calloused over the years to feel no compassion? What kind of monster was I turning into in my old age? I have to get out of this life! I had to make big life changes. Start over at ground zero. I needed to find me, who I was now. I absolutely had to before I thought about tackling the box that held all the secrets of my life.

Most of all, I had to decide how I was going to save my family from whatever was coming my way. This was the perfect time and place to do exactly that: be alone, without the family problems, without any interference from the outside world, and use my mind for my own problems!

Of course, that would have to be after the meeting. I just wanted it to be finished. I was going, as usual, with my head full with worries over Roberto and his health. I guessed I might not be the monster I thought I was. The only bright spot would be seeing Isabella again. I closed my eyes, lay my head back on the couch, and said aloud, "Everything is going to be okay!"

Chapter Ten

The Sunday after I arrived, I was fortunate enough to have dinner with my friends in Citta S'Angelo, and it was wonderful seeing all of them again. Martina was leaving the home, for the first time, to live and start college. She, of course, as Angelica, **had** to return home on the weekends. The family was always so welcoming and warm, and I felt as if they were a part of me.

The next day I received the call I had dreaded. "Missy," said Vito, "looks like the meeting will be Giovedi {Thursday}, but I will be picking you up on Martedi {Tuesday}. You won't get back home until after the weekend. And Isabella said to tell you to bring a party dress!"

I wasn't sure if Isabella said that for our martini hide-away or for a real party; however, I decided I had better take an evening dress. The men were usually in tuxedos in the evening, probably to be ready for any funerals! God, I hope nothing happens this meeting, I thought to myself. "Okay, Vito, no problem. What time will you be here?"

"Early, Missy, morning at seven."

I said, "I'll be ready. See you tomorrow!"

It seemed as if I had just unpacked and here I was again, packing for a trip I wished was already over. I was happy I had left behind clothes. I had the perfect little tea-length dress for the party; however, it was in bright red. The thought had crossed my mind that it would match any blood. Was this another intuition of mine? And if so, where was my spirit friend? I felt secure as long as he did not show up. Nevertheless, he did also warn me of harm to loved ones. I wished he would make up his damn mind and find a tongue to tell me instead of these games of charades.

When finished with my luggage, I opened a bottle of champagne and drank the whole damn bottle. I was feeling very arrogant when the house phone rang. "Pronto," I answered.

From the other end, I heard a small, quiet voice. It was Roberto, and he sounded like death as he said, "I do not know what to do. I do not want to go through with this divorce. In addition, I cannot afford to give you any money! Why did this happen?" I had to make Roberto promise to go to a doctor. I would talk to him later. I could not allow myself to get off track for this meeting. I was leaving the next day for Sicily.

I don't know whether the champagne or Roberto's call was the source, but I did not sleep very well. And when I did happen to doze off, the dreams were just crazy and in color. Great! I thought at one point, I'm probably having a stroke.

I put on the bedside lamp and sat against the headboard to clear my head. If I had Luigi's box with me, I was sure I would have opened it at that point. I was glad I had given it to Gina to put in her basement safe. The black pouch was in a safety deposit box at my bank.

Before this trip, I had thought it better not to find out before this meeting. I did not want anyone to ask questions as to what I found—or, worse, who or what I was. I had an answer for them right at that moment, alone in my bedroom: Nuts! That is what and who I was!

I tried to concentrate on my 'visitor,' hoping he would appear and give me answers, even if I had to play charades. No such luck! I lay back in bed and finally was able to sleep for a few hours.

The alarm went off too soon, and I knew Vito would be on time. He always was! I looked at myself in the bathroom mirror and said, "Asshole. You had to drink the whole bottle, right?" I had just finished dressing when my gate phone rang the house. "Buon giorno, Vito," I said as I pushed the button to open the gate. I then hung up, unlocked the door, and proceeded to bring my suitcase to the foyer.

I returned to collect my make-up in the bathroom and as I turned, I almost screamed as there stood Sergio. "Oh my God, Sergio, how did you get in? Was that you a minute ago?" Sergio walked toward me and I held out my arm full length, "I cannot deal with this right now. I am waiting for a friend to take me to Sicily. You should not be here, especially now. God, if Vito sees you, he'll be furious."

Sergio simply said, "I needed to talk to you. I don't care who sees me!"

I was mad now. "Well, dammit, I do. Do you want to see me in trouble? Tu sei pazzo {you are crazy}. We cannot talk now! I have to leave! They should be here any minute. You have to go!" I pushed Sergio to the front door just as the phone rang again. "Please, Sergio, you have to leave before they come in. Take the stairs, please."

Sergio answered as he left, "Okay, for now. But, I will talk to you when you return. Or, I don't leave now. It is your choice."

I pushed the button for the foyer door. "Just go now, please." Vito exited the elevator, just missing Sergio who took the stairs. However, I knew that Lorenzo was in the car downstairs. I hoped Lorenzo would think Sergio was just a resident. Someone is going to have to save me before I can save anyone else if that happens again, I thought.

The ride to Sicily was beautiful, as usual. I felt safe in that car with Lorenzo and Vito. I should enjoy it now before hitting Sicily! I then asked Vito, "Where is the meeting, anyway? Are we going to Dominic's?"

Vito cleared his throat and said, "No! Pietro wants the meeting at his house this time. You know, Missy, like a dog who takes a pisciare to mark his territory." Vito, who usually is neutral when talking about either Dominic or Pietro, seemed to be annoyed at this.

"Oh, come on! Vito, is there trouble already and we aren't even there yet?" I asked shaking my head.

Vito patted my hand and replied, "You know one accuses the other of never having any morals. Can you just imagine that! In this life of ours, these two fight over who has more morals. Especially after what Dom pulled last meeting with you. I never understood those two."

I had to laugh. I could not help myself and answered, "Both of them believe that moral fiber comes with cereal. I'd dump both of them immediately like toxic waste if I had any say."

This upset Vito and he said, "Elisabetta, don't be starting, okay? We have a long ride ahead of us. Yo, Lorenzo. Stop for coffee."

As we were relaxing with coffee and dolce, I questioned Vito about Don Lazzaro and his goons. "Are they going to be there? Why hadn't I met the Don before the last meeting?"

Vito answered, "Only because it was Luigi's memorial. The Don doesn't go too far from his villa. I doubt if any of them will be there, but if they are, it is not a good sign!"

I almost choked on my coffee and responded, "Well, that makes me calm down a bit. You want me to choke. What kind of a bad sign? Is that why I didn't get your word that nothing was going to happen?"

Vito only gulped down his coffee and said, "Not to worry, Missy. It will all be okay!" Vito handed Lorenzo the bill and we left for the car.

During the car ride to the small airstrip, Vito and I talked. "Missy, I didn't give my word because things often don't unfold the way they are supposed to or the way you want them. You cannot have that many in one room, all wanting to be king, and have everything senza problemi {without problems}. You have always handled yourself with self-confidence in whatever you do. Keep that up at this meeting. You are number uno in everybody's eyes, but things around here have changed. You have graceful strength; use it. Stay focused," said Vito.

I sat quietly for a second and asked, "Vito, how much longer do I have to do this?"

Vito did not look at me. He stared out the car window and answered, "Missy, for the rest of your life!"

I spent the next hour staring out my side of the car as the tears fell. It was the first time someone that I knew loved me had honestly confirmed my worst fear.

Chapter Eleven

We arrived at the air terminal and boarded a little plane, which scared me to death. Out of fear, I think, I fell asleep and awoke only when Vito touched my arm before the landing in Sicily. There was an empty limo waiting for us for Pietro's' villa. After only half an hour, Vito asked, "Missy, want some coffee, sandwich, something? I am starving. I just saw Lorenzo licking the steering wheel. Come on, honey, stretch a little before we reach the villa," said Vito. We left the car and entered a small cafe at the gas station.

I was still kind of groggy and upset over the conversation with Vito. "Get me anything. It doesn't matter."

Vito shook his head and went to the counter where Lorenzo was standing. I felt numb. I had this upcoming meeting on my mind, Roberto, this life, the box, my family and their safety, and my sanity. I was staring into space when Lorenzo sat down across from me. "Ah, come on, Elisabetta; don't let the bastards get ya down. You have to mangia. You need to eat and grow up big, like me," Lorenzo laughed.

I did try to joke. "That certainly takes away my appetite."

Just as Vito sat down, Lorenzo said, "V, Elisabetta just insulted me about being fat."

Vito sat down his food, rubbed my back, and said, "Lorenzo, they could use your ass for a billboard. Eat!"

The drive to Pietro's was with very little conversation. I just wanted the quiet time to get my thoughts together, if possible. However, I did ask Vito if he had found out why Dominic was at the casino. Did Vito think Dominic knew I saw him?

"Missy, I tried checking it all out for you. Dominic was not supposed to be there but in Chicago. I am still working on it. I will find out, believe me! Don't get discouraged."

My thoughts then turned to Pietro's villa and I was hoping I would see Isabella there. I did not want to stay at Pietro's unless I had to. I would rather stay with Isabella.

As we drove up the beautiful tree-lined drive to the massive iron gates, my stomach was fluttering. There goes that damn gut feeling again! Something was going to happen. As I slumped down in the backseat, Vito turned and said, "Missy, trust your instincts. I will be close by. Don't worry about anything."

I said disgustedly, "I know. I remember the rules."

As we departed the car, I started to cry as Isabella came down the steps to greet me. 'Elisabetta, I am so happy to see you! I am calling the AA right now and tell them I quit. My drinking buddy's in town." I hugged her hard and she looked into my eyes, and quietly said, "We'll talk. How about staying at my villa instead? I will clear it with the two boneheads."

I was so relieved. "Isabella that would be the medicine I need. Thanks!"

As our luggage was being unloaded, Isabella and I were so busy talking and hugging I did not see Pietro standing beside me. He greeted me with the same warm, handsome smile he had that many years ago at Guido's funeral. "Benvenuto, Elisabetta," Pietro said as he kissed both cheeks. "Come va?"

I returned the kisses and smiled, "I am wonderful, thank you, Pietro, and for the wonderful invitation to your home."

Isabella leaned in as Pietro gave orders to everyone. "Kiss

up," she laughed.

Pietro then turned and said, "Why don't you two get to your catching up. I will have drinks delivered to the veranda in the back. Andare avanti {go ahead}!"

I had to whisper to Isabella as we made our quick escape, "That's a first! You and I get to spend time together first! Wow! Isn't it fun having a different boss this time around?"

Isabella responded, "Honey, don't be taken in with his pearly whites, they are all the same. One wrong move with Pietro and you become an organ donor!" I was shocked over hearing that because Isabella had never before said anything derogatory about Pietro.

I tried to joke, "I've had enough with the organ donors in my life as it was. Thanks for the heads up!"

Isabella then said, "Pietro will refuse to have you stay any-where but at his villa, so I will invite myself. Dominic, howev-er, will have to stay too, unfortunately."

I was glad to hear that. "Isabella that is great. It did not mat-ter where I stayed if you were going to be there. This should be another catastrophe. Do you think there are hiding places in this huge monstrosity too?"

On the veranda, Isabella and I were looking over the wed-ding album of Maria and Davido; and, of course, I had beautiful portraits of the new baby, Niccolo. Isabella was amazed at how much Rocco and Dominic had grown too.

Isabella asked about her godson, Claudio. I told her he would be marrying in May. Isabella assured me she would attend, with or without Dominic. Isabella said, "Well, he finally found the woman of his dreams, huh? What is her name?"

I told her, "It's Nicole, and she comes from a nice Italian family. She fits right in with us! I like her a lot. Claudio seems to have settled down quite a bit. However, the trick from Dominic had a lot to do with it too! Speak of the devil, Isabella!"

We were just enjoying ourselves, and Dominic appeared car-rying a cocktail. "This looks like a lot of trouble starting here! Missy, give me a hug. I have missed you!" I wanted to jump down his throat! I wanted to scream, 'How, could you have missed me? You just saw me at the casino not that long ago,' but I kept my mouth shut, for a change.

Instead I arose and smiled, "Dommy, you up to no good, as usual? Isabella and I were just looking over the pictures of the wedding. Care to join us?"

Isabella spoke up and said, "No! Go away. I see enough of you. Give Elisabetta and me some time alone. Get!"

Dommy kissed me and said, "I'll see you later, honey. The boss has spoken!"

Dommy went back inside and Isabella giggled, "See he has changed since the last meeting!"

While Isabella and I had the time, we talked about what might happen in the meeting. I was on my own, as usual. Isabella was never invited to attend. "Listen, amica," Isabella said quietly, "These men didn't get this successful, at their ages, by sleeping on the job. They all are still as conniving as ever, including the old Don. Elisabetta, speaking of that, I noticed there have been two dumbbells watching us since we arrived. We could use them to exercise. Don Lazzaro's muscle heads. You remember Thumbs and Tomatoes. Just so you know. I think everyone's afraid you and I will take over."

We laughed. I replied, "I just want out of this mess! They can fight it out amongst themselves for all I care. I want my family protected or I would not be here now!" I sighed and continued, "Speaking of that, Isabella, I did not get an answer from you about the meeting. Do you expect any trouble? What have you heard?"

Isabella leaned closer, pretending to be looking at the album, and whispered, "I would feel more at ease if Don Lazzaro was not here."

I instantly remembered what Vito had told me on the ride here. This meant trouble. "Oh damn," I said, way too loudly. "Vito already warned me of trouble if he was at the meeting. Promise me something, Isabella: if anything bad happens, take me to a hiding place quickly, okay? Stay close by!"

Before we could continue, a butler came to the veranda and requested, "Signori, please join Pietro and Dominic. Follow me. I will take your glasses." Isabella and I both groaned at the command but followed behind like good little girls.

As we entered the main sitting room and took our glasses from the butler, Isabella whispered, "Ever notice how the color of a room affects your mood? With me, it is whether or not Dominic is in it!"

I was smiling as Pietro made his formal welcome to Isabella and me. The one thing that happened that pleased me was both Pietro and Dominic took the time to look at the album and my grandsons' pictures.

Dominic said, "I guess I should start calling you Grandmother!"

Thinking of my ugly grandmother, I quickly answered, "Only once, Dominic, then I'd kill you!"

Isabella got a little nervous because I was brazen enough to say kill. "Elisabetta didn't really mean that!"

I turned and looked at her and laughed, "I certainly did!"

Dominic looked at Pietro and said, "I told you the two of them are trouble. You never listen to me!"

Pietro came back at him with, "Because you are crazy, Dominic!"

I looked at Isabella and said, "They are at it already and we haven't even had a meeting! Does a man ever grow up?"

We both accepted another drink from the butler, and Isabella sat on the sofa. "Pietro," I asked, "scusi, where is the closest bathroom, per favore?" Pietro called his butler to lead the way.

Exiting the bathroom, I ran smack into Joey Thumbs. As I tried to walk by him, he touched my arm and spoke in his broken English, "Elisabetta, I surprise you wit people no good. When with bad, you git bad. You like be in fire!"

I thought, as I stared back at him, He is full of intelligence, maybe double digits if he tried really hard. I took this as a threat. I know my instincts. However, when I tried to pass, Joey moved slightly to the left to block my way. I stepped back and brazenly answered, "And, what, you have the match, I suppose! Get out of my way, now!"

Joey 'asshole' Thumbs then became nervous. "Scusi, scusi, Elisabetta, no trouble me, okay?" He rushed off.

Back in the sitting room, I was wondering if I should say something to Dommy or Pietro. I decided to speak only to Isabella. I might be able to use that little scene with Joey further down the meeting trail! Since the men were still at the other end of the room, I did exactly that.

Isabella was shocked. "Those goons know better than to approach either of us! Are you going to say something?"

I said, "No! I think I might just keep that under my hat. I never know when it might come in handy these next few days."

Isabella handed me my drink and said, "Damn, you're good!" as we clicked glasses.

Chapter Twelve

The afternoon approached, and it was, of course, time to eat. Pietro asked if we would like to freshen up first and both Isabella and I jumped at the chance to get away. Dominic replied, "No! I am okay. Isabella, you and Missy get settled in."

Pietro said, "Take whatever rooms you want."

Isabella and I walked to the beautiful staircase that divided at the top. "Right or left?" asked Isabella.

I laughed. "Anywhere they aren't! Let's just investigate a little first. What do you say?"

Of course Isabella was game, and we found two suites next to each other with connecting balconies. "We will stay on the right side and let the cafonis on the left," laughed Isabella. We settled into our suites, and decided to meet in about one hour.

The scenery from the balcony was marvelous. I did notice many men securing the gate and property. There were also men in boats docked next to the huge house. I said aloud, "Like a freaking scene from the Godfather!"

I finished cleaning up and met Isabella in the hall. "Did you see the guard dogs outside?" I asked.

Isabella said, "I wondered if it was to keep people in or out. There must be a shit load of people coming to the meeting. One of them is Don Lazzaro, I am sure, since his goons are already here! That is probably why Pietro told us to pick rooms first. He wanted to keep us separated." I never gave that a thought.

"Isabella, I must be slipping. That idea never crossed my mind. Are you packing a gun by any chance?" I asked.

As we came down the staircase, Vito and Mano were at the bottom. I was happy to see Mano again, surprisingly enough. I didn't like what he did for the familgia, but I suddenly felt safe. Isabella made a fuss over both as this was the first time she had a chance to talk to them. She turned to me and said, "Remember what you asked me upstairs about packing? I'm not, but there's no worry now. Either one of these two could have a cannon under their coats! Who would suspect?"

I took Vito's arm, Isabella took Mano's, and we walked towards the dining room. I pulled Vito a little closer and whispered, "I had a run in with Joey Thumbs. I didn't like it one bit, but don't say anything."

Vito was furious over the encounter and mumbled, "Stupido! You okay, Missy? He touch you?"

I smiled at his protectiveness and said, "He'd pull back a stump! It's okay, just in case I need that information later!"

When we entered the dining room, there were so many people. I saw all my old friends again, Mauro, Trieste, Lorenzo, Salvi, and a few of Pietro's men I remember from the meeting a few years ago. Then I saw Orlando and Matteo from Venice. They both greeted me and we talked briefly.

This meeting was going to be a circus, I thought. I scanned the room, remembering the rule, and noticed that there was a spot at the long table without a chair. Don Lazzaro must be here!

Isabella and I stuck close together and worked the room being the perfect guests. Just as I started to relax, in rolled Don Lazzaro with his two ass wipes following closely behind.

"Let's go," I said to Isabella. "We need to pay our respects!"

Being nuts, Isabella replied, "Sure. The way he looks today, it might be his last at the dining table."

I whispered, "Please behave! You are as bad as Gina." I purposely stared in the eyes of Joey Thumbs, and it was not a look of admiration. I could see him get flustered that I might say something to his boss!

I was the first to lean down and kissed him on both cheeks, "Don Lazzaro, I am so happy to see you again—and looking so well."

Next was Isabella. "Don Lazzaro, what is your secret? You are still the most handsome in the room."

Don smiled at both of us and said, "I told those cafonis you here only for me. But nobody listen? No!"

Isabella and I got on either side and walked slowly with the Don to the bar. We gave Don a glass of vino and he held it with both hands. He looked into it for a second and said, "Twenty years ago, ahh! I okay with both you." I smiled at Isabella, but we knew the only way the Don could handle the two of us at about eighty years old, twenty years ago, was to have one of us stand him up at the time.

I clicked my glass with his and said, "There is not doubt in my mind!" He smiled from ear to ear.

Pietro announced, "Buon appetite," and, as usual, pranzo {lunch} was delicious, pleasant, congenial, and too filling. I loved when they ate because they did not fight or curse. It was disrespectful to cause trouble at the table during eating.

Just for a second, Roberto's family flashed before my eyes. When his father was alive, there were few dinners where someone did not fight, pound the table, or argue over some discussion going on. Roberto's family loved each other immensely, but discussions were very loud. In Italy, it was very different, especially with this crew of thugs trying to act civilized. It is crazy what comes into your mind at the weirdest times.

I wondered what would happen if anyone of the servers, bartenders, butlers, or house cleaners revealed conversations that went on in this home. I remembered my dad's rule, 'Nothing ever talked within this home, leaves here!'

Vito was sitting between Isabella and I, and she tapped my shoulder. I looked behind Vito and Isabella mouthed, "Look at the Don!" I looked over and the poor man had more on his clothes than in his mouth or on his plate. I wanted desperately to go over and help him.

Vito grabbed my arm and said, "Don't even think about it. You would embarrass him."

I quietly answered, "Do you read my mind now? Vito, you are getting scary!" Pietro invited the men to the smoking room for after dinner drinks. He then suggested that Isabella and I, along with the few women also attending with their husbands or whatever, take a leisurely stroll around the gardens. The other women looked at Isabella and me as if we had just left a brothel and went on their merry way. It didn't matter to me.

Isabella said, "Dominic doesn't like me to mix too much with them anyway. Talk about old school—and just look at those hairy faces. I am not sure they even know that Dom and I are married. Who cares?"

Something told me that Isabella really did care because she was very lonely here in Sicily. She always loved returning to the States. Both Isabella and I were out of place here. We had to take off our shoes to walk around the gardens; either that or the heels would make it look like the fairways I remembered at the country club as a child. Sometimes I would remember the huge holes left behind by golfers. However, it felt great on my bare feet.

We found a bench among the beautiful flowers and sat to talk. "I hate this life too," said Isabella.

"Why do you say that, honey?" I asked as I put my arm around her shoulders.

"No family, children, fun, friends, or much love. I feel like my life has always been a business. Understand, Missy?" asked Isabella.

I knew exactly what Isabella meant and told her a little of what was going on between Roberto and me. Isabella patted my hand and said, "Remember what we talked about at the last meeting? You have to do what you can to get out of this and protect your family. It is harsh, I know, but it just has to be! If I could, I would already be out of here. I wish I was younger and had half the experience I have been through in my life. I would do so much differently."

Before we could finish, some of the women approached us to talk. I tried being pleasant, but it annoyed me.

We all returned to the villa, and the butler informed us there would be music in the grand room around eight o'clock. Dress would be casual. Nice of them, I thought. I only had the one dress for the cocktail party that usually came after the meeting, unless someone died. Bite your tongue, I thought to myself! I had hoped Isabella and I would have more time, but Dominic had other plans. I thought yuck and went to my room to get away from all the testosterone!

I called home to make sure my grandsons and children were okay. I wanted news on the baby too. I was happy to speak with Maria. She had wonderful news. Her examination showed no cancer cells anywhere. Apparently this little wonder cleared up the problems Maria had for six years. What fabulous news for Maria. I said, "The little angel was meant to be born, just like you were! Enjoy Niccolo now, he will grow fast enough!"

I then spoke to Gina, Gypsie, Gracie, Sheri, Rocco, Dominic, and Claudio. It took an hour to get off the phone. I had to rush to get downstairs on time at eight o'clock. As I rushed to open the door, there stood Vito. "Have you been waiting for me?" I asked.

Vito smiled and said, "Just your escort tonight, my lady!" I knew he was worrying over my encounter with Joey Thumbs.

The evening went well, and I was extremely tired when I returned to my room. I was happy there was nothing early the next morning. If we wanted something, Pietro told us to call the kitchen. Isabella laughed, "Dom will be there to answer, I am sure. It is his favorite room! I will see you tomorrow, Elisabetta. Sleep well!"

Chapter Thirteen

I slept very peacefully, even though the meeting was that night. I called the kitchen for coffee at around ten o'clock. I walked unto the balcony with a blanket around me and thought of that morning in Positano with Sergio. Funny I should be thinking of him. I have to get that problem straightened out too with Pietro and Dominic. Sergio would have to work for Pietro now, I would guess.

As I looked down on one of the levels of this mansion, I saw a young woman sunning on a chaise lounge. She was naked except for a small towel over her butt and apparently oblivious to all the people attending the meeting. I did not know if I should say good morning but figured, what the hell could happen? I had not seen her attend any gatherings since we arrive. "Buon giorno," I said.

She lifted her head slightly, put on her sunglasses and replied, scared, "Scusa! Buon giorno! Am I problem here for you?"

I smiled, "No, not at all," as I waved at her and went back inside.

The maid knocked on the door and greeted me with coffee,

dolce, juice, fresh fruit, and yogurt. "Buon giorno, Signora," she said happily.

I answered, "Buon giorno. Gee, I didn't order all this!"

She smiled and said, "Orders from Mr. Dominic."

Great, I thought. Now he even tells me what I should eat.

I smiled and said, "Mr. Dominic is a pain in my culo, but grazie."

The maid giggled and closed the door.

Immediately there was another knock. I thought she had forgotten something. I was surprised to see Isabella rolling her breakfast into my room. "May I serve you breakfast, signora?" she laughed as she removed a large table cover exposing Bloody Marys.

I laughed, "I like yours much better. What's with all that celery?"

Isabella acted as if she was surprised and said, "Signora, that is breakfast!"

We wheeled both carts out onto the balcony and sat down with blankets over us. "I could get use to this life if it didn't involve so much other crap," I said.

Isabella responded, "I will drink to that. However, I drink to mostly anything."

God bless her, I thought. She could always make a scary situation easier to take. If I couldn't have Gracie, Gina, or Gypsie here, Isabella certainly is my friend. I found myself becoming fonder of her every time we were together. Moreover, we had been through a lot all these years.

I smiled. "Isabella, have you seen the new 'scenery' down below".

Isabella looked at me curiously and stood up. "Holy crap! Look! Hurry up!" As I stood, there the beauty was, standing up, butt naked as she walked around looking out over the water.

"If Dom sees her we will need the medic team. She is a baby! How old do you think she is?" asked Isabella.

I replied, "About late thirties, forty years tops! Who is she, do you know?"

Isabella said, "Pietro has no children! It has to be his latest lover. Pietro always has them a fourth his age! Dom told me Pietro loved a girl long ago but her family shipped her off to the States. He never became close to another woman after that!"

I tapped Isabella on the arm as if to say, Watch this. "Scuse! I am Elisabetta and this is Isabella. What is your name?"

She shyly replied, "I am Cecilia, but Pietro calls me Chezi."

I responded, "We are happy to meet you, Chezi. Sometime would you like to have coffee with us?"

Chezi seemed nervous, "Yes, I would. But I ask Pietro first, okay?"

I smiled, "Okay! Just let us know. Have a wonderful day, Chezi!"

As we went back inside, I said to Isabella, "Well, Pietro is teaching her the rules. Shame too, she is so young! Isabella, since I am 'excused' until dinner and the meeting afterwards, you and I should take in the sights of Sicily, and not like that one." I pointed to the young woman.

The enormity of where I was and whom I was with hit me like a ton of bricks. We not only had Lorenzo drive and Vito in our car; but we had a car with two other men following us. Now, that should make my shopping the 'hit' of the day I thought, running from a hail of bullets from one shop to another. "Isabella, is this really necessary. I am afraid to get out of the damn car!"

Vito looked back at us and said, "Missy, everything is fine. It is just I would feel safer watching over you two. Sicily is not a place for a woman to go out alone during the day. At night, it is worse, and you will never do it! You always manage to get into some trouble. And no drinking martinis today. You need your smart brain tonight, don't forget."

I responded, "Yes, sir!" as I saluted him like a soldier.

Lorenzo spoke up, making fun of Vito, "Send Elisabetta to her room, Vito!"

Vito was not amused. "Just drive, pain in the ass!" However, Vito was absolutely correct. Every time Isabella and I exited the car, outside a store, a restaurant, anywhere, the men were crude.

Not like other places in Italy. These men made kissing sounds and moaned as if they were about to have an orgasm. That is, right up until they saw Lorenzo and Vito get out of the car. It was as if they all lost their lips!

After one incident, the men following behind always escorted us. I felt badly for what Isabella would do to these poor souls. She would hold up beautiful bras against them, show her legs to see if they liked her shoes, and went as far as to hold the tiniest thong against the one. His face turned crimson, even under that Sicilian complexion. I asked her, "Aren't you on some kind of meds?"

I have to admit, Sicily is beautiful—the flowers, the little outdoor places to stop and taste their food, and the shops. No wonder Lorenzo wanted to drive. We skipped very few of the outside chefs, some cooking right on the street. However, the food was excellent, even the pasta with sardines, a Sicilian favorite. It was like a food feast, a little of this, a little of that, and the desserts were the best I had ever eaten anywhere!

Also, there was a slushy drink, called granita of fresh fruit and ice, and it was so refreshing, I did not mind not having the alcohol. Before long, Vito told us we had to return to the villa. I had no money to buy anything but certainly enjoyed the window-shopping. Isabella, on the other hand, went nuts on shoes. "I have to buy something!" she laughed. "They won't let us drink!"

Chapter Fourteen

When we arrived back at the villa, there was no one in sight. Isabella went straight to her room to hide all the shoes. I looked at Vito, questioning, and he said, "Their part of the meeting was today. That is why they wanted you two out of the way!"

I was talking to Vito as I climbed the staircase. "I'll see you later, Vito!" Just as I turned the corner to my room, there was Joey coming the other way. I thought, Don't start please. I have enough assholes to deal with tonight. He had no right to be on this side of the villa. Don Lazzaro was on the other.

Joey Thumbs again stood in front of me as I tried to pass. "Elisabetta, please, I sorry you think I no respect yesterday," he said in his horrible English. "Will you speak out?" He pointed outside through the window.

I answered sarcastically, "I don't think so, Mr. Thumbs!" However, when I tried to pass again, he put both hands on my shoulders. If he knew my life with men putting their hands on me, he would have thought better of it! Here I frigging went off again, as I kneed Joey in the balls. He only grunted slightly but did not go down! He was like a wall! Either that or Joey had no balls. "Get the frig out of my way!" I yelled loudly. I heard someone coming up the stairs and hoped whoever it was would be on my side. I couldn't take two of them, but I'd take this bastard! One harder knee, and I hoped Joey would go down.

Luckily I did not have a chance to as I saw the fear in Joey's eyes at what was coming at him. Mano came around me quickly as he picked Joey up, his feet dangling, and slammed him against the wall. "Joey, I know you are handicapped because you are stupid, but do you have hearing loss too!" Then, Mano went through a series of filthy Italian words as he kept banging Joey against the wall. "Never, ever, go near Missy again! Don't even look in her direction. Do you understand that, or do I have to make you an example? Do it again, Joey, I swear."

Mano choked him harder and said, "Your father was always in the concrete business, si? Well, did you know that concrete can be formed into any shape? But, ya see, I have a problem with it! The blood stains it and it's a bastard to get out. Now, only 'cause of the Don and I amico to your father, you walk away now and no andare all'altro mondo {not go to the other world}. Not a second time, ha capito {Understood}?"

Before another second went by, Vito came behind me, Isabella came from her suite, and it was like a parade. Vito just quietly said, "Elisabetta, go to your room! Isabella, go with her!"

I tried to talk to both Vito and Mano, "It's okay! I can handle myself. Joey didn't mean anything!" I was scared something would happen to Thumbs. I could not live through that again.

This time Vito asked, nicely, "Please, you two, go. There will be no trouble here! Go!"

Isabella and I entered my room. I turned to look at her in her robe, "What the hell? Is this Joey a nut case? What does he want from me? I kneed the sucker in the balls and he didn't even wince!"

Isabella gave me a hug and said, "Honey, he knows better. I don't know where his head is. It was a stupid move on his part, but nothing will happen, honest. The Don is here and it will be up to him to handle Joey Thumbs. The guys have too much respect for Don Lazzaro to step on his territory or his men. It will be okay! Let's call the kitchen for something small to eat and something large to drink!" I was certainly willing to go along with that!

"Isabella, no hard liquor, please. I need my faculties for tonight!"

About fifteen minutes after Isabella called the kitchen there was a knock on the door. The maid wheeled in antipasto, pane {bread}, and Bloody Marys. As she was leaving, I saw Lorenzo in the hallway; no one else was around. I sighed deeply and asked, "Lorenzo, did you smell food?"

Lorenzo laughed, "Didn't I tell Vito earlier, he should send you to your room! It's okay, Elisabetta. Relax."

I closed the door and looked at Isabella, "Didn't you start yet? Pour me a drink, please, with lots of ice! Isabella, why is there always problems involved with these meetings? It is like a damn circus out there. Do I attract all these idiots? It's like a fly to crap!"

Isabella laughed, handed me a drink, and said, "These cafonis don't see a woman like you often. What do you think Joey wanted? Have any idea?" It surprised me that she was insinuating it might be a come-on by Thumbs.

"You've got to be kidding! After what we saw naked running around the property! Joey is, like, maybe thirty years younger than I am. No, I think it had to do with business. I have to go with my gut on this one, Isabella. There was something else to this. I did not get those vibes from Joey. It has to do with business, I am sure. I just go on the defensive with men, especially if they put their hands on me. Old hurts never go away."

Isabella and I sat and enjoyed our little snacking on the balcony. I knew she was trying to calm me for what might go on tonight, and I was thankful. Isabella looked at her watch and said, "It's time to get ready, honey. Dinner will be right on time because of the meeting. I believe cocktails are at six o'clock. Dom and I will knock when we are ready to go down."

I thanked her, closed the door, and fell back on the bed holding my head. My thoughts instantly went to my family and Roberto. "No! I said to myself. "You cannot even go there right now," and I smacked myself in the head. Now if that wasn't stupid! I gave myself a headache. I said as I stood up, "Thanks a lot, Pops, for that little advice a hundred years ago! Damn, that hurt!"

The long soak in the tub was exactly what I needed. However, I will never get used to these narrow tubs. The only bitch who could fit stretched out in this would be Isabella's sister, with the perfect hips.

I lay out the red dress, jewelry, shoes, accessories, and then thought, Okay where is that mind of mine? It has to be here somewhere. Aloud I said to myself, "Elisabetta, you are losing it again! Knock the shit off!" I then applied makeup to this person I hardly recognized any more. I hoped Isabella was not wearing black. I would stick out like a sore thumb. Speaking of thumbs, I wondered what had happened to Joey.

I went over my paperwork for the third quarter of the year, and, as usual, (pat myself on the back) everything was in order. Now, if I could get my brain that organized, I could run the frigging country! I was out on the balcony when I heard the knock. To my delight, Isabella was in a beautiful, bright shade of green. With Isabella's red hair and green eyes, she was a knock out.

I looked at Dommy and simply smiled. "You ought to be glad we even allow you to be seen with us!"

Dommy snorted, "Get the hell out here before I beat your ass! You ready for the meeting, Missy?"

I closed the door and shook my head, "As ready as for any of these damn things! Isabella, did you ask Dommy about our naked beauty?"

Isabella smiled, "Just as I thought. She is Pietro's, literally. She is not allowed to come to the functions. She is here for his disposal, only. Not a bad life, I would think!"

Dommy was annoyed, "She is stupid. What kinda life is that for a young girl?"

Isabella just hugged his arm and said, "Do I hear a little sour grapes, my dear husband?"

Dommy stopped dead in his tracks, looked at both of us, pointed his finger, and said, "The two of you, I swear! You two are always trouble. Don't start, either of you!" Together, as if we practiced, both Isabella and I laughingly bowed to him.

When we reached the main ballroom for cocktails, Dom strutted like a peacock with Isabella and me on each arm. Pietro approached us and laughed, "Dom, now how did you capture such beauties? And don't give me that stuff about one shoe bigger, either."

I took Pietro's arm much to Dominic's dismay. "Buona sera, Pietro. Everything okay?"

Pietro patted my hand through his and replied, "No problems today at the meeting. Tonight might be another story. Come on, let's get champagne. Dom, you come too, only because you have beautiful Isabella!"

Pietro stopped a server, took two champagnes for Isabella and me, and asked Dominic to go to the bar for a man's drink! Isabella whispered, "Finally, now is our chance to run fast!"

I whispered back, "I don't need to be tempted. I am ready."

Vito and Mano approached us and Vito asked, "No whispering secrets, you two! I want you in view at all times tonight!"

Mano chimed in, "It could be a worse view, V! You two have it all, beauty and brains. Hey, remember one of those girls of mine, the one who thought the chef drowned the lobster?" Both Isabella and I finally relaxed as we laughed over that whole story.

"Her name was Chick wasn't it?" I asked Mano.

"Only because she forgot her name," laughed Mano. The rest of the cocktail hour was pleasant, but the night was young.

Before we knew it, the butler announced, "Attenzione. Dinner will be served in the dining room in fifteen minutes." Isabella and I found a waiter to take our glasses. Mano offered his arm to Isabella, "My pleasure?" Isabella took his arm as Dommy was nowhere in sight.

I then turned to Vito and said, smiling, "Your pleasure?" He laughed as we walked to the dining room. As we found our place at the table, I noticed instantly that Mano and Vito were on either side of me. A good or bad thing? I wondered. Well, I tried to joke with myself, both men being the size they were, I certainly have enough coverage for anything coming my way! Sometimes humor was the only way I got through these meetings. I also realized I had been talking to myself, aloud and quietly, a lot lately.

The dinner was enough to feed Africa, again. There was a huge antipasto, three kinds of pasta and meat, every fresh vegetable in Italy, two kinds of salad, and so many desserts and fresh fruit I got sick looking at it. No wonder the men are the sizes they are! The antipasto and bread would have satisfied me. Maybe they were hoping I would die of a heart attack before the meeting. Come to think of it…no, I did not mean that, I thought.

After the dinner liqueurs, the men excused themselves to go to the smoking room. Isabella and I instantly received orders from Vito to "stick close by." After he left the room, I asked Isabella, "Let's go outside to the garden. What the hell could happen there?"

Isabella took my hand and said, "A breath of fresh air would be good for you before the meeting. Come on, I never follow their orders anyway."

I smiled, "Unfortunately, I always do, along with all those frigging rules!"

Isabella and I found a beautiful place and sat down. The air was crisp and clean and I wished it were tomorrow. The biggest meeting would be over. "I am getting way too old for this Isabella," I said as I sighed.

"I know, honey," agreed Isabella. "Me, too! You will be great tonight. I promise I will be close by if I have to hide behind the curtains. Look! Vito and Dommy are there with you—and who can forget Mano! It would take the Italian army to bring him down."

I had to laugh. She was right. Mano was powerful and as

big as a building. "Isabella, they were at the meeting two years ago and all hell broke lose! I just have a bad feeling. I have to go with it!"

Isabella leaned over and put her arm around my shoulder for a hug. "Then go with it and be prepared. I know, after all these years, to not go against those feelings of yours," said Isabella.

We sat for a second, and then she asked, "Where has our dapper neighborhood spook been? You haven't said much about him lately." I laughed at how everyone in my life knew of him. He had become a part of all my friends' lives.

"I really don't know. The last time I saw him was right before Luigi died. I don't see him around here, unless he is hiding in the bushes. I guess I should take that as a good thing?"

Just then, the butler approached to ask us to return. "Here I go," I said to Isabella.

Chapter Fifteen

This meeting seemed different somehow. Not everyone sat at the table, as always before. Vito sat behind me with Mano behind Dominic. Don Lazzaro and Pietro were at one head and Dominic at the other. It looked like the gunfight at the O.K. Corral. I felt small and lost for the first time. I did not feel as if I was entirely among friends.

Then it started. Pietro brought the meeting to order by saying, in Italian, "With the permission of Don Lazzaro, we will start this meeting." The Don nodded as if that was good enough for him. Pietro continued, "Again, God bless our families all gathered here tonight. I welcome you all to my home. I hope I speak for all the families in welcoming Elisabetta to our family here in Italy."

I did not like that! It was like ownership, and I looked toward Dommy. His eyes told me to behave. I then thought, I hope this is not one of those blood things, where they take a knife to your hand or some other ritual like that! I squirmed a little and Vito leaned forward and just touched my back to let me know it was okay.

My hands started to sweat. I definitely was getting way too old for this! Pietro continued, "Most of our business was handled earlier, and I will ask if Elisabetta is ready for the work from Lou". He looked in my direction. It took me so by surprise; I lost my train of thought. After all these years, I thought, everyone knew about Lou.

Apparently Pietro did not want to reveal that bit of information to the Sicilian side of the family. Quickly, I responded, even though my head was on pause, "Grazie, Pietro. I am ready!"

I took a few minutes to arrange the accounts on the table and to give myself a few seconds to control myself. I never had to do that before! As I methodically went over every entry, every month, ending with the final report, I could see the amazement in the Don's eyes. I thought he was impressed; however, when I finished, the Don asked, looking around the table, "Lou, io non so Lou {I do not know}! Chi {Who} Lou? Italia? Stati Uniti? Dove Lou. {Where}?"

I prayed for someone to answer him quickly before my irritable bowel kicked in. Talk about getting the crap scared out of you. Finally, Pietro and Dommy both started to talk at the same time. Pietro waved Dom to go ahead. Dominic stood up and asked permission to speak. I thought I would go into shock! I never saw Dom ask permission for anything. Who is this Don Lazzaro, and where can I hide right now?

I was proud of Dominic as he explained, in very short detail (without giving away any important information about 'Lou'), my family's involvement with Pops, my grandfather, my dad, and Guido. Dommy also spoke of 'Lou' as if he was a real person who only would deal with me. Both these men were lying to the Don.

I saw Don Lazzaro put his head down for a second, and then he looked sharply at me. In his broken English, Don Lazzaro tried very hard, speaking very slowly, to get his point across to me. "As old man, I remem many things. No remem Lou but, these men you speak, good men. Men with honor, respect. Stories true. Elisabetta, you make heart proud, think Sicily familgia. You honor, respect. Raramente bella Donna..." the Don then looked to Dominic to translate.

Dominic quickly looked at me and said, "rarely beautiful woman."

Don waved him to be quiet and went on..."intelligente!" (I knew that word and thought this must be the original chauvinist pig.) "Men permessa lavorare."

Okay, I thought to myself, whose gun could I borrow? In the States, most men want a woman to work and they certainly do not wait for permission! The Don was certainly old school, like the wooden hut, brick fireplace, and share-one-book kind of old school. I hoped he finished talking, but he took a sip of wine and continued, "You meet with me, capito, and domani?" I knew that meant tomorrow and it was not a request but a command. He then waived for the meeting to continue.

Pietro stood again and thanked Don Lazzaro for his wisdom and acceptance of a woman working with the family. I almost gagged. Up yours, I thought to all the men at the table. I was mad. Accept this, I thought as I stuck my napkin in my crotch on my lap. I was still fuming when Pietro interrupted my thoughts with "Elisabetta?"

I replied, "I'm sorry, Pietro, I was just making sure I covered everything in my head!" That was good and fast thinking! I guess the old mind still works. "What did you say?"

Pietro smiled and looked at the Don, "See, molto bene con lavoro {Very good with work}."

Pietro continued, "At the meeting earlier we discussed the problem with Joey Thumbs. The Don decided Joey needed to make an apology to you here and now." Don Lazzaro made a hand motion and Frankie Tomatoes opened the door for Joey to enter the room. The old man stared accusingly at Joey and I could see the poor young man shake.

Distressed, I looked behind at Vito, and whispered, "I've got to do something!" I was scared to death this would be another smack in the mouth with a large object like in Rome. I was almost ready to stand and run. Vito only shook his head, No!

As Joey came beside the Don, the old man raised his hand as if to say to Joey, "Do It!" Joey kept his hands at his side like a robot, stood straight, and said, "Signora, I am sorry to make you not happy. I no want you not happy by Joey Thumbs. I wrong speak you. I no mean hurt no body. I beg you take me apology. Per favore!"

I felt horrible for this poor soul. I looked in Dominic's direction, and he winked and nodded ever so slightly. "Yes, Joey, I accept your apology!" I was going to say more but the Don pushed Joey towards the door. He and Frankie Tomatoes left closing the door silently.

The Don looked at Dominic and Pietro with both palms of his hands in the air as if to say, Was that enough? Pietro thanked the Don for handling the problem, and Dominic nodded and put his hand on his heart. Can I go now? I was screaming in my head! I did not have to wait more than a second when Vito pulled out my chair. "Have I been dismissed?" I whispered to Vito.

He said quietly, "You must ask permission first!" At first I thought Vito was joking, but he held the chair against the back of my legs so I could not move.

I then asked permission, "May I be excused, Don Lazzaro?"

The Don motioned for me to come near him, Vito following closely behind, as the Don kissed my hand saying, "Domani e buona notte!" I answered good night also and took Vito's arm as my legs were shaking!

As Vito and I exited the room, I took a deep sigh. "Was that all okay, Vito?" I asked. Vito hugged my shoulder and said, "Perfetto! And, I was to tell you Isabella has been waiting on the veranda for you."

I smiled broadly, "Thank God! I'll go meet her, okay?"

Vito said he had a few things to handle but we were not to go too far from the veranda. I kissed him on both cheeks and said, "I am so glad that is over! It is over, isn't it?"

Vito said, as he shrugged his shoulders, "I hope so, honey! But I am not sure your part of the meeting is over. Remember;

do not wander off! I'll meet you both back here at the veranda." He watched as I walked quickly and opened the huge double glass doors to the veranda and my friend.

"Yes," squealed Isabella, "Are you finished? Did everything go without a hitch? Anybody get hammered in there? Come on, tell me, tell me!" I sat down at the table and Isabella took my hand, "Well?"

I laughed. "Give me a minute. You are getting like the big D. Pour me a drink, please, and give me a second to unwind."

As Isabella poured champagne for the both of us, she said, "I was so worried. I do not like waiting as an outsider. If it was only Dom, I could give a rat's ass; but I was really concerned about you with Don Lazzaro in there!"

I took a deep breath, a sip of champagne, and said, "My part was fine, perfect according to Vito. However, that had to be one of the scariest meetings. Of course, not topping Rome, but it was close! The Don made poor Joey come into the meeting and apologize in front of everyone! Can you imagine?"

Isabella looked around and said, "That was a severe punishment for the poor guy to apologize in front of the men—and to a woman of all things! You can bet he will learn this lesson well. The next time there will be no getting off easy!"

I knew I could not say any more to Isabella about what actually went on behind closed doors; however, we did get off the subject and talked about our last day together. "I don't know when we can take off for a while. I was commanded by Don Lazzaro to see him tomorrow. I have no idea why or what time. I am sure I will find out soon enough." I sighed and continued; "Now that little get-together scares the hell out of me. I am hoping Dom will have some idea why, before I am cornered. I swear Isabella, if it's something I don't like or an order from this man, I'll roll his ass so far down the hallway in that wheelchair he'll think it's jet-propelled."

Isabella laughed hard just as Vito came to check on us, "I would feel better if you due gocce d'acqua {two peas in a pod} take this to your rooms. How about it?"

I looked at Isabella and said, "I would love to get into my robe. How about you?" Isabella agreed and we were escorted to our suites.

"Isabella, come to mine so we are not disturbed by the big D."

About thirty minutes later, Isabella came knocking. It was as if we were having a pajama party at our age. We bundled up with our robes, blankets, socks, and slippers and went to sit on the balcony. It felt cooler on the balcony, and Isabella joked we might need antifreeze, just for medicinal purposes, of course! She went inside and called downstairs for "hot toddies."

I had to laugh, "Do they even know what that is?"

Isabella just nonchalantly said, "Whatever warms me up." Isabella never really drank as much as she had this time around. I was hoping she had been joking about the AA thing when I arrived.

The motor mouth in me asked, "Isabella, how is everything with Dominic? Really."

Isabella closed her eyes for a few seconds and said, "You know him, Elisabetta! You have known him longer than I have. Dominic will not change, and I really do not expect him to at his age. Moreover, do not get me wrong, Dom was never a physical abuser as I saw you go through those many years ago. Just the same, Dom has changed for the better since the last kick in the ass, thanks to you. It is just that I am so lonely all the time. Elisabetta, aren't you lonely sometimes?"

I had to respond with the truth. "Isabella, I have never spent an unlonely day in my life!"

Isabella sighed deeply and said, "I know of Dom's indiscretions, but I choose to look the other way and mix the martinis. Elisabetta, are you trying to ask me about the drinking? I know I am starting to have a problem. Sometimes I look for anything to pass the time and warm me up when there is nothing or nobody around. It is the life I chose, I guess." That last sentence sent me back immediately to my conversation with Dad after Mom died.

"Isabella, you keep telling me to get out of this mess. That it was not my path of choice as a young girl. Yet you cannot leave either. What is going to happen to us old, wrinkled farts, ten years from now?" I smiled.

Isabella just rocked back in the chair and said, "Just save your family from this life. Whatever you have to do...." Just then, Isabella was cut off by the maid's knock on the door with the Italian version of a hot toddy. We dropped the conversation as we both looked into this large pot of whatever and argued back and forth like children, "You try it." "No, you try it!"

Finally, I poured two cups and Isabella talked me into tasting it first. She watched with quiet curiosity waiting for a sign. Well, Isabella got it quickly. "Holy shit!" I gasped at whatever it was! The liquid warmed me from my lips, stopping off to make my crotch sweat, and immediately dropped to my feet. Isabella laughed! "It's not funny." My throat started to burn. "This is like instant menopause. I am having hot flashes, my crotch is sweating, but my hands, and feet are now freezing. What is in this stuff?"

Isabella took a sip from hers, swished it around as if it was expensive wine, and swallowed. "Its antifreeze, straight from the garage!"

Many hours passed and Isabella went to her room. The meeting still had to be going on, and that made me wonder if everyone was still alive.

Chapter Sixteen

I awoke late and wondered if everyone had already gone downstairs for *colazione*. As I started to jump in the shower, my phone rang. "Hey, Elisabetta!" laughed Isabella. "That was some good stuff last night, huh? I slept like a log. I never heard Dom come in. We have to find out the recipe of whatever it was so we can bottle it and take it back to the States. How are you?"

I had to smile, "I was just getting into the shower. I never slept so well myself. Yes, make sure we find out what it is! Did you and Dom have breakfast yet?"

Isabella answered, "I have no idea where he is. Dom probably smelled something cooking though. You know what? He might not have come to bed. I don't remember seeing him, and his usual pile of clothes are not hung over the chairs. When will you be ready?"

I answered, "Give me a half hour and knock. Whoever is done first?" Since I was finished, I went to Isabella's room. She was almost ready and I sat on the bed. "What can we do today after I am finished with Don Lazzaro?" I asked.

"Do you know what time or what it is about yet?" asked

Isabella.

"No! I sure wish I did though. Maybe I should not eat before, if it is going to be early today. My luck, I will have pains in my stomach, not have time to ask permission to leave, and get shot to death." I laughed.

Isabella said, "That's simple. Just tell the old man you have plans and to get his old ass in gear!"

I closed my eyes and shook my head at her. "I can see why they make you wait outside the meeting rooms! Between you and Gina, it's a wonder I'm not already dead!"

Isabella and I entered the smaller dining area for breakfast. We were alone. "Are you sure Dommy is okay?" I asked Isabella.

"Now you have me worried, Elisabetta. Usually if Dom has eaten, there is nothing left. It looks like Vito or Mano haven't either. Not a good sign, I would say." Isabella answered with a puzzled look on her face. "Come on, honey," Isabella said. "Let's eat. I am sure they will show up eventually. They cannot still be in another meeting. After we eat, let's just sneak by the big dining room and see if we see any bodies lying around." I had a look of horror on my face and she quickly rescinded, "Elisabetta, I am joking!"

I had to say it. "Isabella you remember what happened in Rome two years ago. I returned home in terrible shape. I never want to feel that way again!"

We started to take our plates outside and the maid came rushing over to assist. "I do that, please. My pleasure. I bring espresso!"

I had to ask, "Please, what is your name?"

She seemed shocked that anyone would want to know and quietly said, "I am Carla."

Isabella and I sat down on the veranda and I said, "Thank you very much, Carla." Isabella and I both caught each other looking around for someone, anyone, to appear. "This is just too strange, Isabella. It is as if we are the only ones left. I am going to ask the maid when she returns."

Within five minutes, she returned and I asked, "Carla, do you know when the meeting ended last night and where everyone might be this morning?"

Carla seemed shy and meekly replied, "Signora, we finished cleaning up around three this morning. I am quite sure there is another meeting, a smaller one, here at the villa. An Americano arrived very late last night. Would you like me to find out?"

Isabella immediately replied, "No, thank you. That will not be necessary. We will just enjoy the peace and quiet for now." Carla giggled and left.

Isabella and I were busy talking and laughing. We were just enjoying our espresso when, out of the edge of my vision, I saw someone strange! It was in a place in the garden where no one would need to be unless they were up to trouble.

"Isabella," I said, "There is someone watching from the garden. I cannot see who it is, but I believe we should get our asses out of here quickly! Just move as usual and don't spook whomever. Maybe we can find Vito."

You could tell Isabella was used to this because it was as if I just said 'it is a nice day.' Isabella was very calm, blotted her lips, and said, "Should I pretend to fix my thong and give him a good show?"

I grabbed her by the arm and we slowly walked inside. "Normally Vito is everywhere I look!" I said.

Isabella replied, "Let's go upstairs. We might be able to see more from the balcony!" However, when we did reach my room, we saw no one.

Isabella could not resist, "Your spirit friend is back, has turned gay, and likes pretty things around him!" I was very uneasy. We walked back to the small dining room, and there sat everyone, as if by magic. I told Dom and Vito about what I had seen outside and Mano was out of the room before either of them could move.

Vito looked at me and said, "I am sure it is no problem. Here, sit and have coffee with us." Isabella and I took a seat and Vito informed me that the Don would be waiting in the library in exactly one hour.

I had to ask, "Did the meeting take all night? Was there another one this morning? And who was the American who showed up late?"

Vito was surprised, looked at Isabella, and said, "Is that damn spook around her again?" He looked back at me and said, "How the hell you know that? Come on, Missy, tell me. Is that bastard back again?"

I laughed at Vito, who was this huge and afraid at the same time. "No! I haven't seen him, but Isabella thinks he turned gay and is playing in the flowers outside!"

Dom just continued to eat as he looked up at us as if we were ready to be committed. "Missy," Dom finally said between mouthfuls, "as soon as I am done here, Vito and I want to talk with you before you see the Don."

I could not resist. "That should take a week or two. I can wait!"

Dom never even looked up from the plate and muttered, "Smart asses. Everyone's a smart ass anymore!"

When Dommy finally finished eating, Isabella excused herself to call her family in France. "Elisabetta, I'll meet you upstairs when you are finished," said Isabella.

Vito spoke, "Dom, you wanna tell Missy why you were at the casino? Missy, believe it or not, it isn't a bad thing!"

Dom put his napkin on the table and responded, "Missy, I wasn't sure you even saw me. I knew you and your friends would be there, but I had a meeting and that was the best place to do it. The visitor last night was who I met there. It has nothing to do with you. You have to believe me. I had nothing to do with your seating partner on the ride here from the States. That really was a coincidence. Freaky, if I think about it long enough!"

Dommy continued as he pushed his chair back, "Anyway, before you meet with the Don, I wanna straighten that out. I did not want you to think I was up to no good. My promise after Luigi's funeral, I meant. Honey, you will not have any problems from me. I learned my lesson. You are a damn good teacher! Anyway, I want you to meet this man, again!" I looked at Vito as if to say, What the hell is this now? Dommy snapped his finger at the opened door to the dining room.

As I looked towards the door, Mano walked in, followed by Mike, of all people! I was shocked. Mike, the renegade FBI agent who had sat next to me on the airplane! No wonder I felt he wasn't hiding anything against the family. He was with the family! I said, "I don't believe it!"

Vito shook his head and said to me, "Honey, I didn't know about it either until we arrived in Sicily. Dom had no time to talk to me before we left the States. But, Dom, I would have had an easier flight here if you didn't go off half-cocked all the time. You should have told me!" I knew Vito was aggravated with Dommy.

Mike approached my chair and said, "Elisabetta, I did not have a clue! Talk about fate stepping in! I am as shocked as you are. It absolutely was a freak coincidence. It is a damn small world, isn't it? I never expected to meet you again! I was walking around the garden, smoking some butts, and couldn't believe my eyes."

I looked at both Dom and Vito and said, "Is this for real?" I felt much better when Vito assured me it definitely was real. No bullshit attached to this meeting with Mike, again! However, I did not want to know why Mike was there. The less I knew the better I would be. I had a very uneasy feeling about this Mike character that I could not shake.

Dom dismissed Mike as fast as he called him in! He then turned to me and said, "Let's get down to business before you meet with Don Lazzaro. Missy, he might try to get information from you about the operations with Lou. Be aware. He is old but a sly volpe {fox}. But Missy, be respectful and talk only when he asks something of you".

I looked at my watch, it was time to see the Don. "First, Dom, I hate the fact that Mike saw me here and knows my name! Couldn't that be dangerous? What about all that talk of protecting my identity? However, do not worry; I will be careful with the Don! Where will you be when I am finished?" I asked.

Vito answered instead, "I will be waiting outside the door. Dom, you go to your room with Isabella, and we will be there as soon as the Don leaves!" It was apparent that Vito was in charge, and I felt a little safer.

Chapter Seventeen

Both men walked me to the library. I took a deep breath and knocked on the door. "*Entrare* {enter}," was the response from Don Lazzaro in his weakened voice. Dom and Vito stepped away from the door so the Don did not see them, and I walked inside.

"Buon giorno, Don Lazzaro. Come va oggi {how are you today}?" I asked.

The Don smiled widely, shook his head as if to say he was good, and motioned for me to sit. Here we go, I thought. The Don put his hands together. "Che bello {how beautiful}."

I caught myself blushing and answered, "Grazie, Don Lazzaro."

He brought his electric wheelchair to alongside me and continued, "Complimenti, Elisabetta! You very good work of Lou. Mai {never} I met woman like you and sono vecchissimo {I am extremely old}. You remem what I say you?"

I had to think for a minute, "To get out of it?" I asked.

"Si, si," he replied as he shook his head very slowly. "You think it, si?"

I smiled, put my head down, and said, "Always!"

The Don smiled. "I happy you think! Luigi say si, want you out! Capito." I just nodded yes. Don Lazzaro took my hand and sadly said, "Sorry, Elisabetta, walls stand 'tween are tall for you. You baby, young, essere solo come un cane." I did not understand the Don. It sounded like he said I was to be like a dog. I did not think that was a complement and it showed on my face.

The Don, becoming flustered with his English, said, "No! I think. You be soul alone in world now. No good, no good!"

I sat for a second as he wheeled around me and thought, The Don might be very old but he certainly could see through to my soul. How did he put it? A soul alone in the world? He was a smart old man! A knock came to the doors and Don cursed under his breath in Italian, "Who?" he demanded.

From the other side, I heard Carla, "Don Lazzaro, I have your medicine!" He grunted an acknowledgement and Carla entered quickly. She was holding a small tray and she was shaking. He took the water and pills and made a face at me.

"I no like!" he grunted again. I winked at Carla and she seemed to relax slightly. She left us just as quickly. The Don then turned to me, stuck out his tongue as to say the pills were terrible, and continued, "I think, whadda I say you before you come Sicily. Familgia not together no good. I think men like brothers, so many gone now. Then, familgia believe omerta. Never want me cause man to fall. Old omerta, no more. No respect. Son Vittore, oh Dio, no respect omerta. Same men today. But I do my terms, not nobody. I do my schedule, not nobody. Cosi {so}, I live old. I think not so good to live long time." The Don hesitated briefly and said, "No good you do work. How old you when work this?"

I answered, very slowly, "Too young, nineteen years. But, Don Lazzaro, then it was not like this. It was my way of life. Today, I don't like it! I am getting old, too. You, please, tell me how I get out. What will happen when I do? I worry for my family and if they will be safe! I worry will I be safe?" The tears started a little and I became angry with myself for showing the

Don such a woman's thing. "Sorry, Don Lazzaro. I worry for my loved family and friends, you understand?"

The room suddenly had gotten so silent I could hear noise in my head. Ever have that happen? It becomes so silent you almost hear your mind working. It was scary, especially in my current mental state. For a few seconds, I thought the Don had either fallen asleep or died. I was almost afraid to breathe. Therefore, when he finally said something, I jumped a mile. "I think problem. Listen to old man, Si. You no work maybe problem. No can cheat honest people. Man now like rat in sewer. You no work, and me die, maybe blood will be shed. You see in box from Luigi, maybe face to face with enemy, joined by blood." I nodded yes and he continued, "What box Luigi for you? You see what?"

I assumed the Don meant what was in the box. Talk about playing charades, I answered, "I have, yes. I did not look yet."

Again, the damn silence. Maybe I should remember the old rule of Pops and take a two by four to the Don's head to restart him. However, I waited. Show respect, Dom had told me. Don Lazzaro's next response really came out of nowhere, "You let me see box, si."

I gulped as I refluxed into my throat. I thought, Go with your gut and head, Elisabetta. Go with it!

"Sorry, Don Lazzaro. I mean no disrespect, but that box was kept for me by Luigi and it concerns my family not the familgia here. I want to keep that just for myself. It is my only connection now with my family. I hope you understand."

The Don turned his wheelchair so his back was to me. Talk about flashes of lightning in my head. I thought that meant either, get out, you are dead, you are stupid, or any of the above. However, I had not asked to be excused; so, I waited for some sound, something from him. I thought, Maybe I should see if there is a plug on his wheelchair and plug him into a two-twenty socket. I sighed way too loudly and he turned around. "Sorry. I think you good teachers. Luigi no want you show. Only you box. But, what think you if is familgia Sicily?"

Okay, I have to decipher again, did the Don mean I should not show the box from Luigi? I was either being tested or the Don really wanted to see the box. I had no idea! And, what was that crap about 'if familgia Sicily'. I have been through many tests. I had hoped if it was a test by Don Lazzaro, that I passed this one with flying colors.

"Elisabetta, I find answer for you. Dimme, {tell me}, if you, ahh, Pietro or Dominic, who you feel familgia you? Who you trust, here?" He pointed to his heart.

My answer amazed me because I said it without thinking it through, "Dominic!" I replied.

Don Lazzaro said, "What if blood different? Why no Lou?"

I was caught off guard for a second and said, "Lou very old!"

The Don then shook his head, "Good. I find answer you. Go now. I say ciao you when go villa."

I pretended I understood completely. However, was I to say goodbye to him or he would to me before going home? I would worry about that later. I asked permission to be excused and he nodded. I shook his hand and Don Lazzaro kissed mine.

I closed the doors, stood facing them for a second, and sighed deeply. Just then, someone touched my shoulder and I thought, Don't let it be Joey Thumbs. At this point, I was so wired after that meeting, I would take him down with one knee. Luckily it was Vito, just as he promised. "Let's go upstairs. Dom and Isabella are waiting!"

Chapter Eighteen

Vito took my keys and unlocked my door. I heard him talk to Dom, in Italian, from my room. I kicked off my shoes and lay across the bed. What the hell was that meeting all about? The Don asked a few questions about Lou but seemed only to be interested in my life. What did he mean, whom did I consider family? I thought they *all* were family. That is what they wanted me to believe at the freaking meeting.

I heard them enter, and Isabella flopped on the bed next to me. "You know what, Elisabetta, if there were mirrors on this ceiling, and you had a fat man on top, it would look like you were anorexic because you would be completely covered."

Dominic became angry and yelled, "Isabella!"

She just snickered. "Dommy, you have no sense of humor!" Isabella and I got off the bed and sat on the couch.

Vito picked up the phone and ordered drinks and antipasto for the room.

"Missy, how did it go? You okay? Mostly, did you behave?" asked Dominic.

"Dommy, I cannot even explain it. I am glad the Don speaks

some English, but there were a lot of things that got lost in translation. One time I thought he said something about me being alone with a dog."

Before I could finish, Dom said the exact words, "In Italian it is translated differently. What the Don was probably saying is 'to be without a soul in this world.' But, you are right, the English version sounds that way, with a dog." Both Dominic and Vito laughed at this.

Vito was next, "Missy, go on. Just give us the short version of what you understood." I explained the conversation as best I could. More importantly, Don Lazzaro had asked about the box from Luigi. He was interested in who I considered my family within the familgia. How the Don mentioned blood, both my blood from family and blood from bloodshed. I felt the Don wanted to know, if I found my blood was different after opening the box, would I change my mind about family?

Dom pulled at his neck collar and asked, "And your answer was?"

I answered, straight-faced, "I told the Don I hated all of you and the only family I felt close to was Isabella. Therefore, the Don made her the head of your family. Did I do okay, Dommy?"

Dominic looked at Vito and snorted, "See! See, what did I say this morning? All smart-asses!" Isabella had a good laugh.

Dom and Vito went out on the balcony to talk, and Isabella told me of her family. "I called Rosella in France. Mama said my sister is in the hospital for stomach and bowel problems, I gave Rosella a call. I tried joking, but you know her, Elisabetta, Rosella does not joke."

I laughed, "I feel sorry. I hope she will be okay; but, what the hell did you say to her?"

Isabella said, "Rosella has just returned from the rain forests in Costa Rica and thought she picked up some kind of alien bug. When Rosella told me her symptoms, I told her she was probably trying to pass a square fart through those perfect hips. Rosella got pissed at me!"

I started to laugh. I really did not mean to, but I could not help myself. "Go on, nutcase!" I said.

Isabella smiled, "It was like the phone call from hell. They need to give her drugs. Rosella asked if I just called to annoy her. I told her, yes, of course, I have a whole club in Sicily, and we meet once a week just to see how we can annoy her! I then told her the whole world does not revolve around her and her perfect hips."

I felt badly but still laughed. "Isabella, the poor thing is in the hospital!"

Isabella replied, "Poor thing, my ass. Rosella then told me that my life was so wonderful. I never worry about anything because Dominic takes care of it. Rosella then told me I was jealous of her because the one thing I could never be was thin! Can you imagine that bitch?"

Isabella paced and continued, "Then Rosella went on to say I am too Americanized and have forgotten my roots. I shave my legs, get the false nails, wear too much makeup, and dress entirely too sexy for my age!" Isabella was livid but continued, "I had to come back at her, impacted farts or not! I told her if anyone wanted to see a rain forest, they should look at her legs. Now, that is a rain forest that could use some pruning." At this point, I was hysterically laughing.

My insides were saved by the bell, or in this case, the knock on the door. Vito came in from outside, looked at us laughing on the couch, shook his head, and opened the door for the butler. As Vito was making drinks, Dominic said, "Isabella, you should be nicer to your sister. She is the only one you have."

Wrong time to mess with Isabella as she came back at him so quickly, Dommy backed away, "You want to get into this now, Dommy? Bring it on!"

Dom grabbed his drink and said to me, "I don't get in her way when Isabella is like this. I'll wake up tomorrow with a Mohawk in my private area!"

Vito put his hand on Dom's shoulder and they went back outside to continue their conversation.

I tried to change the subject. "Isabella, is there something we can do today? I am supposed to leave tomorrow for home. That is, if I get permission to be excused by Don Lazzaro."

Isabella was shocked, "You go to the States tomorrow?"

I answered, "No! My home here. I have a lot of work to do before I leave for the States."

At that moment the men entered the suite again. "Dom," Isabella asked, "do you think it all right for Elisabetta and I to go somewhere for a bit before dinner?"

The men looked at each other and, in unison, answered, "No!"

Isabella, as well as I, became very annoyed. Like a comedy skit, we both said in unison, "Why?"

Vito answered, "Missy, until Dom and I figure a few things out, I would like you to stay around the villa. God, there is so much here. You two can get lost. Name it and I will make it happen. Just you and Isabella. I know how you like your little sessions together! Do we have a deal?" I looked at Isabella and she made a face but agreed. Dom said nothing. My old intuitions were screaming from inside of me. I was in danger. I knew it!

Isabella started giving outrageous orders, and I thought she was desperately trying to force Dom to let us go off the property. "We would like to start with a total spa treatment and detoxification so we can fill back up with alcohol. Then, we would like to sit through a showing of the current designer fashions, including shoes and jewelry."

Just then Dom yelled, "Wait! I need someone here to take this all down!" as he picked up the phone for the butler.

Isabella winked at me and said to Dom, "Have him hurry up before I come up with too many ideas!"

Chapter Nineteen

As it turned out, Isabella and I had the most wonderful day. We had our spa treatments, complete with mud baths, body wraps, exfoliation of dead skin, massage, hair, nails, the works. We were then ushered, in our robes, to a large room. Waiting for us was champagne, strawberries, chocolate, and other delights; and, the show began of the new fashions of Italy. It amazed me that all this was thrown together in a few hours. It takes me weeks to handle a one-night open house.

Isabella and I could pick anything we wanted to wear for the evening dinner party. As Isabella and I went through the gowns, I had to smile, "I always take the small soaps, shampoos, anything I can get my hands on from hotels. Think anyone would miss these?"

When Isabella and I returned to our rooms, we were exhausted. We decided to rest before the cocktail party. I felt wonderfully relaxed. In fact, maybe that is why I had a visit from my dear friendly spook.

I had gone into a deep sleep and dreamed he was sitting on the couch in my room. It was, again, very real. He was holding something similar to an opened billfold with what looked like a license. There was a bright shiny object on one side. Brightly illuminated, it hurt my eyes badly, and I could not see the photo.

I remember trying to sit up, or wake up, but I could not. In my sleep, I said to my spirit, "What is it you are trying to tell me?" At that moment, the billfold turned to fire and he disappeared. It was then I awoke with a start! My eyeballs were hurting and he was gone. Whatever my spirit friend was trying to say left me with an uneasy feeling and my first instinct was of Mike at the villa. "Go with the feelings," I said to myself.

Both Isabella and I had picked the most gorgeous dresses for the party. Of course, they had to be returned the next day, but for that night, I felt amazing. Both Isabella and I chose designs by Roberto Cavalli, both black. Isabella's dress was softly flowing with umpire trim of gold braid. My dress was form fitting to the knee and flared out slightly with a very small train, trimmed in silver. We both had our hair done up instead of loose and my 'do' was studded with diamonds. Isabella had gold braid weaved into her red locks.

There were escorts waiting to walk us to the ballroom where the men were meeting. When we entered, you could hear a pin drop, and Dominic beamed from ear to ear. Dom walked to greet us, and Isabella whispered ever so quietly, "I make him look good, huh?"

I answered, "You always did! I feel like Scarlet when she entered that party with the curtains as her dress." We were like fly paper. I looked around to see if the Queen of England might have arrived after us. A fuss was made by all the men as their wives, or whomever, looked with distaste.

I remembered my training and scanned the room. I was only remotely aware of the sensations in the palms of my hands. This was always an indication of something not being right. I noticed that Don Lazzaro was not present, and out of the edge of my vision, I saw Mike.

Pietro approached us then with champagne and said, "Wow! You two add class and life to this old villa!" as he kissed us both.

Pietro then gently pushed me at arms length and just stared into my eyes for what seemed forever. It was a confusing moment for me! Pietro then said, "Elisabetta, for just a second, in this light, you look like a beautiful girl I once knew. I never noticed it before!"

I smiled, said thank you, and then asked Pietro, "Where is Don Lazzaro?"

Pietro answered, "The Don was very tired after the meeting this afternoon and decided to spend the night in his suite. You might see him tomorrow before you leave. Come on, you two, mingle, talk, and make these old men smile!"

As Isabella and I looked around, we saw all the women grab onto their old husbands. I laughed and said, "Please! These women are kidding, right, Isabella?" We definitely were not after their husbands!

The cocktail party was amazing, as usual. It still was hard to understand the old Sicilian women and men because of their dialect. However, Vito was never that far away from me to interpret. It was unusual for Vito to be that close the entire night. Also unusual was catching Pietro's constant glances. Most of his glances seemed with great sadness.

I also noticed that Dom glued himself to Isabella's hip. At one point, Isabella and I got together to talk. "Finally! Dom is so far up my ass, I cannot fart! What is it with these two men tonight?" she asked.

"There's trouble, I know! I had a visit, dream, or whatever this afternoon. It has something to do with that Mike. But I awoke with such pain in my eyes!"

Isabella got louder, "What! You had a visit? Oh, come on, what did he say?"

I laughed, "That has always been the problem, the sucker never speaks. However, I have become very good at signs and charades."

Chapter Twenty

The next morning I awoke both excited and sad. I wanted to leave for my *casa* but did not want to say goodbye to Isabella. There was a knock on my door, and I thought it had to be breakfast. I was surprised to see Vito. It was early and he usually was involved with the men. *"Buon giorno,* Vito. What's up?"

Vito said, "Sorry, Missy, there has been a change in plans. You cannot go today. It seems Don Lazzaro needs to see you again; so, rather than be rushed and drive at night, we will leave tomorrow, I hope."

I was annoyed. "Dammit! Vito, do I have to go through another meeting with him? I want to go home!"

Vito stepped inside the bedroom and closed the door, "You don't have much of a choice, honey. Just think of it as another day to spend with Isabella, okay? Come on, you are really grumpy today! What else is wrong?"

I tried to joke, as usual, to cover up my disappointment, "I have to poop!"

Vito laughed, "You do too much of that! The truth now! Tell me!"

I sat on the bed and started, "Besides the circus here, Roberto and our problems, money headaches, and these freaking meetings? The advice from old men I do not even know; not knowing whom to trust; the talk of blood and not knowing who the hell I really am; the fact I hate this life; having someone waiting for me to make a mistake and fall. You telling me I cannot get out of this life; but the Don in Sicily telling me he will handle the problem to get an out for me. That makes me think all this talk from him about blood could be my own. Let's see now…pick one, Vito!"

Vito was taken back by everything I had just spieled off! "You never mentioned all that about the conversation with the Don," yelled Vito. "You listen to me, Missy. The Don might run things here, but he will not control your life. When or if you get out of this should be on your terms and not his. To find peace for yourself and your worry over the safety of your family will come from friends. Use your good sense! You know the Don is too risky for you to trust. The only one you need is me! No one else if you don't want to. Understand! I usually get what I want. You should know that! I stay in the background, but I am not an outfield player. I will not have anyone force my hand before I am ready," said Vito softly.

I flopped back on the bed, and Vito could see the stress taking over. "Missy, look at me!" demanded Vito. "There is no one in this world that cares more for you in this business than me. If you stop trusting someone in this life of yours, you will go down. I won't stand by and have you second guessing yourself now. I know there may be an out coming up soon, but not on anyone else's terms, especially in Italy! I am going to call Isabella to come and stay with you. I will return soon!" Vito picked up the house phone.

Isabella knocked on the door in a flash. Vito said to Isabella, with hurt in his voice, "Isabella, you talk to her. She trusts you!" Isabella closed the door and said nothing.

She pushed me over, stretched out on the bed, and waited a few seconds before saying, "When you are ready, we can talk.

But just one thing I will say first, there went one of the two men in this whole place that I trust completely, Dom included."

Isabella reached for the phone and called the kitchen, requesting breakfast be delivered immediately. She turned and said, "You need to eat something!"

We lay in silence until the knock on the door. Isabella jumped up, "Good! If I am lucky, Carla will remember I like to drink my breakfast along with some food for you!" she smiled. I lifted my head slightly to see.

There were two different trays, one with a ton of food and the other with Bloody Marys and plenty of celery. Isabella laughed, "I knew I liked that girl from the very beginning. Get your ass up and eat. Don't make me call Mano!" she threatened.

I smiled, "Okay, okay! I am getting up. Mano would eat everything anyway!"

We pulled our chairs together, set up our breakfast, and Isabella broke the silence. "Come on, honey, tell me what I can do to help. What has been going on these past few days that turned your brilliant mind into sponge cake? Damn, if you can't talk to me after all these years, you'll go crazy!"

I poured myself a Bloody Mary and smiled. "I passed crazy about fifteen years back and am moving forward rapidly to lunatic. But, if you don't mind, we will talk after we enjoy this. I don't want my stomach acting up again!" We both agreed and talked about everything else but my problems.

Later we took our coffee outside and sat overlooking the beautiful gardens. I thought for a minute and asked, "Isabella, I wrote down seven names on a piece of paper. What I would like you to do is number them according to how much you trust them. Will you do that for me?"

Isabella smiled, "No problem. But I was hoping it would be a list of who we thought had the biggest one!"

I yelled, "Behave, please!" but had to smile.

Isabella got up, went inside for a pen, and sat down to start. I already had been thinking about it long before my talk with Vito this morning. I was anxious to see Isabella's take on these men. After all, she knew some of them a lot longer.

It did not take Isabella long. She folded the paper and held it in her hands. "Now you tell me why. And this is who I believe. Some of these men think differently of you. You are like their sister or little girl, for Christ's sake. I am only Dominic's wife. There is a big difference. I honestly will tell you my answers, but it will be different for the two of us. You have had a more intimate closeness than I do with the business and family all these years. I came into Dom's life later. You all have a long history."

I then took my paper out of my robe pocket and said, "Let me see yours first, okay?"

As simple as Isabella can be, she replied, "Are we playing doctor?" I broke up laughing, but she knew how to ease my stress. Isabella handed me her list. Listed from number one through seven, Isabella had Dominic, Vito, Pietro, Mano, Lorenzo, Salvi, and Don Lazzaro.

"I am surprised to see Dommy as number one, Isabella. Tell me, how did you come to this order?"

Isabella replied, "Dominic is number one for trust. He is my husband and, asshole or not, he does love me. Vito is number two because he is a loving and honest man, even in this life of ours. Number three is Pietro only because in Sicily you never hurt another's family. Besides, I know he always liked me just for myself, as a person. I think Pietro is honorable but maybe only here in Sicily. Okay, number four is Mano. He is a protector, a fighter, but I never could get close to him. He was always the enforcer and scared me a little. Where was I, oh yeah, number five is Lorenzo. Again, I do not have much contact with him except as my driver. He is harmless though. I would have no need to have to trust him, if you know what I mean. Number six is Salvi. I do not know him that well—again, no need to have to trust him. I have little contact with Salvi as he is usually in the States. And, last but certainly not least, the Don. He is old, and the reason I have him dead last is that he would go after Dominic in a New York minute. I would have him in that spot for that reason. I would not be worrying about myself, only my husband. Okay, give!" Isabella said.

I gave her my list. There indeed was a difference in our trust. Therefore, we did the exact same thing. "Tell me why," said Isabella.

So, I started, "Okay. I have Vito as my number one because he has been with me since I was a child and I've never feared him. He is loyal and more like family to me. I put Dom second because of what he did to Claudio. I have Mano at three because I do believe he would kill for me, enforcer or not. I have Salvi at four. He has been a friend with and without the families on both sides, personal and business in the States. He is trustworthy, loyal, and a confidant. Now, what is next, number five is Lorenzo. I agree with you he is a good man, somewhat slow, but definitely nothing to not trust about him. Pietro comes in at number six. I know he was a friend of Guido's, but that was a million years ago. I also know that he saved Luigi from God knows what. I trust him, but he is here in Sicily and I am in the States. I still do not feel like 'family' here, if you understand. And, dead last, like you, is the old Don. We only agreed on two, numbers five and seven. We should go to a casino or bet the numbers."

Both Isabella and I looked at the sheets and she said, "Elisabetta, this is what I meant. The only differences are where we live. Pietro would never make a move. Dom is number one as trust in the family business, not in his indiscretions. He is my husband. He would die for me. When you think about it, our lists, in their own way, are the same. Number one and two are the same, only reversed and for valid reasons."

I agreed and it helped me think straighter. I needed to apologize to Vito.

Chapter Twenty-One

Isabella and I were quietly thinking and heard a very light knocking on the door. I looked at Isabella, "It sounds like a child. I'll get it!" Isabella had turned to see who it was as I opened the door a crack. Of all people, it was Joey Thumbs.

Isabella flew up out of her chair and into the bedroom like a banshee, "Joey you have to be stupid! What the hell are you doing here?"

I pulled him inside the bedroom before anyone saw him. I was furious, "Talk Joey. What the hell are you trying to say to me?" Joey looked like a mouse caught as he stared worriedly at Isabella. "Don't worry about Isabella! You can trust her. Now, what the hell do you want—before Vito returns?" I asked.

"Sorry, signori, please, hear Joey. Only me want you speak Dominic. I no want be here. I want go America for work. I love girl and familgia make her go America school. I no can go from Pietro, only if work Dominic. If no, I die if leave familgia Sicily. I think you okay speak with. I think maybe I see her, if okay her, then I stay America. If she say no speak, no want, I return to Sicily. If I run, very bad to run from Pietro. Men come after me.

I no stupido. You help Joey?"

Isabella and I looked at each other, and she was the one to speak first. "Joey, so the problem is you love this girl who was sent to America, and you want to work for Dominic? Have you spoken to Pietro or the Don?"

Joey became nervous and said, "No, signora. I no can speak Pietro, only Dominic. Say he need for Joey to come. No problem Pietro." Joey then went on to speak the rest in Italian. How his family was all for him going to marry her. Joey also had the approval of her family in Sicily. However, since he was young he had worked for Don Lazzaro. Joey could only go to work with another family but not leave the 'businesses.' Isabella was explaining as Joey continued to talk too rapidly in Sicilian.

I became frightened for him and said, "Listen, Joey! You go now and we will talk of what we can do to help; but you cannot be here if Vito returns. Okay? You go now and we will talk later tonight at the party." Joey kissed our hands and backed out of the room. I was so relieved when he left. There was no one in the hallway. I turned to Isabella, "We have to help the poor sucker. What can we do?"

Isabella thought for a second and said, "We need to put our heads together on how to get Dom to request Joey from Pietro. Maybe Vito will help you?"

In the back of my mind, through all this new crap, I was thinking of the meeting with Don Lazzaro. Now what was that supposed to be about this morning? "Isabella," I pleaded, "please try to think this out alone this time. I have that second meeting with the old man this morning. I cannot take another thing on right now, okay?"

Isabella gave me a hug and said, "No problem. I will come up with something and I will keep you out of this. I will think of an excuse why I want Joey Thumbs. It keeps you safer and raises no suspicions from Pietro or the Don." I kissed Isabella as she left for her room. I had to be downstairs for a short meeting with all the men in ten minutes. I had no idea when I was to meet with Don Lazzaro alone.

As I was approaching the meeting room, Vito met me. "You okay, Missy?" He kissed me on the cheeks.

"Is it okay if I bitch a little in there and tell them I want to go home? I am tired of their faces!" I joked.

Vito took my arm and quietly said, "You need a good beating. Behave!"

As we entered, Vito pulled out my chair, and I said, "Buon giorno. I am sorry if I am late." They assured me that I was worth the short wait. I smiled so sweetly it upset my stomach. I had no idea why this meeting was called since I had completed my end of the work. I was hoping it was a little coffee-klatch.

As I looked around the room, I realized the Don was missing in action. I looked at Dominic and he winked. Okay, that did relax me a little. Should not be a problem; and, besides, Vito and Mano were sitting in the background. Pietro started the meeting. I was daydreaming a little when he called my name. "Elisabetta, we are meeting this morning for a short time. However, we decided this conference would continue for one more day, and Don Lazzaro would like to speak to you after this meeting. He is not well today and wants to remain this evening. Therefore, we will have a cocktail party tonight. I am sorry for any inconvenience. I know you wanted to leave for home. I hope everything is fine?"

I looked around the table and said, "No, I am fine with that. Thank you for your consideration." I was thinking to myself, You are going to get sick if you do not stop the nicety, nicety crap.

The rest of the hour meeting was horseshit that I really did not need to attend until Pietro asked me, "Elisabetta, have you decided who you will train for your well deserved retirement eventually?" I caught myself stuttering by that unexpected remark. I shot a look at Dominic! It surprised me that he did not drop dead on the scene, falling face first right into his pastry!

I started to sweat, dabbed my face with my napkin, and my stomach was killing me. I took a deep breath and answered, "Pietro, I haven't really decided yet only because I feel I have plenty of time. I do not plan to go anytime soon. As my broth-er Claudio always said, 'Heaven doesn't want me and the devil thinks I'll take over.'" With that all the men laughed.

Pietro saw I was flustered, "It is okay, Elisabetta. No prob-lems here, and we certainly do not want you to go anywhere! It was just brought up at one of our meetings. I was to present it to you. We certainly do not want to lose such a beautiful addition to our meeting table. Let us know whenever you are ready."

I just nodded my head and looked directly at Dominic. Did he start this crap at the meeting to force my hand again? At that exact second, I wished I had opened the box from Luigi. I now knew I would do just that when I returned home. There could have been something to use at this last meeting. My son was not getting involved! I did not care how many old farts in wheel-chairs came to the meeting!

Chapter Twenty-Two

When I was excused to visit with Don Lazzaro, Dominic motioned for Vito to go with me. However, Mano followed right behind, a little worrisome for me! As soon as we were out of hearing range, I asked, "Do either of you know who was the one questioning the work? Who asked Pietro to bring it up, do you know?" as I looked at both men.

Vito responded quietly, "We will talk later. And, I know you! It was not Dommy. Right now, get ready for Don Lazzaro. I have to do something quickly, but Mano will be right outside the door." Vito motioned for Mano to wait as we walked to Don Lazzaro's suite.

I looked at Vito and whispered, "It's like a virgin being taken for sacrifice to King Kong!"

Vito shook his head and said, "Oh, Dio mio!"

I gently tapped on the door and Joey opened it for me. Don Lazzaro was sitting up in bed, "Buon giorno, Elisabetta. Come." He patted the bed. Okay, I thought, if I want him to go quickly, I could get under the covers instead.

Behaving, I replied, "Buon giorno, Don Lazzaro, I hope you

feel better! I understand you need to speak with me?"

The Don snapped his fingers for Joey to leave us alone. I leaned down, kissed him on both cheeks, and he asked, "You like coffee, dolce?"

I responded as I patted his hand, "Grazie, no!"

Don Lazzaro sat quietly for a second and I thought, Please don't fall asleep or die now, I'd be blamed. He then spoke, "Mia mamma speak me, no use fighting life, life always win." I thought, What the hell does that mean? But, I smiled and shook my head as if I understood. He continued, "You! You fight life all time, si. I have in life, one time, many men of law look for me. Ahh, I was no good. Me luck good, a volte {sometimes}. Now no can fight more. No fight life, man. Per favore, Elisabetta, do for me when Stati Uniti?"

I answered, "Of course. What, Don Lazzaro?"

He took my hand and, in a demanding tone, replied, "You see box! No wait! You see pronto when return! You blood old like me!" That certainly rocked my head. Did he mean I was related somehow? God help me, I had enough nuts in my family tree! However, I nodded my head, yes.

Don Lazzaro rested a second and continued, "Ahh, Luigi, bravo! Today men idiota. No good! I remem you familgia you speak when baby. I no remem Lou! Other men you speak buona! You know who good, here." He pointed to my heart again. Okay, that was the second time he did that. Maybe the old man just liked cheap feels. However, I smiled and shook my head.

The Don shifted around in his bed and said, "When die me, I speak Pietro for familgia Sicily. Pietro bravo, you no afraid. I speak Pietro…who work you when no Lou? When you old?" I took from that conversation, Pietro would take over the families in Sicily. But Don was wondering who would take my job, or 'Lou's,' when he died. So, he was the one who put the bug in their ears.

I smiled, "Don Lazzaro, it makes me happy to know Pietro will be boss after you are gone. I trust Pietro in Sicily. He was a good friend of Luigi and Guido's. I am not afraid of Pietro. But, I do not know who will do this work. I thought I had time."

The old Don immediately said, "Si, si, si! No problem me. I want know now. You figlio {son}! You tell me?"

I could not resist, and the mother instinct in me rose like the hair on a cat's back, "That is a serious request!"

The Don came back, without blinking an eye, "I am serious man!"

I put my head down and slowly said, "I do not know, honestly. I have to think about it and speak with Lou. My training will help me get through it fine. I have had no problems all these years. I will make the right decision. I do not want you to worry about it." I tried to say this gently, as if I really gave a rat's ass what this old man thought.

"Elisabetta," the Don said in a weakened voice now. "I want man here, Sicily! No America!" There it was. The 'nasty' everyone was warning me about when the old man dies. Sicily wanted control over me or whoever might be doing the work. Not control in the States, as it always had been. They wanted all money transactions going through the family in Sicily and eliminating, one way or another, all my friends, and family, in the States. The old Don showed his hand, and I was more than pissed.

Vito was right! This old man was a fox. I did not intend to involve my personal family; however, I was not turning my back on the other family that had been close to me all my life. The old Don was screwing with the wrong person if he thought for one second I would abandon them. I would not leave either family out to dry.

The Don saw my anger on my face and said, "You open box. You then know who familgia."

I had to ask, "Don Lazzaro, do you know what is in that box?"

I felt he was not honest when he said, "No. I think then you know who work here or Stati Uniti when see. Blood first."

Okay, the Don was so sure I had bloodlines with him in

Sicily; he thought I would turn my back on the only family I had known in the States. He was underestimating me as a woman. Maybe a Sicilian woman could be talked into what she should do. I was not Sicilian—or at least I did not think I was. I would follow the rules, as always. The old Don could just go shit up a crooked stick; come to think of it, there was a horrible odor coming from under the sheets. It was then I asked if I could be excused. His response: "No, presto, wait!" as he tapped the bed again as if I was a lap dog to lie down and obey.

I had to sit for more than twenty minutes before realizing the Don was sound asleep. He had his hand over mine. I gently pulled my hand out so I could leave. Permission or not, I was not waiting around. He was not my boss, even though I had the feeling he thought he was. I walked quietly to the door and slide outside to the hallway. Mano was waiting as he promised. "You okay, Missy? No problem with Don?"

I rolled my eyes and said, "Yes. Problems up the ass. Where is Vito?"

Mano answered, "I'll go find him. You go to your room."

I closed my bedroom door and Isabella came in from the balcony. "Boy, you look like you could use a drink! How did it go? Rough, huh? I can tell by the look on your face. Do you want me to call Dom or Vito?" asked Isabella.

"Mano went to find Vito. They should be here soon. What a cluster F that was! That old fart is conniving. Let's pay Carla to put something in his meds!" I joked.

Just then, Vito knocked and asked, "Okay if Mano and I come in?" Vito immediately came to me, put his hands on my shoulders, and said, "You look like a bag of ugly fell on your head! Talk to me, you have to trust me!"

I then apologized about the conversation earlier, "Of course I trust you, Vito. God!"

Mano then chimed in, "I can just go across the staircase and drill a hole in the old man's ass if you like?"

Vito looked at him to go away. Mano kissed me on both cheeks and left the room. Vito made me sit down and asked

Isabella to call for food and drinks. "Do you want Dom in this conversation, Missy? It is entirely up to you. I am okay with it," said Vito.

"I think that is a good idea." I answered. I already, unconsciously, knew what family I would go with if push came to shove.

The trays arrived from the kitchen right before Dommy walked in the room. "Mano just said I might be needed here. What happened Missy? You don't look very well."

I had to smile, "All these compliments will give me a big head. You are the third person in this room who said I looked like hell. Knock it off!"

Chapter Twenty-Three

Isabella was busy making drinks. Vito and Dommy pulled up chairs to the sofa. When she brought the drinks to us, Dom asked her to leave the room. I was mad, "Absolutely **not**, Dom. Isabella is to stay. This is going to stop. I am going to tell her everything from now on anyway, so get over it."

Dommy, of course, came right back at me, "I can carry any problems you have. No need to involve Isabella."

I smiled, patted his leg, and said, "The only thing you can carry is an over inflated ego, Dommy. Isabella has always been your strength."

For once Dommy agreed, "You are right, Missy. There is no need for Isabella to leave. It is hard to get over the old ways. Come on, tell us about the meeting!"

"First, Dom," I asked, "who was the one at your meeting who questioned Lou, my work, and who would take over?"

Dom answered quickly, "It was Don Lazzaro. He could not accept the fact you, a woman, were at the meeting and not Lou. He requested Pietro to question you this morning. Vito and I were annoyed that the Don never asked us about your business.

He cut us right out of the conversation. That was a show of disrespect. That part of the business has always, all our lives, been handled at our end. Pietro even apologized after the old man left!"

I then filled them in on my end of the meeting, "The Don wants me to use a man in Sicily to run the business instead of the United States. I have the feeling he also wants to appoint a man for me to teach. Pietro will head the families when the old man dies. He questioned the box Luigi kept for me and what was in it. He asked me to open it as soon as I returned to the States, before I make up my mind about my end of the work, as if the Don suspected what it might contain. He told me I was blood, whatever that means, in Sicily. In a sly, around about way, the Don was asking me to choose a family for the business. The other bad thing was, he mentioned having my son continue. I told him I had to speak with Lou, that I was not ready to think about that right now and had no plans to quit soon."

Dom sat back in the chair and said, "So, the old man wants it done and done huh?" I had not heard Dommy say that for a long time. 'Done and done' was usually followed with some kind of big trouble!

Vito spoke, "Listen, Dom, at least we know what is in the old man's mind. We can plan for this and keep Missy safe at the same time. Now you and I need to have a meeting with Mano, Salvi, and the other guys before we leave here. Who knows, maybe Pietro. We will have to feel that one out a little."

Vito looked at me and said, "I promise, we leave here tomorrow. Just hang in there one more night. Dommy and I will handle some damage control and get our minds together. You pack up before the party and dinner. Isabella, are you staying upstairs now?" Isabella assured him she was hanging out with me. Vito and Dommy left to handle God knows what!

I looked at Isabella and we both came to the same conclusion. "That is the perfect solution for Joey Thumbs. He can move to our family and use the excuse to train him for the job. Although, that is entirely out of the question. However, Don

Lazzaro and Pietro do not need to know." I said to Isabella.

"That is exactly what just went through my mind. Now you and I need to have a little meeting before the dinner party," agreed Isabella.

Whenever Isabella and I put our heads together, it never took as long as the men. We had a plan worked out within an hour. To think that old fart thinks women are not good for the meetings. He would not know what hit him! However, we both knew we had to run the plan past Vito and Dom before tonight.

Then the real problem hit: I only had one dress for a party. The red dress I wore the first night. Isabella and I had given back the other designer dresses.

Isabella announced, "We can kill two birds with one stone. I will ask permission for Joey Thumbs to take us to my casa. We can get two dresses for tonight and have time to speak to Joey before we are noticed at the party." I agreed with her, but we needed to talk to Vito and Dom before Joey. "You start to pack; I'll get it straightened out and be right back. It feels good to be doing something, instead of you doing everything all these years," Isabella said excitedly.

Before I had time to finish packing, Isabella and I were on our way to her casa with Joey driving. At Isabella's home, we told Joey what we hoped would work. We asked if he was willing to go along with the plan. Joey was more than thrilled and said he would do anything he could to live in America. We had set our plan in motion. We left Isabella's with clothes in hand. I had taken a sapphire blue gown and Isabella an off-white one.

The dinner party was as usual. We would mingle and be perfectly behaved. Don Lazzaro made it this time, and I was very surprised to see Mike still there. Right before we were to sit for dinner, Mike approached me, "Quite a few people here, at one time or another, were on the most wanted list. Were you aware of that?" he asked.

I ignored his comment and instead answered, "I am surprised you are still here. I thought you said you wanted to see the sights?"

Mike came back again with a come-on remark, "I kind of like the sights I have beside me, thank you!"

I said, "Thank you. But, really, why are you still here, may I ask?"

Mike replied, "You never know where you will see me again, at a meeting, or an airplane, or from the looks of this gang here, a courtroom! I need to catch a smoke before dinner!"

I smiled through my teeth and said, "Those things will kill you. Give them up!" Mike just smiled and walked away. I did not like Mike!

Dinner was wonderful, but I noticed the Don barely ate and excused himself to go to his suite. Pietro snapped for the servers and requested the Don had coffee, water, or whatever else, delivered to his suite. As Frankie Tomatoes helped him from the table, every man stood. Isabella and I did not! After Don Lazzaro left the room, Pietro announced there would be a short meeting for last minute business with the family from America. He then promised everyone it would not take long. I looked at Dommy and he shook his head no. What a relief. I did not have to attend.

Isabella and I left for my suite; however, we were not alone long. Dommy and Vito entered and said, "The meeting is in fifteen minutes for only Pietro and our guys. No others were invited. We are going to approach Pietro about your work, Missy." Just then I had to tell them about Joey Thumbs, the whole story of why he wanted to come to America, how we were going to say it was to learn my books, however, never really giving him any information. Joey would only know one small job of the entire transactions, be a decoy of sorts. This would appease Sicily and keep the business where it is supposed to be, with Dom. It was a real cliff note of the whole story, but Vito and Dom got the picture. They would handle it at the meeting and congratulated us on our plan.

When they left, Isabella was in shock. "That is the first time, except what you, me and your friends did to bring down my lovable husband that I actually got to do something. I loved it. That is exactly what I need. I need to be involved," said Isabella. She had no idea I was planning on her becoming very involved. That was for another night. This day and night had enough in it to deal with.

What was that saying I learned as a young girl, about waiting for the other shoe to fall? I was just about finished with most of the packing when Vito came to the door. "Missy, I am sorry. Pietro would like you to step into the meeting for a few minutes only. However, you have to follow Dominic's lead, okay? Apparently, Pietro trusts you more than Pietro trusts any of us here. Think you can do this?"

All I could say was, "I want to go home, dammit!"

Chapter Twenty-Four

As I entered the small library room, all my 'friends' were there. The only person from the Sicily family was Pietro. "Thank you so much, Elisabetta. I am sorry to have you return tonight at such a late hour. May I get you something?" asked Pietro as he pulled out a chair for me.

I smiled and answered, "No, thank you, Pietro. What is it you want from me?"

Pietro looked directly into my eyes and said, "What is said now stays here, but I am sure you know that rule by now!"

I laughed as I said, "My dad's favorite warning to us as children!"

Pietro settled into a chair and started, "Dominic and I have made decisions about the business you handle. I know what Don Lazzaro would like to see happen, but he has never worked with you over all these years. I know better in this particular situation than he does. I have no problem with the way things have been done. We have had no problems. Dom and I have made the decision without Don Lazzaro. Of course, we want your input and approval of these decisions. Is that okay with you? If there are any questions afterward, please tell us here behind these closed doors."

I nodded yes as I looked toward Dominic.

Pietro continued, "The Don is totally against your work staying with Dominic. We have come up with a few solutions, until the time comes when I will take the position of Don in Sicily. First, we would like Joey Thumbs to move to America with Dominic and work with you on the books. I have talked to Joey; but the Don has not given his permission yet. You let Joey know as much or as little as you wish. Or, nothing at all. That is totally your call. I understand Joey's problem with his love for this girl. In my life, I have been exactly in that position Both families here have given blessings. It is Don Lazzaro standing in the way. Joey has gone to talk with the Don now and beg for his permission. Assuming Joey goes with you, and that friend of yours who was doing work with Dominic, what's his name?"

Dominic answered before I could, "Sergio. His name is Sergio!" I thought I would get sick. I did not plan for this! Was this Dommy's way of getting Sergio out of my life?

"Yes," said Pietro, "Sergio will work for me in Italy. He will be protected as I was told you have feelings for him!" Again, I felt sick. How could Dominic just speak about my personal life that way? However, I did bring Sergio into this mess when I brought Dommy to his knees. Was this Dominic's way of getting even? I had to speak my mind!

"Excuse me, Pietro, may I say something?" I asked.

Pietro nodded, "Certainly, Elisabetta, you know that. Go ahead!" There goes that mouth of mine again, I thought.

"Well, I would like to know is this a form of power struggle? I do not like these power struggles between the families, especially if I am in the middle. It seems the universe tosses them at me on a regular basis, but I have learned how to defend myself lately, as Dominic will testify after the meeting last year. I try to remember this when people enjoy pushing my buttons. If this is some ploy to use my friends as a pawn over me, I will fight it!" I continued.

As I was talking, Vito was slowly walking to stand behind

me. Dominic looked annoyed, but mostly hurt over my statement. Pietro spoke, "Elisabetta, I told you before, your personal business is yours alone. I will not interfere if it is personal; however, if it involves another person in either family, I feel we must talk about it."

I sat for only a second and retaliated, "Let me get this straight. If I see Sergio, who is only a friend, I have problems with you, Pietro. I have Dominic telling me I cannot leave my husband because he knows too much! What was that all about a few years ago, Dominic, scaring me when I filed for divorce? I only wanted to keep my husband safe, but it wrecked Roberto and I wound up going back to him to hurt him more. Was that a test? I did all that for a test? Now both of you are trying to make me believe all this is my choice. You will not interfere with my personal life? That is a laugh! It is exactly what both of you are doing and I don't like it!" Vito put his hand on my shoulder, but I was not going to shut up now!

I continued. "I am so far up the creek without a paddle with you two, and I cannot swim! What is next? You are going to tell me how to run Lou's end of the business. I would never use Joey Thumbs to do a thing involved with me. I will not mess with what works, the number one rule to remember. In addition, while I am on a roll here, how do I know my family will be left alone? If I decide to work with you, Pietro, what insurance do I have that my family will be safe? I have everyone in Sicily except the street cleaner telling me to 'get out of the business,' to 'save my family,' to 'protect them even if I have to leave them'! What do all these people know that I don't?"

Vito again put his hand on my shoulder and squeezed slightly, but he would have to hit me with a stick to shut me up. I was getting angrier. "After all these years, especially now at my age, you all should know I refuse to have someone control me with threats; it only manages to really piss me off! The one thing that seems to slip everyone's mind here is you need me—I do not need you! I will do my job, as I always have with never making a mistake, and pass it on to whomever I want when, and only when, it is necessary. You can ship a boatload of young men to America with Dominic 'for the business,' but it is my call. In the end, it is my call only!"

Pietro said to everyone, "Let's just take a little break. We will continue this in half hour. Okay, Elisabetta? I just want you to calm down before we continue. You are absolutely correct in what you just said to us. I just think we need a little break for now. Vito, go with Elisabetta!"

Vito and I walked around the veranda for quite a while before I apologized, "I am sorry Vito. I was supposed to follow Dominic's lead and I blew it!"

Vito smiled and replied, "Missy, we do know you after all these years. Dommy and I knew exactly what your reaction would be to Pietro's requests. And, as usual, you came through with flying colors. It was exactly the retaliation we expected from you, and it was perfect!"

I was in shock. I thought for sure Vito was going to read me the riot act. Vito and I sat down and he continued, "However, however, I say, when we get back in that meeting, go with your gut again. But, please and try to follow a little of Dominic's lead, okay? The meeting is going exactly the way we want it to. Pietro thinks the world of you, even more so, it seems, the past few years! He will go along with whatever you decide for your end of the business. Remember that, okay?"

Vito and I were walking back to meet again with Pietro. Joey Thumbs came running out of nowhere and almost knocked us down. Joey was moving damn fast to make Vito rock a little on his feet! "What! Joey, what the hell…!" yelled Vito. Joey tried to run and Vito grabbed him with one hand, "Okay, Joey. What the hell is up? Who are you running from?"

Joey kept looking behind him, visibly shaken. I said, "Vito let me! Joey, look at me. What happened? Whatever it is, Vito and I will help. You do not want to screw things up now when you are so close to leaving here. Tell us." I pleaded.

Vito grabbed Joey by the arm and we went under the veranda where no one could see us. Vito put a tighter hold on Joey and demanded, "Speak, dammit!"

Joey was stammering, "I ask Don. I beg him. Don want Joey stay Sicily. I say no! Don no like. He speak me, get Carla. Don malato {sick}. I say, no! I say, Don say me yes, then I speak Carla. I no want Don morire {die}. I wait long and Don no speak. Don morto adesso!"

I knew those words as I looked at Vito, "The Don is dead now?"

Vito shook Joey. "Did anyone see you with Don Lazzaro?"

Joey shook his head no and said, "I go. No person find!"

Vito sternly said, "How far do you think you will get? You won't make it off the grounds. It was not your fault. The old man was sick. Joey, look at me! You are going to go back to the Don's room and find him dead in bed. That is all you will say. He died when he slept. Capito {Understood}. Joey, you have to do this, or no America. It was not your fault."

It had crossed my mind that Joey could have killed the old man; however, I then had to intervene my two cents as my mind was wheeling, "Vito, no! Joey has to be with us, here, outside. Let Carla find the Don when she goes for his medication. Didn't Pietro just say Joey was asking the Don's permission? It would look too suspicious if the Don died with Joey in the room. Let someone else find the Don, and Joey was with us," I repeated.

Vito took a step back, a deep sigh, and said, "You are right, Missy. Joey, you walk in with us so everyone sees you. You were with us this past half hour. It will be okay! Do not worry!"

Vito, Joey, and I then walked back to the meeting room. Fortunately, everyone was milling around. Of course they turned when I entered after my hissie fit. At least they saw Joey with us. Pietro approached. "You ready, Elisabetta? You okay to finish? It's okay if you need more time!" I thanked him and said everything was fine.

"Let's get it 'done and done' as Dommy always says." I smiled as it occurred to me that Dommy always said that when ready to choke someone.

Pietro then asked Joey to check on the Don. As fate would

have it, Carla excused herself as she climbed the stairs, "That is okay, Joey. I am taking Don Lazzaro his medication." Vito and I stepped aside to speak a second as everyone entered the meeting room. Joey took off almost at a run, probably to hide.

"Vito" I said, "It is better this way. Joey is young, and we can keep him in line with this little bit of guilt. It wasn't his fault the Don is dead but Joey feels responsible." Vito nodded his head and we entered the meeting.

We did not have time to get comfortable when we heard Carla yelling for Pietro. She then went off speaking in Italian, screaming at the same time. I never saw a room clear as quickly as then. A few of the men had their guns drawn. I sat very still away from the stampede. It was like two tons of men trying to get through the doorway. Dominic looked suspiciously at Vito and me as he tagged behind. I whispered, "You go, Vito. Everyone will wonder why you stayed." Vito left behind Dominic, and I slowly moved towards my bedroom suite.

Chapter Twenty-five

As I approached my door, Isabella came running out of her room. "Elisabetta, is everyone okay? What happened? Is Dominic hurt?"

I grabbed her by the arm and pulled her inside. I could not help myself, "Isabella, another fucking meeting, another fucking death! I am beginning to feel I am the black cloud! The Don is dead! But we aren't supposed to know that yet. Wait until Dominic and Vito return." Isabella was confused, and I think she believed I had something to do with it. I could tell by the look on her face. "Isabella! Don't even think it! I will explain later. I have a lot more people on my list who need to go way before the Don!"

Then it hit me like a ton of bricks. I would not be able to go home now until after this funeral. "Isabella, I guess we have to stay another day, huh?"

Isabella rubbed my back and said, "Looks that way, honey, unless the old man is playing possum. However, you know it is only one or two days until it is over. I am sorry, honey! But, I am glad you are in Sicily, because now the shit will hit the fan.

Did the meeting go without any problems?"

I laughed, "Plenty of problems, and then the old man picks tonight to die, God forgive me." I blessed myself.

There was a knock on the door and Isabella opened to see Vito. "You two okay?" he asked as he stepped inside my room.

I whispered, "Vito, what is happening? Is Don Lazzaro dead?"

Vito acknowledged that by nodding his head, "They are waiting for the priest and doctor right now. Nevertheless, the old man is definitely dead. He has no family, so Pietro will handle the funeral. I am sorry, Missy; you know we have to stay for this!"

I shook my head disgustedly. Vito continued, "It couldn't have come at a better time. Don Lazzaro was over one hundred years old. It was his time! That is life. But, Pietro will be in charge. It is a whole other baseball game now." I looked at Vito with sadness over his talking about a person dying with such a matter of fact attitude. Nevertheless, Don Lazzaro certainly had lived a full life. I still blessed myself anyway!

Dommy then walked in. "They are preparing the body now before the doctor gets here. The priest is with him now. Pietro is handling everything, but apparently the old man already planned his funeral about twenty years ago. He had a mausoleum built, a casket picked out, and the whole nine yards. We have to go soon and pay respects!"

I was shocked, "You mean we have to go into that bedroom and see his dead body?"

Vito patted my back and replied, "It's not as if you haven't seen about a thousand already in your lifetime. It will be fine. We four will go together. Missy, this is going to be a lot different from Luigi. The old man does not want to burn. They will bury him in the mausoleum. He is going to hell anyway."

Mano called my room and Vito answered, "Hey, V, you can come to the Don's room now. Are you with Dominic?"

Vito answered, "Yes. We will be right there!"

I grabbed Isabella's hand and said, "I wish I didn't have to go through this!"

Isabella replied, "Just hang onto me. You are more used to this than me." I had to shake my head. How can anyone ever get used to this? We left the room, Isabella and I following Dommy and Vito.

I never had seen an actual funeral in Sicily. Since Luigi was cremated, after we viewed him there was only a memorial. This was certainly different. As we four entered the bedroom of Don Lazzaro, there were many people just sitting and standing around. I remember walking on something crunchy under my feet. A priest had just finished giving last rites. I thought at least this way it would not take twenty years for the confession. Don Lazzaro, I was sure, had a lot to confess.

Isabella and I stood in the background. Vito and Dominic went to the Don's bedside, kissed him on both cheeks and his hand, blessed themselves, and walked back to us. Dominic said, "You two go now! Just kiss him on his forehead, bless yourself, and back away."

However, when Isabella and I approached, I was shocked to see there was a bowl of salt on his chest, sprinkled around his body, and on the sills of every window. That was probably what I stepped on when I entered. I looked at Isabella, did what we were told, and returned to Vito and Dominic.

Vito knew me and said, "Don't even ask. I will tell you later".

I, however, never listen. I whispered, "Isn't it too late to have him pickled? Don is over one hundred years old!"

Vito whispered, "The salt is on the heart, all around his body, and at every opening throughout the villa, to prevent any evil spirits from entering him. We believe a soul is vulnerable between death and burial and needs to be protected from attack of evil spirits."

I replied, "He already is an evil spirit!"

Vito looked at Dominic and said, "Andiamo" {Let us go}! He held onto my arm.

Outside the room, I quietly said, "What did I do?"

Vito shook his head and said, "Dio mio! Missy, this is going to be a big deal. His funeral will be very public. Everyone will come. We have to go to Mass, drive around Sicily, all before the Don can be buried."

He could tell by the look on my face, I was not a happy camper. Vito said, "I know, I know. But, we have no choice. Everyone will stay and probably a lot more will be showing up."

I had to joke, as I always do, to keep my sanity, "I am running out of underwear!"

Isabella cracked up and Dom said, "V, let's get these two to the room and you and I will take care of business. And, you both have to wear all black until we leave here! And no make up!"

I looked at Isabella and could not resist. "That should kill a few more people before we leave!"

After the men left us, Isabella and I had to make another trip to her house. Joey was more than happy to escort us! "I like this kind of shopping," I laughed to Isabella. "Just shop at Isabella's Closet. My daughter, Sheri, does the same thing, especially when I am away. She crosses the street and shops at Mom's Closet." We again left with clothes in hand. I had a long black sweater dress with matching coat. Isabella had a one-piece dress, which she called her funeral dress. We returned to Pietro's before anyone knew we were gone!

Chapter Twenty-Six

When the Don was prepared, whatever the hell that meant, Isabella, and I were commanded to stay in our rooms. This was only a man's time to respect the Don. Women were not included. I had to laugh at Isabella when she said to Dominic, "Don't get any ideas from this old tradition when we return to our *casa,* or I will be pouring salt around your sorry ass!" It did not matter to either of us though; we had more time to spend alone just talking and relaxing.

After a few hours, Vito called my room and said we should be ready the next morning at six to leave for the church. After I hung up, I told Isabella, "They must be trying to sneak the old man into church before God awakens. Why so early?"

Isabella said it would be a packed Mass and then the long ride following the hearse around Sicily would be an all day event. Isabella and I spent the rest of the night sitting outside and talking about everything over the years, my brother Claudio, my children, Guido, Gemma, my friends, and her family. It was peaceful, but I wanted to go home.

The next morning, it did not take long to get ready since I did not have to apply makeup. But it was scary, and certainly something I never do. Venture outside without my face on! Vito knocked on my door, and I met the three of them in the hallway. "What now?" I asked everyone.

Dominic answered, "We see the Don again. He is in the casket and ready to go. This is one last visit of respect. There were a hell of a lot of people filing through all night. We then go to Mass!"

When the four of us approached the casket, it was magnificent. It had to cost tens of thousands of dollars. The lining looked like liquid gold. Don Lazzaro was in a black suit, a red rose in his lapel, and looked a lot younger than his one hundred-some years. I saw Dominic and Vito both put Euro into his jacket pocket. I leaned over to Isabella and said, "The angels must not be coming for the Don, I guess he has to take a taxi!" Isabella took out her handkerchief as if she was crying so no one saw her laugh.

Dom told us to go with Joey and wait outside. Vito and Dominic would be out shortly. Apparently, both of them, along with Orlando, Matteo, Pietro, Mano, Lorenzo, and Trieste, were pallbearers. When Isabella and I stood near the car, I said, "The Don weighs about fifty pounds with his clothes on. These eight men together could move the Leaning Tower of Pisa. Why so many?" I asked.

Isabella said, "Another sign of respect. These are the men that the Don handpicked and trusted completely to safely deliver him to his final resting place. The Don had all this written down. They will be along. We have to walk behind until the Don is put in the hearse."

I looked around and there were so many women, all in black, crying, covering their mouths, some beating on their chests. Isabella said, "Dear Lord!" as she fumbled in her handbag! Put this on your head." She handed me a black lace doily and I did as I was told.

Up until that point, I could not imagine why the women were staring at us. We needed to cover our heads. I then asked

Isabella, "What about the red Italian horns they all have?" These other women had these enormous red horns around their necks or pinned onto their coats.

The men finally came out of the Villa, black bands on their arms, and Don in hand. However, the funeral car was parked about a block away. Everyone then touched the casket as it passed by. Isabella quietly said, "Just follow me. Do as I do and we will get out of this alive."

Everyone followed behind until the casket was in the hearse. We then all walked back to the cars to follow. Isabella and I got in the back of the car, and I was wondering who would be driving. "Isabella, in the States, sometimes the women drive the cars if their husbands are pallbearers."

Isabella smiled, "Not in Sicily, God forbid! Dom and Vito will be here soon."

As Vito drove at two miles an hour behind the Don's hearse, it took us forever, as many people had to touch the car. We stopped at two or three piazzas where more mourners joined, walking behind the cars to the church. Dominic was explaining everything to me as we drove.

This was a very public funeral, and when we entered the church, it was standing room only. Isabella and I followed to the second row and slid into the pew. "Stay standing!" whispered Isabella.

I whispered back, "Either Don Lazzaro was very popular or everyone was scared to death not to show up!"

Isabella answered, "Mostly the second thing!"

What amazed me the most about this Mass was an outside person would think this was the holiest man in Sicily, not a man who was on the most wanted list at one time or another. I was thinking to myself, Be a real bastard, do rotten things all your life, and you get a Mass like this? Only in Italy! I wondered how much the Don donated to the church all his life in order to have this grand good-bye. As I looked around the church, not one person was dressed in anything other than black. Isabella's bright red hair and my blond hair, even with the doilies, stuck out like sore thumbs.

Finally, the Mass was over; however, we had the long ride again through the streets on the way to his mausoleum. I could not believe the size of this monstrosity, and of course, it was the biggest in the cemetery! It was bigger than some homes we passed. I said to Dominic, "Why didn't the Don just build a pyramid and take everything with him?"

Vito had to laugh a little, "As powerful as the Don was here in Sicily, he hated bugs and anything that crawled. Can you imagine that?"

What a spectacle with some of the women dropping to their knees and wailing as if Don Lazzaro was their long lost child. "What is that all about?" I asked Vito.

Vito said, "Most people in this part of the town owed much to Don Lazzaro. He kept them working, helped them with any problems, paid for doctors, hospitals. He was not all bad, Missy! Pietro will have some shoes to fill with the people here. Don Lazzaro was here before half of them were even born! I'm old, and he was in charge before me!"

Chapter Twenty-Seven

On the way back to Pietro's, I asked Vito and Dominic when I could leave. Isabella answered, "Elisabetta, now there is a feast. Every person you saw along the way, at the house, and in the church, will bring food to the house. And don't forget, we cannot take off the black!"

I answered, "I am going to have to buy another seat on the airplane, Vito, like you. This eating all the time has to stop!"

Vito smiled through the rearview mirror and said, "In Sicily you look like you have one of those eating problems. You are too thin now!"

I grabbed Isabella's hand and said, "I knew I loved that guy!"

Well, Vito was right on the money. Whatever kind of meat, seafood, vegetable, salads, pasta, pastry, or fruit you could imagine was showing up at Pietro's door. Most people only stayed a few seconds and left, backing out of the door, as Pietro personally thanked them all.

I also noticed that the men kissed Pietro's hand. I had to smile as I said to Isabella, "I thought that was only in the movie Godfather that it was done!"

Isabella knew I felt out of place and came back with her

usual joke, "Dominic one time told me I had to kiss his hand. I told him to kiss my ass! But I might have like that, not the kissing his hand, the kissing of my ass!"

We sat like perfectly behaved women, crossing our legs at the ankles, and nibbling on small pieces of food until Pietro approached us. "I thank both of you for all your respect. Elisabetta, thanks to you for putting up with the old traditions; but, we have a few minute meeting left. Vito informed me you would leave very early tomorrow. I am very happy you were here for this and met Don Lazzaro!"

As Pietro kissed Isabella and me on the cheeks, I asked jokingly, "Do I kiss your hand now, Pietro?"

His answer was surprising, "Elisabetta, you never have to kiss my hand. It should be the other way around. You two can sneak away if you want now. I know you are dying to go! Go ahead! Elisabetta, I'll see you shortly before you leave." Pietro then turned and snapped at Joey Thumbs, as Joey moved quickly to Pietro. "Walk these beauties to their suites, Joey. Return here so we can talk!"

When we reached our suites, Joey kissed Isabella on the cheeks and he turned to me, "Joey much thank you!" as he kissed my hand.

Isabella joked as Joey left, "I am insulted. You and I are going to talk now. Get on your bathing suit, and I'll meet you in the Jacuzzi outside on your balcony."

What bathing suit? I thought. Okay, there is a first for everything as I kept on my underwear and bra. Isabella laughed when she approached the Jacuzzi with her towel. "You are a prude! You need to take some lessons from Chezi!"

I poured champagne for both of us and matter-of-factly answered, "You are my friend. I do not want to blind you and have to pray to Saint Lucy! Anyway, this covers more than that dental floss you have on!"

As we relaxed and enjoyed the hot water, I asked Isabella, "How long have you and Dommy been married now?"

Isabella took a large gulp of the champagne and smiled, "It

will be forty years soon. Can you just imagine that! I did not try to kill Dominic in all that time! It amazes me what control I have!"

I knew it was long before Roberto and I but had not realized it was shortly after I took over the business for my dad. "We go back a long way, Isabella." I answered. "Pour me another, too, please! So, I guess you and Dommy are in for the long haul, huh?"

Isabella stuck her finger in her glass, thinking, and replied, "After all these years, Dom is starting to come around. I waited too long to hand him over when I, or we I should say, got all his wrinkles ironed out!"

My mind then drifted to what I was going to do with my marriage to Roberto. I absolutely had no idea! I certainly was seeing a change in Roberto, and for the good. And then there was Sergio. I had to handle that problem before leaving Italy. I asked for the whole bottle of champagne!

"Isabella, I have been toying with an idea but am not sure yet if that is the way I want to go. This is in regards to my end of the business. I might want to talk to you soon and get your input. Is that okay?" I asked.

Isabella started singing a real oldie as she answered, "Anytime, you're feeling lonely, anytime you're feeling blue...."

I closed my eyes, drank straight from the bottle, and laughed, "Isn't there a radio here or something else for music!"

Again, when Isabella and I finally went to our suites and to bed, I am not sure if it was the events of the day, too much champagne, or that my mind was like sponge cake again, I woke up by the freezing coldness and my 'friend.' This time I sat up in bed and he was just standing alongside. I said sleepily, "I hope you are my old friend and not Don Lazzaro. I have enough visitors without his starting too!"

My head hurt from the champagne and I tried to clear my mind. Whatever he wanted to say, I needed to think a hell of a lot clearer than at that moment. I yawned and asked, "What? Let's see, now. It could be about the old Don, Pietro, my meetings, Roberto, Sergio, my job, pick one please, and let me get back to sleep!" I was being a smart-ass, and I immediately said, "I'm sorry!" Now I knew I was a bona fide nut case! I was apologizing to a spirit for hurting his feelings. Where are my meds?

I pulled my knees to my chin and sat for a moment to attempt to gain some control over my head. My old, friendly, spook, father, whatever he was, did not leave. I panicked a little and asked, "Not my family, please!" However, I knew instantly, somehow, it had nothing to do with them, and quietly said aloud, "Thank God. Okay, give me a hint!"

The room became colder and I pulled the covers up to my shoulders. "Well, you didn't warn me about the Don's death; I did not see you at any meetings; it must have to do with Roberto, Sergio, or that Mike character, right? Or maybe me?" Just then, my 'friend' touched his eyes and held out his hand; it was red, like blood, and vanished. I then knew whatever the problem was had to do with my eyes. I put my hands over my eyes and said, "Shit!"

I did not sleep the entire night. I kept thinking that before I left for Italy I had wanted to go to the eye doctor. Those fibromyalgia eye migraines were too often. I was tired of buying the drugstore glasses and knew it was time for the glaucoma tests. It was not that I had a problem seeing distances; however, I did need glasses for reading. I did not want to make a mistake on the books, God forbid! I just never took the time. I knew, after my little visit, I definitely would see an optometrist when I returned to the States.

I decided to call Gracie and talk to her. She'd had the problems with her eyes for years because of the aneurysm. Maybe she could ease my mind. I felt relief when she answered as it wasn't too late in the States. "Honey, I have been worried about you," she said. "I was hoping you would check in with me. How is everything? When will you get home?"

We talked for a while, and then I told Gracie of my visitor. After describing the pains in the eyeballs, which I realized unconsciously I had had for quite a while, Gracie became concerned.

"Maybe that is why you get those 'lightening bolt eye pains' instead of headaches," Gracie said. "You thought they were from the fibromyalgia, but maybe they are not, Elisabetta. When you return I will go to my eye doctor with you. He is the best, and you have it checked out. That will ease your mind as well as mine!" I agreed and asked Gracie to set up an appointment a few days after I returned home.

I then decided to call Gypsie to see if she knew what was going on with Sergio. I was lucky to call when Gina was visiting. "We were just talking about you!" said Gypsie.

I cut her short and asked, "What is going on with Sergio, do you know?"

Gypsie said, "I talked to Momma yesterday. The family knows you are in Italy, so I would imagine Giovina has the poor sucker chained in a dark basement somewhere! Why? Are you worried?"

I told both Gypsie and Gina what had happened with the Don dying and about my visitor. It was Gina who went off, as usual, "That black-capped bastard should go somewhere and jump some woman's bones, literally speaking. I always worry about you alone in Italy let alone his tagging along. And, on top of all that, another man dies? When you get home, Gypsie and I will take the evil eye off you. And a nice bath in holy water wouldn't hurt either."

Chapter Twenty-Eight

The next morning, the phone woke me, "*Buon giorno, amica mia*," cheerfully said Isabella. "Our presence is requested for breakfast in the dining room before we all leave. Are you ready?" I grunted, and Isabella laughed, "Okay, I'll give you thirty minutes tops and then I'll be over, ready or not!" I pulled my sorry ass out of bed and was ready on time. I was anxious to go home.

True to her word, Isabella knocked on the door in exactly thirty minutes. As I opened it I said, "You are a pain in my ass! Do not get like Dommy, or I will have you put to sleep. How can you be so cheery every single morning?"

She grabbed me, kissed me on both cheeks, and said, "I just got laid!"

I looked directly at her and said, "Bitch! Number one, with Dommy—yuck; and number two, go ahead rub it in!"

We joined Dommy, Vito, Mano, and Pietro in the dining room. Pietro wished us good morning and signaled for Carla to bring us juice and coffee. Pietro then said, "Elisabetta, we only need to talk for a few minutes. Is right now okay?"

Before Dommy could say a word, I responded, "Isabella stays!"

Dommy looked at Pietro and said, "Missy doesn't do mornings very well!"

Pietro smiled at me, "The way the meeting ended, with the Don's death, you were having a problem with us. So, if you would let me tell you the plan before you yell, I would really appreciate it." Pietro then pointed to Carla and said, "Lots of coffee, please, and something sweet with chocolate!" I was surprised Pietro remembered.

When Carla came over with coffee, I said, "Carla, I am sorry for yesterday. I feel terrible that you had to find the Don. Are you okay?"

Dommy looked at Pietro and said, "See, Missy's coming along now! Coffee and something sweet brings a smile to her face!"

Carla smiled at me and said, "Thank you. I was afraid, but I have seen many men dead. It is a way of life here!" She then left quickly.

I could not resist, "I heard you, Dom! Maybe that is why I don't smile at you! I need something sweet!"

Isabella and the men cracked up as Dommy smiled at me and replied, "V, what did I say, smart asses, all of them!"

A few minutes later, Pietro went over the plan. Vito was right. My little fit before Carla found the Don dead went exactly the way it should have. It could not have unfolded any better if we planned it ourselves. Joe Thumbs would come to the States under the assumption that I would involve him in my work. Not! I thought to myself. The business would be entirely up to me, with no interferences from Italy or the States! That was a demand and not a suggestion. Both Pietro and Dominic agreed. I had done a wonderful job so far and for many years. They did not plan to interfere with my system or ask me to hand it over.

I knew what I was going to do with my system and who would be my second trusted person with the job. I was thrilled that I did not have to reveal any of my plans. That would take quite a while, and I was not ready at this second. I had plenty of things to handle at home. This alleviated a lot of stress for me. At least for the time being. Further down the road, with my plan, the crap would hit the fan again. As usual, I smiled okay to everything Pietro said and planned to do whatever I wanted anyway! Pietro did surprise me, however, with a huge hug before I left the room. Again with that loving stare!

After the breakfast meeting, Vito and Mano collected Isabella's and my luggage. We snuck away for a little personal time before we all left. The men always became uncomfortable if Isabella and I cried when saying goodbye. Isabella told me she was returning to the States and would call me when they arrived. "Dominic has to stay for a short time for businesses with Pietro now that the Don is dead. However, it should not take long. I would like to see the family—and the baby, of course!"

I was excited Isabella would be close by, well, in the States anyway. There were quite a few things I wanted to talk with her about, and everything was falling into place. Now, if my life did that also, I would be in great shape! Isabella asked, "Did you know that Mano was also staying in the States and not here in Sicily?" That scared me, but I was glad for that piece of information. I had hoped it had nothing to do with Roberto or Joey Thumbs.

"Shit!" I said aloud. I should make that my mantra.

It was such a relief to get on the road with Lorenzo, Vito, and Mano. I had to ask, "Mano, how come the pleasure of your company too? Not that I mind at all, it just surprised me!"

Mano turned around from the front seat and said, "I am coming to the States with Vito. I guess you'll have to get use to seeing this ugly mug more often!"

I looked at Vito for some kind of explanation but knew he would say nothing until we were alone. "Well, Mano, it makes me happy!" I lied. Vito squeezed my hand and smiled out the car side window. I joked, "It might keep Dommy in check, what do you think, Mano?"

Mano surprised me with his off-the-cuff answer, "Done and

done, isn't that what the little bastard always says?"

From that little remark, I realized Mano was still upset with Dommy over the trick with my son. I sat and thought for quite a while as the men talked back and forth in Italian. It might not be a bad thing for Mano to be close by. I had no idea what I would be facing with my life in the States. I was sure Mano was there also to keep an eye on Joey Thumbs. However, the idea of his interfering with Roberto and me scared me quite a bit.

Vito broke my concentration when he said, "What's your take on it, Missy?"

I felt like a deer caught in headlights, "I am sorry, Vito. I was not listening to your conversation. My take on what?"

Vito laughed, "You must be at ease. Your mind never stops working. What was the rule of listening to everything around you?"

I shot back at Vito quickly, "Not when I am among friends. I am, aren't I?"

Vito joked with me, "You need to be beat! Dom was right, smart ass!" Vito continued, "What's your take on Joey Thumbs and the situation with Pietro as Don in Sicily?"

I thought for a second, "Well, I won't work with Joey. He is not smart enough and I would never have someone I do not know involved in my end of the business. Second, Joey is young and in love and that is the reason he wanted to come to America. Joey might not be anything more than a gopher for you guys, but I do not want to deal with him one on one. Third, I like the fact that Pietro is Don now. He is much more in tune with today and I think he will be a fair and honest Don, if there is such a thing! Don Lazzaro asked me who I felt was family. Of course, I said Dommy; but I have no problem dealing with Pietro. Just something I cannot put my finger on. However, I just do not want to have to answer to him. I like the way things are and have always been. At my age, I am not up to a big change. However, I do trust Pietro, to a point, at least where I am concerned. I would do work for Pietro without a problem but want my part of the job to stay in the States. That is just my take on the situation!

However, I would like to retire!"

Mano turned quickly to look at me. "Missy, you know the only way out of this pile of shit is to go like the Don!"

Vito became furious with Mano and yelled, "That is not for you to say, Mano. You overstepped a little there, amico!"

I touched Vito's arm and asked Mano, "Am I going to have a problem with you, Mano, after all these years?"

Mano seemed actually hurt, "Missy! Never! I think you took that wrong! Never!"

Nothing more was said about my job. However, we did stop at least three times to eat before we reached the airstrip. Whenever we stopped, people would move aside and look at me as if I were the Queen. I could see people talking about who I might be. One woman asked Lorenzo, in Italian, if I was a movie star. I got hysterical laughing. However, I was surrounded by about one thousand pounds of flesh with these three men. I am sure it looked scary.

When we approached the airstrip for that little plane, I did become worried. This was a tremendous amount of weight to get off the ground. All three men took up two seats each. There was one thing, however, that always made me feel terrific: I felt so emaciated next to them. Fortunately, there were only a few more people on with us. I still kept my eyes closed as it took off.

As usual, there was a car waiting and Lorenzo slipped in behind the wheel. On the travel to my home, I was trying to think if I had anything left in the house to serve these three. "Vito, will you all come into the house? I need to stop at the store for some supplies. I have plenty of booze, just nothing to eat."

Lorenzo yelled from the front, "Don't worry, honey, I'll run into a market before we get you home."

Lorenzo found a market, went inside while we waited, and came out with four bags of God knows what. When we reached my home, I realized it was the first time Mano had seen the inside. "Missy, it is beautiful. You did a hell of a job on this place. We used this place a few times to just, ah, get out of the way, if you know what I mean. It looked nothing like this. My compliments, Missy, my compliments." Mano walked from room to room checking everything.

Lorenzo went right to the kitchen and told me to "Go sit." Mano made drinks for everyone, and Vito and I sat down at the table. I felt useless as they took over. "Can't I help out?" I asked.

Both men answered, "No!"

As they were busy, Vito said to me, "The remark in the car bothered you. The remark from Mano, huh? Missy, not to worry! Mano was talking about us as men in the business, not you. Mano would never do anything to hurt you!"

I answered quietly as the men came to the table, "It's not me I worry about!"

Chapter Twenty-Nine

When the men finally left, I dropped on the couch. *What an adventure that was*, I thought. I was exhausted and immediately got into the shower, put on a lounging outfit, and settled in to relax. That was when the gate bell rang. *"Pronto?"* I asked.

"Baby, ciao, is it okay?" asked Sergio.

I thought to myself, Dammit, not today, please. However, I said, "Yes, it is okay. One minute." I pushed the button to open the gate.

Within a few minutes, Sergio was at the door. "Elisabetta, I am sorry, late. I work and go back in one hour. Okay you and me talk?" As I walked away from him, Sergio touched my arm, spun me around, and gently kissed me. The hug that followed was like the best massage, like a summer breeze, comforting and warm. I had to back away from him.

Over the next hour, I tried to explain to Sergio that he would be working for another man in Sicily. I told Sergio he would be contacted by Pietro if he were still interested in working. Sergio seemed thrilled as he asked, "It is okay for you and me to see again? Oh my God, I am happy. No problem Dominic?"

I had to lie to him. "No. Everything is same. I cannot see you if you work Pietro. But I want you to work with Pietro. You can make a lot of money!"

Sergio laid his head back on the couch and tears came to his eyes. "I do not want money. I want you in my life. You no understand!" I wanted to say just how much I did understand, but I could not bring myself to do it. Sergio was on my list to be protected. If anything happened to him, I would never be able to feel anything again. By way of Dominic's manipulations, I got Sergio involved in this mess, and it was my own fault. Sergio just kept hugging me as I tried to talk.

I knew deep inside there was no way Sergio could get out now. He knew too much; Dominic had made sure of it and would not hesitate to eliminate that problem. Sergio had to have a meeting with Pietro before anything could go further with the work. I would blackmail Pietro if I had to so Sergio would be safe. I had enough to worry about with Roberto and my family in the States.

I became more frustrated as I tried to explain all this in one hour. Sergio had to return to a hotel near by, pick up a private group, and return to Rome. Between the feelings we had for each other, the time limitation, and my exhaustion, it did not go well. Before I made Sergio leave, we both were in tears. "Please! I will see you again before you leave?" Sergio pleaded.

I said, "Yes. I will call Pietro and then we can talk more!" Sergio kissed me with such gentleness. I closed the door, soaked in perspiration, and immediately changed my clothes. Every time I was around that man, I got the same reaction. My feelings had not changed and that worried me. "No wonder your life is going to hell in a chamber pot, asshole," I said aloud to myself. I flopped on my bed after changing and said, aloud, again, "I need help, stronger medications, something! Maybe if I just plan to stay here and hide from everyone that would work." But I missed my family so much, especially my grandsons.

I needed a plan, again! I would have to talk to Pietro because that part of his plan was not exactly discussed. I wanted to know about Sergio. Pietro knew apparently that I had feelings for Sergio. Besides, Pietro knew how Dominic used Sergio to keep me in line. I could use that advantage if I needed to. But something told me I would have a better time with Pietro than dealing with Dominic when it came to Sergio. Dominic was overly protective of my personal life. With Pietro, it was solely business. However, what would I do if Sergio absolutely refused to work with Pietro? Could Sergio be protected?

Could I have any more on my mind? I took my medication and slipped under the covers. I became angry with myself that I wished I were not alone. I started feeling sorry for myself and cried. I knew Sergio and I had to be over. I wondered what kind of monster I had become. I would put on my clown mask and love just as they do with big tears in my eyes. I was afraid loves masquerade was over and so was true love for me. I was glad that I finally had the chance to feel what it was like with Sergio. It kept me sane many times with the crazy life I led. What would happen now, and how could I go through every day, every hour, with not one thought of Sergio?

Chapter Thirty

The next morning I received many calls. Isabella, to make sure I was at my *casa* and safe; Vito, to give me a phone number where I could call him; Melissa, Cassie, Gracie, Gypsie, and Gina, all at different times and all worrying about me. I had wonderful friends, and for that, I was so thankful.

I then received a call from Claudio, who chastised me for what I was doing to his father. I could not believe it. Roberto had gotten the children involved, and that was horrible. I was hurt. I was the only parent, those many years, available always for my children. Where was the "Hello, Mom, I love you. How are you doing?" Nothing. If that wasn't bad enough, I then received a call from Roberto. It was five o'clock in the morning in the States and he was depressed, sick, and crying. Out of self-preservation, I told Roberto I could not deal with it at that moment. I was ready to jump off my veranda.

That very thin line my mom always told me about between sanity and insanity was being stretched like a rubber band. I had a lot of work to do before I left for the States. I needed my mind clear. There were many times the phone rang and I was afraid to answer it. Honestly, I knew how vulnerable I was at that moment, and not being strong frightened me.

I had no idea when Sergio would pop up again, so I telephoned Pietro to straighten a few things out about the work in Italy. One of his men said Pietro was very busy; however, when Pietro heard it was me, he answered, "I am sorry, Elisabetta. You can call here anytime and I will inform the men of that. It doesn't matter how busy, okay? I love you, and I think you know that! What is on your mind? Are you okay?"

I thanked Pietro and answered, "One thing we did not discuss in detail before I left is bothering me. We talked only briefly about this man in Italy named Sergio. Do you remember, Pietro?"

There was a short pause and Pietro replied, "Of course I remember. Sergio was the man old pazzo Dom tried to give work to behind my back, am I right? What is the problem? Is Dom up to tricks again?"

I assured Pietro Dommy was behaving but joked, "It is still early, Pietro. However, what is going to happen to Sergio now? Does he contact you or the other way around? Are you planning to have Sergio work for you? It is important to me; Sergio is very important to me. Do you understand? He is family too, and I do not want him hurt in any way. And if Sergio decides not to work, will you protect him?"

Pietro was silent for just a second and said, "I'll treat this Sergio like I do my other men! I don't know what you are asking, Elisabetta, tell me!"

I thought to myself, You have gone this far. Get it all out now before you leave Italy. "Pietro, there is one thing I hadn't mentioned to you and Dominic, and I really should have! However, I planned to talk to Dommy myself after I talk to you. I know Dom and Isabella are still here, and I would appreciate your letting me tell him, okay?"

Pietro agreed, "No problem, Elisabetta, you know that!"

I continued, "I don't mean any disrespect when I say this, but I want my family at peace. I want to be at peace! If any member of my immediate family, or Dom and the family, are attacked in any way, financially, physically, anyway, I am in a position to retaliate. I have learned a lot over the years. The one rule my Dad taught me, that I never disclosed to anyone, is to keep documentations of accounts, bank records, all transactions, and names of people I have dealt with since I started this mess. The paperwork is in a safe place."

I felt the sweat pouring down my armpits, but I could not turn back now. I continued, "If anything happens, a copy will be forwarded to the FBI, CIA, IRS, every official you can imagine in both countries. I know it would bring down Dom and the family too; but, if it comes between my personal family and any loved ones in Italy, there is no choosing. I have paperwork that all of you have long forgotten; however, I did not! I apologize for not saying this sooner; however, when it meant dealing with Don Lazzaro, I knew I would have a lot of trouble. Pietro, I hope you understand. I never will use this unless I am forced. I hope we still can go on as always, even though you know this information now. Am I wrong?"

Pietro immediately answered, "Elisabetta, I know you and I knew the men who trained you. I never for one second thought you did not have your back covered. I assumed all along that would be a rule you would follow. After all, the first priority of everyone involved was to keep you safe. I am new as the Don but not naïve. I saw what you could do to bring Dom to his knees when he tried his little power trip. It does not change a thing between us. I know you. However, you talk to Dominic. He might be a problem. Dom might feel betrayed. But do not bullshit a bullshitter. Tell Dominic straight up exactly what you just told me. It will be fine. I expected nothing less than that from you. That is why you are so good at the job. I never want you to hand the job over, if I have a say!"

I thanked Pietro for his consideration and apologized again for handling this little information over the phone. I knew it was a form of blackmail but did not care. "Pietro, all that happened with the Don, I just didn't have the time to meet again with you, one on one. I will talk to Dominic as soon as he is through in

Sicily. I am hoping I will have no problems with him."

Pietro replied, "If you do, honey, call me; we will handle it together on a three-way conversation. I will work it out, do not worry. You are family, and I take care of my own. Whatever you want to do with this Sergio is up to you. He does not know anything right now. Let it be Sergio's choice if he wants to work. However, you know where I stand as far as you and him together. It makes for bad business if Sergio decides to work only with me in Sicily. I hope you understand that. We will talk when we hit that bridge. Take care, and safe flight home."

When I retired that night, I thought of what I would say to Dominic. I needed to talk with him directly but wondered if I should run this past Vito first. My mind was also on the box. I had decided that I definitely would open it when I arrived home. Everyone was telling me I was family, but no one knew for sure what the box actually contained. Maybe that would also help me in the protection of everyone, including myself.

Chapter Thirty-One

The next morning, or should I say afternoon, I awoke much rested. I wanted to pull the covers up over my head and just stay there all day. Since I got back to my *casa*, it had been brutal for me with confronting Sergio, Roberto, Claudio, and Pietro. Now, the problem would be talking with Dommy before he heard it second hand. I decided to call Vito and asked to see him. Vito would know just how annoyed Dommy would be when I tell him I blackmailed the new Don of Sicily! With that thought, I did pull the covers up, more to hide than anything else.

When I had the strength and courage to get myself together, I telephoned Vito, "Ciao, Vito, how are you today?" I asked.

"Missy, everything okay?" asked Vito. His voice had changed to concern, "You sound very tense! What happened?"

I then asked if Vito could come to see me. I needed to share something with him. I wanted him to come alone.

"Missy, I'll be there in an hour. Is that okay? Lorenzo can wait in the car, no problem," said Vito. I needed the time to dress anyway. I was glad for the little delay. I knew I had to go with my initial impulse and talk with Vito first.

It took less than an hour for Vito to show up. He had to be

staying very close to my house. When I heard the knock, I took a deep breath before opening. "Thank you, Vito," I said. I am sorry to ask for this meeting now. I have a problem, or better yet I probably caused one."

Vito kissed me and said, "Coffee on? I brought dolce!"

I immediately went to put on coffee and proceeded to set the table. "I need your input this time on how Dommy will react to my blackmailing Pietro?"

I thought Vito would choke, and for a second it scared me. I kept banging Vito on the back. "I am so sorry, Vito! You know me I can never stop the lips from flapping at the wrong times. You okay?"

Vito wiped his mouth and said, "Sit down! What happened? What did you do?" I explained the entire conversation with Pietro to Vito and awaited his response. "And, Missy, do you have the paperwork to back that?" Vito asked.

"Vito, I am sorry. That was one rule I learned from Pops on down and never revealed it to anyone. I never had to before this. Yes, I do have it all, exactly as I told Pietro. I should have talked to Dommy first, huh? He is going to be pissed at me!"

Vito blew out his air, exhaling, as if he was trying to blow up a balloon. He shifted in his chair and said, "Well, first, you are right! Dom will not like the fact that Pietro knew this bit of info first. That problem we have to correct somehow. Second, why didn't you ever share this with me? That is dangerous, Missy, for you to have kept all this documentation on both families. It might just backfire if you do not handle it right."

I caught myself apologizing again to Vito, "That was one rule from Pops and Dad that was never to be revealed. That kept me safe at a very young age. Then, I didn't know you men from Adam. I knew nothing about trust lists and where the whole mess would lead my life!"

I stood up and said, "I am going to call Dommy now. Neither will tell the other, and I will stay on Dommy's good side, if he has one!"

Vito agreed it was the thing to do, and now, since I just talked with Pietro last night. "Missy, show Dominic the respect he deserves! I think it is best!"

I felt terrible then and replied, "Vito, it never was my intention to show Dommy disrespect. Honest!"

Vito kissed my cheek and handed me the phone, "I know that, Missy. Call Dominic while I am here, but do not tell him I am, understand?"

I felt my hand shaking as I dialed the number. Caterina answered the phone and I said, "Caterina, it is Elisabetta. Come va?"

Caterina seemed pleased with that little acknowledgement, "Grazie, Elisabetta, sono bene!"

I continued, "Is Isabella or Dominic at home?"

Caterina answered they were and proceeded to get Isabella, "I miss my drinking partner. Elisabetta, how are you? You ready to go back to the States?"

I cut Isabella short and asked, "Isabella, I could use a few martinis right now! Is the big D around today, honey?"

Isabella's response was, "Oh, boy! This cannot be good. You actually want to speak to him! Yes, honey, he was here a minute ago. Dom leaves a lingering odor. Hold on, I'll get him right away!"

A second later, Dommy was on the phone, "Missy, you miss me, huh?"

I had to smile, "In your dreams! But, I do have a problem we need to discuss, now. How is your mood today?"

Dominic became worried and said, "Spit it out! According to you and my wife, I am never in a good mood anyway! What's the problem?"

"Dommy, I need to tell you something that should have come out with the meeting between just the five of us. Remember, Pietro, you, Mano, Vito, and I. Well, now is the time. All these years, the one golden rule I learned from Pops, Dad, and Guido was to keep all my business in writing and safely tucked away for protection. I have every single transaction, such as bank numbers, names of people, and the whole nine yards. I have many copies ready for mailing to so many authorities in both countries, it is scary. It is something I felt should be done, but it was also the way I was taught. Now, I understand why that rule was so important. When I was young, it did not mean much. After I met the old Don, I realized how necessary it really was! Dommy, you still there?" I asked.

There was such silence I felt we might have been cutoff. Finally, Dommy spoke, "Missy, I need time to take this all in. Let me get this straight. You can bury any of us by a short trip to the mailbox! Do I have that in a nut shell?" Dommy was not taking this very well, and Vito could tell by my expression. Dominic continued as he got a little louder, "Cazzo! {fuck}! Let me call you back. I...I'll call you back," and Dommy hung up the phone!

Vito took the phone, hung it up, and said, "Missy, Dom always needs to process stuff before he speaks. I just told him that after the problems last year. Dom never thinks before he speaks or acts. Maybe he is finally listening to my advice. Give him time. Dom will call back soon, but I am waiting here until that time. Go get more coffee. This might take a while!" Vito knew I was upset and arose to hug me. "Come on! Missy, it will be okay. Dommy's just not used to anything getting by him. Honest! Trust me!" Vito looked at his watch and said, "I will give Dom half hour, tops, and one of us will get a call! I know the short shit!"

I hated waiting for a phone to ring, a pot to boil, or for some-one to return home. It makes you feel hopeless and helpless. Who is the Saint for that? Saint Jude. Saint Rita? At that moment I could not remember. Therefore, when Vito's cell phone rang, I jumped. Vito looked at me to be quiet and answered, "Pronto! Hey, D, where are you?" From that point, for at least three min-utes, Vito said nothing but grunts. "No problem, D" replied Vito finally. "I will go over right now."

Vito looked at me with a smile and said, "I am on my way over here now! Put on the coffee! Dommy is calling you in about one hour. It is fine, believe me!"

Here, all along, I thought the one man I would have problems with, seriously, was Pietro. I never expected Dom to be upset. Vito removed his coat and said, "Missy, you know Dommy. He has that Napoleon thing going on—you know who I mean, that short dictator."

Chapter Thirty-Two

I tried to do 'busy' things while Vito and I waited. It seemed like a lot longer than one hour until phone rang. "Missy," said Dominic in a quiet voice, "is Vito there with you?"

I answered, "Yes, matter of fact, he is! Do you want to talk with him?"

Dommy replied, "No, but I need to talk with you. How old was I to be before you filled me in on this little surprise? I have to hand it to you, Missy, old Don Lazzaro was right. Very rarely do you see a woman who is beautiful and smart. You took me off guard. You were right in telling me. I only wonder what you intend to do with these papers?"

I immediately answered, "Dominic, you know I would do nothing unless I was forced to. I have to worry about my family. When I learned this rule, I had no children, no grandchildren, and almost everyone I loved was involved with the family anyway. However, now, I have some people I love dearly who are not with the families, and that worries me. After I met Don Lazzaro, I realized how nasty things could become and I promised myself I would tell you. I went against every rule taught me by Pops, Dad, and Guido. However, the rules were for a different time. Not today with the idiots coming up behind you men."

Dominic said, quietly, "You seem to have a lot of Pandora boxes ready to open around you, huh? Well, this little information of yours rocked me back a bit on my heels, but it could work out for the best. My first impulse was to choke you. I hung up the phone and scared Isabella to death. I did my usual ranting and raving until I came to my senses. I know what you have can bring many families down; but, on the other hand, Pietro is the new Don. With Don Lazzaro, you knew what you had. Who knows for sure what kind of Don Pietro will be."

There was a slight pause and Dommy continued, "Missy, I know how you feel about all of us. Through everything we have thrown your way, you never wavered. I was the worst of the lot! However, I knew everyone of your teachers. This should not have come as such a surprise. It just did!"

I was relieved, "Thanks, Dommy!"

He was not finished with me yet, "Missy, this is dangerous shit you have control over. Did you tell Pietro?"

At that second, I looked at Vito so he could hear me, "Did I tell Pietro?" I was waiting for some kind of sign from Vito. Immediately, Vito shook his head and mouthed, "No!" I was surprised but trusted Vito completely and answered, "No, Dommy, I did not tell Pietro."

Dommy seemed happy and answered, "Okay! This could be a very good thing for the family in the States. The more I think about it, Missy, the happier I become. There will be no problem. I will see you when I return. Put V on now, please!" I gladly handed the phone over to Vito.

Vito and Dommy talked for quite a while, and I became concerned it was about me. However, when Vito hung up I joked, "Is there a problem with me? Did Dommy tell you to drop me off my balcony?"

Vito poured another cup of coffee and said, "Yeah, right! That will never happen! But we have a problem with this cafoni in Sicily. You know the young one with the old Don. Not Joey

Thumbs, the other one?"

I thought for a second and said, "Frankie Tomatoes? What is the problem with him?"

Vito told me about the conversation with Dominic. "This Frankie had his hairs twisted because Joey was coming with the family to the States. Frankie felt they overlooked him even though he was older and had been with Don Lazzaro since a teenager. Pietro had told Dommy to handle the problem since Joey was under his family. Pietro and Dom needed to try to appease Frankie. Pietro did not want to start out alienating any one in Sicily with what could be a serious problem. Frankie came from a loyal Sicilian family line; however, Frankie was making threats around town of not honoring omerta. Pietro had heard Frankie was considering selling out the family with the authorities and trying a power play. This move with Joey was trouble from the beginning. Nevertheless, we had made a decision for Joey to be with our family and now need to figure out how to handle Frankie!"

I became nervous and asked, "How to handle him? What does that mean? Not what I think it does, right?" Vito ignored me and called Mano. There was my answer! Whenever Mano became involved, it was serious!

Vito said, as he was leaving, "Lorenzo, the poor bastard, has been waiting all this time. I have to handle a few things now! I will be back. Missy, you up for dinner tonight with Lorenzo, Mano, and me?" I said yes but felt very uneasy about the whole idea of being in public, gunfire, that kind of crap, especially with Mano!

I sat quietly for quite a while just trying to absorb everything I did in that short time. I needed to up my medications! I had to be crazy to hit the two of them, Pietro and Dommy, over the phone with a form of blackmail. I proceeded to dress and waited for the men to pick me up for dinner.

When the gate bell rang in the house, I thought for a second it might be Sergio. I was relieved when I heard Lorenzo. "Come down, Missy. Are you ready?" I said I would be there in one minute and gathered my handbag and jacket. I was happy to see the men laughing with each other in the car. As I approached, Mano got out and opened the back door. I thanked him and slid next to Vito.

"Buona sera," I said. "Everyone okay this evening?" They all seemed to be in a good mood.

Vito touched my hand and said, "There is something we need to do before the restaurant, Missy. It won't take long and you can wait in the car, if you don't mind!" I felt a little anxious but agreed there were no problems. We drove to the seaport near my casa, where there were gorgeous yachts. It looked also to have a private members only club.

I asked, "Are we eating dinner here?"

Vito said, "No, Missy. We need to check something out. You wait, please. It won't take too long!" The three men slid out of the car and walked down along the boats.

I waited about ten minutes and decided, what could it hurt to see some of these boats? They were enormous and I was surprised to see a lot with American names. So, never listening, I got out of the limo and strolled down the pier. Within five minutes I passed a yacht that was rocking as if someone was having wild sex. I smiled until I heard the yelling of Italian men. I then realized it was Mano and Lorenzo. I knew then I should have stayed in the damn car. When am I ever going to listen!

Remembering my training, I took note of the number on the yacht and the name, My Alibi. I had to shake my head. Perfect! I guess I am supposed to be their alibi tonight. What an appropriate name for this crew! Suddenly, I froze when I heard Mano swear in Italian and say, "I said take off everything!" Whoever was with them I hoped was not a woman?

Then I heard a voice I did not recognize. "Go fuck yourself!" I cringed as I thought, that was stupid if talking to Mano! The yacht started to rock, and I had the feeling the poor man, whoever he was, was being undressed! I then heard Mano again, "Don't break my balls! I am worried now. You cooperate now while still breathing, or we can do it another way!" Things got quiet for a while, and I almost wanted to go inside the yacht to stop whatever was going on. I knew that would be stupid. I should have listened to Vito and I would not be in the middle of this crap. However, something was holding me there.

I then heard Lorenzo say, "V, He's clean. No wire! But I see why Frankie did not want to take off his clothes. Look at that tiny dick!" With that remark, I took off like a bat out of hell and got back to the limo before anyone saw me. The poor sucker had to be Frankie Tomatoes!

As soon as I got into the limo, I wrote down the number and name of the yacht. I waited at least another half hour before I saw the men returning to the limo. They seemed okay, but I had to ask, acting dumb, "Vito, do any of you own a yacht here? They look beautiful."

Mano was very proud to announce that he had his yacht docked at this pier. Mano turned around to look at me and said, "Missy, guess the name of my boat!"

I tried to be a smart ass and replied, "I don't know! Puttana {whore} or another dirty Italian curse word?"

Mano smiled. "It's My Alibi. Great name, huh?"

Before I could say anything, Vito said, "Who spelled it for you, Mano?" Mano laughed, gave Vito the finger, and turned around.

We finally stopped at a quaint mom-and-pop restaurant on the beach. Apparently, the family who owned it knew these men. You would have thought a few sheiks had just arrived. I settled in for the long haul. These were serious eaters, and I knew the rest of the afternoon and night would be feasting and drinking.

It was hard for me to hear these men laugh and actually feel happy being with them even though I knew the other side of the coin. Mano told everyone a story about a trip on his boat when he managed to wind up in the hospital. "I took this dame from Sicily to Calabria for a romantic ride. I had Orlando drive and we were enjoying champagne. I had been trying to get to her— oh scusa, Missy—for a long time. Well, everything was going great. I knew I had it made. Just as I was ready, the water got wild. I come down real hard to ahh, you know, and it slips and hits the side of the bunk. The dick bends right in half, when it was hard, and the pain shot up into my eyeteeth!

"When I screamed, she screamed, Orlando comes running, and I am curled on the floor holding my own dick. Now, talk about embarrassed. I start yelling at her, what the fuck. Is the hole sewn shut for Christ's sake? Anyway, we take the boat to the medics on the water and I had to explain what happened. They knew better than to laugh at me. I thought I broke the damn thing. And because I yelled at her, she would never speak to me again. In fact, she would not get back on my boat!"

The men were laughing at Mano when he explained it hurt for two weeks just to piss. Mano continued, "Now, I don't worry about nobody; but, when I see her in Sicily, I hide. Dammit, don't laugh. I was embarrassed. Missy, I was trying to be debonair. Now, fuck that!"

Vito then spoke up, "Okay, Mano watch the mouth, basta {Enough}!" Mano apologized to me and continued to marathon eat.

When we were returning to my casa, I quietly asked Vito, "What was decided about that guy in Sicily? You know, the one we talked about today?"

I was almost afraid of the answer, but Vito usually never ignores me. "Missy, Frankie is tied up a little right now, but I am sure he is learning his lesson as we speak. Speaking of that, Mano, don't you need to stop at your boat before we take Missy home?"

Mano did not turn around but merely answered, "Yeah, V. I will sleep there today. Lorenzo can pick me up in the morning. Sorry, Missy, I'll see you in a day or so."

I just shook my head and Vito looked at me strangely, "Missy, is there a problem?" I wanted to say, of course, there is again, but kept my mouth shut for a change.

Chapter Thirty-Three

The next morning when I awoke, I knew I had to make some life changing moves. I also knew I would be honest with Vito and ask what happened on the boat. Over the years, suppressing my feelings only brought me pain. I liked the me who needed anger management classes when in the meeting with Pietro and the men. However, I did not have the time to call when my phone rang.

"Missy, how are you today," asked Vito.

I replied, "You are getting scary, Vito. I was just thinking about you. You have ESP too?"

"Missy," said Vito, "you decided not to wait in the limo last night, am I right?"

I had to be honest, "Yes, I did! You know I never listen, and at my age, I am not going to start now! I am sorry, Vito. I was going to tell you anyway today. I wanted to know if the guy was Frankie Tomatoes and what happened to him. After all, I am involved! I was with you three last night. And, on that subject, I did not appreciate being pulled into a job while going out to dinner! Everyone seems to forget I am a freaking bookkeeper, not a gun maul!"

Vito tried excuses, "Listen, Missy, please. This Frankie character was to meet with us on the boat. We never expected he had the balls to be there. When he was, it took all of us by surprise and we had to make sure he was not wearing a wire or something for the law. Anyway, Missy, Frankie is fine. Nothing is going to happen to him. You have my word!"

I had to dig further, rather than leave it alone—always a stupid move on my part! I asked, "Vito, why did Mano return to the yacht then last night, to play cards with Frankie? I swear, if I find out Frankie was hurt, how do I look at myself again in the mirror? I never got over the Rome incident. How many ways can I say that I don't want to do this part of the business?"

Vito understood completely, "Missy, I have never lied to you and won't start now. Frankie is fine. We made him a counter offer to work with both families. It seems he likes the idea. This is a bit of information you needed to know anyway with your end of the job. Are we okay, now?"

I assured Vito I was and that I trusted him. However, my mouth flapped again, "Vito how do you know to which family Frankie will be loyal? I get very bad feelings about this; however, I will keep them to myself."

Before I could finish my talk with Vito, my gate bell rang. "Vito, I have to go. Talk to you later!" I picked up the phone and answered to hear Sergio on the other end. "Ciao, I am surprised," I answered. It was Saturday and Sergio never came to see me on the weekend.

When I opened the door, I was shocked to see him casually dressed and not in a suit. "Aren't you working today?" I asked. Before Sergio answered me, he took me in his arms and hugged me as if today was the first day of forever. When Sergio kissed me, I felt my legs weaken. I backed away and said, "Wow!" Sergio was confused with this word and I had to smile. I took Sergio by the hand and led him to the living room. "Why are you here?" I asked.

Sergio seemed hurt, "Elisabetta, you no want I here?"

My mind was racing with all kinds of thoughts, as I would like to find a huge chest with a lock on it to keep you here, kind of thoughts. However, I smiled, "Of course. Tell me, is there a problem? Have you talked to Pietro or Dominic? Have you made up your mind to work?" I eventually would have to tell Sergio, either way I could not see him again; however, it had to be Sergio's decision. I did not want to sway him.

Sergio just sat on the couch staring at me for the longest time. He finally said, "Oh, my God! I love you so much. I cannot have a life without you. What can we do? Can't you speak to Dominic for me or have him telephone me?" I closed my eyes and tried to think. So much had happened since I arrived in Italy. I was not sure what to do! I still wanted to see Sergio happy. After all the crap Sergio had done to me, just like Roberto, I had to be crazy. It is amazing to think when I love someone, I put up with a thousand things I would never tolerate from anyone else! Moreover, I had to admit, I did love them both.

Finally, I asked, "Sergio, do you mind if we take a ride? Get out a little in the sun. Maybe I can think a little clearer!"

Sergio was willing to do anything for me. "If we are together, I don't care what we do! Where do you want to go?"

I had no idea why I answered, "I would like to go to the pier and see the yachts."

It seemed wonderful to be outside with him in the daylight. God, sometimes I felt like a vampire only seeing Sergio after sunset. When we reached the pier, Sergio stopped to buy water and we strolled down to the yachts. I knew, unconsciously, why I was there and walked directly to where Mano docked his yacht. Just as I thought, it was gone! I tried rationalizing it in my mind. Maybe Mano drove Frankie back to Sicily. I had hoped that was the reason!

Sergio asked to sit on a bench and I snuggled in close to him. Neither of us spoke for the longest time. We both were content. I was the first to speak, "Sergio, did you know I was afraid of the water. I cannot swim; yet sitting here is so peaceful." I then learned that Sergio was in the Italian army and spent a lot of his enlistment on a boat. We loved each other but neither of us talked much these four years about our past.

Sergio took my chin and kissed me, pulled me closer to him, and said, "Ti amo!"

As I touched Sergio's face, my eyes noticed two men walking in our direction. The old rules, I thought. Be aware of your surroundings. However, when I saw it was the rogue FBI Mike and Frankie Tomatoes, I became frightened. I did not want them to see me. I quietly told Sergio, "Big problem coming. You kiss me so they do not see my face."

Sergio leaned me lower against the bench back and wrapped his jacket around me as he kissed me eagerly. I heard them pass by and a little of the conversation as Mike said, "You do what I want and there will be no problems".

When they were far enough away not to see us, I told Sergio, "We need to get back to the car. Something is not right. Those men are no good. I need to use your phone!" Sergio gladly did what I asked, no questions. As I watched the two men from the car, I asked Sergio to give me privacy. Again, Sergio never questioned me.

Unlike Vito, after I told him where I was. "Why are you at the pier? Missy, Mano is not there."

I said, "No shit! But I guess who is here? FBI Mike and Frankie Tomatoes. Do you know this already or is something wrong?"

Vito's voice became two octaves higher, "Missy, don't mess with me! True? Are you there now? Who is with you?"

Now, that was one question I wished Vito had not asked but said, "That doesn't matter. Is this a problem?"

Vito calmed down a little and said, "It certainly isn't anything we were aware of. Mano was supposed to be gone with Frankie. Something stinks here, and I think they have to be up to no good. Thanks, Missy. Your know your job, that's for sure. I will call you tomorrow. Just get out of there now!"

Chapter Thirty-Four

When Sergio and I returned home, he told me he could stay until late. We talked and laughed so much for such a long time about everything. Sergio assured me he was coming to the United States as soon as his children were old enough to leave for college. Just another three years and they both would be gone. His father, still alive, was the other problem. Until his father died, Italian law forbade the sale of any of the properties.

It had been over a year since we had made love, and I was not sure Sergio wanted it. I felt like it was the first time. I was still self-conscious over my body not being good enough! Sergio might hate sex with me after all this time. I was so different from European women. However, I so wrong!

Such love from this man, he astounded me. The guilt I felt when we entered my bedroom soon dissipated, and I was in a whirlwind of passion and love. Sergio is such a passionate and gentle man with me, I felt so wonderful. I knew what was happening was wrong! I had to end this with Sergio and my heart was broken. I kept saying in my mind, At least you knew what love really is. Just go with it for now and let tomorrow worry about itself.

When Sergio had to leave, nine hours later, I felt so empty. I was leaving in a few days and that would be the end! Although Sergio would never agree to it, I knew for his safety it had to over. Whenever I tried to reason with him, Sergio would not listen. "There is a way for us!" said Sergio, "I will not accept anything else. I will not work if you no see me!"

I said, "Sergio, you are a damn hard-headed Italian. You never listen to what I am saying about this family. It is not that easy. I want you to take the job with Pietro! You and I cannot see each other again!"

As I opened the door for Sergio to leave, he kissed me gently and put his finger over my mouth. "No! No! I love you, and I will talk to Dominic or any man in Italia. No man tell me no see you. Impossible!" I sighed deeply and let him go. I had hoped Sergio would take a tour or something so I could leave the country without seeing him again. It would be so much easier for me!

I slept like a baby, no stress, no headaches, just peace and happiness. Sergio was my best medication. Now, how do I go through the withdrawal of Sergio, cold turkey! Compared to everything else I had been through this whole time in Italy, that would be the worst for my heart!

The phone woke me early and I stumbled into the living room. "Pronto," I said sleepily.

It was Vito, and his comment not only upset me but also took me by surprise! "Missy, I waited last night hoping your friend would leave early; however, when he did not, I went home. Is it okay if I come over now, or are you still occupied?" Vito was upset with me and I was embarrassed.

At my age, I could feel my face turn red! "Of course, Vito, come on over and bring chocolate!" I timidly said. I hurriedly got dressed and made the bed. I felt like a teenager just caught by her parents! This was silly, and I was not going to allow Vito to lecture me at my age. I was ready for a fight when Vito arrived.

"Buon giorno, Vito. What is going on with what happened yesterday at the pier?"

Vito ignored me for a second and said, "Missy, changing the subject will not work with me. Tell me you and this Sergio were just talking yesterday and I will believe you. You never lied to me yet!"

I left the room to put on coffee and Vito followed behind. I said too loudly, "Vito, I won't lie to you. I do not have to! I am not a child and whatever I did last night is my personal business. Am I right, or is part of my job description now a part-time nun?"

Vito became angry with me. "Missy, you can act as tough as you want, but I can see through you after all these years. This Sergio is important to you! Dammit! That complicates things on so many levels; I cannot begin to tell you. You are smarter than this. I was hoping the whole thing was just an infatuation."

I had to laugh, "Vito, have you looked at me lately? I am not a little girl. My years of infatuations stopped when I married Ron! That bastard destroyed me! And, each year after that, until now, I have built another layer to those walls. This man takes them away. Do not tell me what I can do or who I can see. I have enough problems right now, okay?" I then kissed Vito on the forehead and walked to the dining room.

Vito was shaking his head as he sat down at the table. "Vito, tell me what happened yesterday! Did anyone know about this meeting with Mike and Frankie? Was it part of a plan Dommy put in motion?"

Vito replied, "No! It was amazing that you were there! Were you still thinking about that spooky bastard's visit of this wallet thing in Sicily? Going with your gut again, Missy? Well, whatever it was, I am glad you were there. This is the story, and Dom is more than pissed! He went ballistic!"

I sat to listen and was glad the focus was off Sergio and me. Vito started, "Mano was to keep Frankie busy until Dom could come up with a plan. Frankie wanted to work for us but had to show his loyalty first. He would stay in Sicily until Dom felt he could be completely trusted. Frankie was good with this. Mano returned that night to the boat where Frankie was waiting. Mano decided to go to a bar to eat with Frankie, runs into an old woman of his, and tells Frankie to go to a hotel for the night and return to the boat early in the morning."

Vito opened the dolce and continued. "Frankie leaves the bar, walks one block to the hotel, and runs smack into Mike. Apparently Mike had been watching Frankie, but not on Dom's orders. Mike tells Frankie he can make him a better deal than either family. Mike tells Frankie it is either that or go to jail. Mike reminded Frankie he would not survive in a prison, a young man like himself. Mano left Frankie alone and screwed up big time!"

Vito poured more coffee and continued, "Mano had gone to his boat, took a small cruise out, and returned the next morning with this dame. When this Mike left, he told Frankie he would only give Frankie until night for an answer or be arrested. This Mike apparently thought Frankie would be easy to manipulate. Frankie took off for the pier to get Mano. Of course, the asshole Mano was not there! Frankie was walking to a phone to call me and Mike showed up at the pier. This Frankie needs many lessons before he works with us! Anyway, Mike reinforces how easy it would be to nab Frankie anytime, anywhere, and continues to offer Frankie anything to turn on the families."

Vito sternly said, "That is when you and your friend spotted the two together. Frankie never knew you were there. When Mike left, Frankie hung around about an hour before Mano docked. Mano now knows he was caught, and Dom is not very happy! Now, lucky for us, this Frankie is older and much smarter than Joey Thumbs. Growing up in Sicily, Frankie knew there would be no place on this earth for him to hide, maybe the moon, that would be it! Frankie still wants to work with us and Pietro. Of course, keeping us informed of Pietro and his business!"

It was at that point, I had to open the mouth of mine, "Vito, I do not like the fact that this is going on behind Pietro's back.

He is my friend. This could lead to a real problem. In addition, you told me I had crossed the line with my records of evidence all these years. Pietro even was willing to go along with that. What is up with Dommy? Another power play by him—and for what? Dommy promised me he would not cause trouble again. Now I wish you hadn't told me that whole story!"

Vito took my hand across the table, "Listen, Missy, Dom really lost on this one. He brought an undercover FBI agent into Pietro's home! This has to be corrected if Dom is to keep his credibility with the men. On top of that, Pietro cannot know. Maybe Dom is slipping, I do not know. First time for a while Dom screwed up this badly. Well, except for the trick with Claudio and jail. However, it is our problem, not yours. My problem is this Sergio!"

I became belligerent again and said, "Sergio is not your problem! And, another problem you all seem to have forgotten: Pietro believes I am working with him. I will feel as if I betrayed him if I don't warn him about Frankie. I will not be put in the middle, Vito. You better talk to Dommy and straighten this mess out. I think Dom has to come forward with all this mess with Mike and tell Pietro. If Pietro finds out somehow, Dom will look like he is setting up something—which I am not sure he isn't!"

I sat back in my chair as some thoughts came rushing into my head. I realized just how much I had been giving orders to these 'older' men now and not the other way around. When did I become the adult in this group of nuts? It was as if they were my parents and the roles were now reversed in their old age. I was becoming the voice of reason with them. Maybe they all were starting to slip. However, I did not want that promotion!

Vito asked, "Missy, what's the matter? You look like you saw a ghost." He turned to look behind him. "Your friend here?" I assured Vito my spirit friend was not, but the last visit was starting to make sense. I still planned to have my eyes checked; however, something was going to happen to Mike. I saw it and it had to do with fire.

I had to ask, "Vito, what is going to happen to Mike? Do you have any idea?"

Vito was honest, "Missy, no, I do not. That was never my department but Mano's. I know something has to quiet this Mike, but I don't get involved in that solution."

I became angry again, "Vito, how can anyone say that. Whether or not you actually do the act, you are involved, as am I unfortunately. I hate it all! I hate this job! I hate the rules! I hate knowing anything! I wish I were stupid and naïve. Maybe I would sleep at night without medications. Maybe my spirit friend would leave me alone when my mind was at peace. Vito I need to be out of this mess! You know it and I know it! Just how I am going to accomplish that is a different pile of problems!"

Vito sat very quietly for a few minutes as I lay my head down on the table. I did not mean to go off on Vito, but it had to be said. Finally, Vito said, "I will check into a few anger management classes as soon as I return to the States!"

I lifted my head and had to smile. "I am sorry, Vito. It is just the way I feel and I am not keeping things inside any more!"

Vito stood to leave and said, "When did you ever? I don't remember that time! Maybe I was asleep." Vito leaned down, kissed me on the top of my head, and left. I sat at the table thinking. I needed to talk to Isabella.

I walked out on the veranda, and it was a beautiful night. It was peaceful here. Now, if I could have my children and grandchildren closer, it would be heaven. I heard the phone ring and it was Sergio. "Ciao, baby. I am return from trip and want to stop see you Friday evening. Is that okay?" I was leaving the next morning so I did need to talk with Sergio about the work. Excuses? Maybe!

Chapter Thirty-Five

The next morning I was busy packing and getting the house in order. Each thing I did I could feel my heart get heavier. I had been through so much in my life, being alone was not a problem for me. The one thing that kept me going was the thoughts of my grandchildren and seeing them again. Roberto was going to be a problem! I hated myself for what I had done to him. The realization that I still loved Roberto ate at my heart.

I telephoned Isabella, "Buon giorno, my drinking pal, how are you?" I asked.

Isabella was happy to hear from me. "Elisabetta, you leave tomorrow, huh? Damn shame is all I have to say!"

I broke into her conversation and asked, "Isabella, I need to speak with you privately. Is Dominic around?"

Isabella assured me he was out with Mano and asked, "Honey, what is it? You have me believing now that I can do anything. Did my lovable husband cause more problems?"

I continued, "Isabella, did you hear about this FBI Mike? How could Dommy have been taken in like that? It is not like him! Have you noticed something different about the big D? If this Mike truly got by Dominic, I am worried. Is Dommy slipping?"

Isabella replied, "Honey, give me a minute. You are throwing these questions at me! I did hear about this Mike and Dom went nuts. It did get by him. I have no idea how or why. Maybe it is in Dom's plan. You know I cannot ask. Anyway, the only thing I noticed about Dom was he is a much nicer person since last year. I do not believe he is slipping. He usually has a method to his madness. What else is going on?"

This was my time to vent, "Isabella, listen. Are you willing to talk with me on the sly, you know, without Dommy knowing? I mean, it has nothing to do with hurting the family, but we need to talk and compare notes at least once a week or if something comes up in the meantime. Just like when I talked with Luigi once a week. Is that a problem for you?"

Isabella assured me it was not. "You and I are better with our minds anyway! Tell me what can I do to help. However, first, Joey will be my driver and we know how we can control him. Second, I plan to keep a close tab on Pietro. I have become a confidant with his maid, Carla. What is the plan? I know you have one!"

Indeed I did. Now was the time to break it to Isabella. "Isabella, how would you like me to train you to do part of this job? This, of course, would be without telling any of the men, especially Dominic. Would you be willing to do that? I remember you said you hated sitting around and loved being more involved. You know I am never passing this on to my son. We need to work together with complete trust. It means hiding things from everyone and living a separate life. Believe me it can be a pain in the ass; however, I am used to it. What do you honestly think?" I asked.

There was only a short pause and Isabella answered, "I have always told you, anything to help! Hey, if we cannot stick together, we have nothing but these idiot men! If there is one thing you have taught me, Elisabetta, is I can be my own person. The two of us have been to hell and back over all these years. I will do whatever you need!"

I knew Isabella's answer already but needed to hear it from her. "Listen, honey," I replied, "You would be a great help in using Carla and Joey to keep an eye on Pietro. Plus, you have Dommy under your feet all the time to watch. But, again, I cannot stress this enough, no one can know. I would not tell even Vito. I will continue business as usual. Only I know the system. You would be the second in line, only. Then, I would keep my family safe, both of them. At the same time, if anything happened to me, Dominic would be in charge of the money here in the United States and not Sicily. However, if you do not want to be in the middle, I certainly would understand. We have to completely trust each other, and you know I don't do that easily!"

Isabella answered, "Sounds like a plan to me, Elisabetta. It is not a problem. After all, you are only protecting everyone you love, including my dumb husband. I am really, truly flattered that you trust me with this. We could literally kick ass and take names as a team. Just tell me when, where, and how, and I will be there as soon as we return to the States. Honey, you know I love you like a sister; oh sorry, I mean more than that!" Isabella laughed.

I had to ask, "Isabella, where did Mano and Dommy go, do you know?"

I hated her answer. "They took off late last night for Rome for a few days. However, unfortunately, so did Mike from what I understand. You and I know that can't be good!"

I was silent for a second and said, "Not again! I know it cannot be good! Isabella, I have lived with so many secrets deep in my soul, how do I mend my wounded spirit this time? Do you actually think this Mike will make it to the plane?"

Isabella sighed and answered, "Let's not even go there! It is out of our hands!" That is exactly what was preying on my mind!

Just then the gate bell rang and I had to cut my conversation short with Isabella, "Isabella, someone's at the gate. Honey, I will talk to you in the States. You and Dom have a safe trip back!" As I answered the gate phone, I heard Vito. I had hoped it was Sergio! Boy, did I need a hug from Sergio now.

"Missy," said Vito, "open the gate. We need to talk!"

As I pushed the button, Vito could hear me say, "Shit!"

As Vito entered the house, after his usual kiss on the head, I had to ask, "I would guess from the tone of your voice you are not here to talk about my trip to Rome tomorrow, huh?"

Vito walked me to the couch and said, "Sit down!" I braced myself for what I knew, deep in my heart, was coming my way. Vito said, "I am almost afraid that this will be the straw that breaks the jackass's back! Not that you are that," Vito said flustered.

I looked directly in Vito's eyes and said, "I'm all ears! Just spit it out and get it over with!"

Vito took my hand, "Rumor has it that our friend Mike has met with an unfortunate accident in Rome."

I did not want Vito to know I spoke with Isabella, so I acted stupid and said, factiously, "Oh, yes, I am sure it was an accident! What happened?"

Vito continued, "Mike had a 'tour guide' take him to see the sights in Rome before leaving tomorrow for the States. He was staying at an apartment of a friend. Apparently Mike fell asleep in bed with a cigarette. The fire was bad and they found him dead. The charred FBI badge found among the ruins immediately identified this Mike. Didn't you warn him at Pietro's about his smoking?" I could feel it coming and I ran to the bathroom. Afterwards, I sat on the edge of the tub, and my mind was spinning. My spirit was right again. Why did I not do something to stop this? Did it happen because of what I saw from the spirit or because I told whoever did this what I had foreseen? Was I the marionette master now instead of the marionette?

When I came out of the bathroom, Vito's concern was all over his face. "Missy, I am sorry. I wanted you to know before you heard it at home tomorrow."

I looked at Vito and said, furiously, "I am leaving both families and I plan to survive it before I lose my mind completely!

Vito, it is not an option! My mind is made up! I cannot and will not go through this again!"

Vito kissed my forehead and said, "I'll leave you alone. Just call if you need me. Lorenzo and I will be here tomorrow morning at seven o'clock. But, Missy, you have your work cut out for you if you actually think that is an option!"

Chapter Thirty-Six

There was no sleeping that night. The medications could not turn off my mind. I had hoped Sergio would be true to his word and stop before I left, but he never did. Lorenzo and Vito were there early with coffee and *dolce*. No one said a word to each other as we walked around like robots. I was crying off and on, and Vito finally stopped me in the kitchen and said, "If it makes you feel any better, your friend was here last night and I told him to leave you alone".

I was shocked. "And just how was that going to make me feel better, Vito, just how? Sergio would have been the one person to help me out of this depression. I need to protect him from all the crap of the job. Dammit, I got him involved! Vito, is it that I won't be able to trust you now either?" Vito was hurt, but I did not care. My job as the marionette was back!

The trip to the airport was just as silent. Sometimes silence makes the biggest noise! I knew Lorenzo was upset as he kept watching me through the rear view mirror. Most of the time I kept my eyes closed just so I would not have to be nice. I was very happy Vito was not returning with me to the States. I did not like Vito very much today. In addition, I did not like myself at all! I could feel my mind slipping badly. Just how was I going to deal with Roberto and the family on top of all this?

I walked away from the two men at the airport without saying good-bye. As I walked to the area gate, I thought of meeting Mike on the trip here. You never know when you wake up in the morning what life will hold for you. Right now, wherever he was, I bet Mike wished he had knocked someone else down instead of me. Why did I have to be on that damn pier with Sergio? I probably caused Mike's accident. Well, it will be easier when I return home to go with my head and gut. My heart was a big ugly hole in my chest.

I stopped to purchase a paper, hoping to see something about the accident. Unfortunately, there were no articles. Maybe it just was too early for this edition. My mind then drifted to Mike's family, or loved ones, back in the States. I found a quiet spot alone and waited the two hours for the flight. I was in shock, rapidly losing my mind, and was in and out of the bathroom constantly until it was time to board.

Just as I entered the line to board the plane, my cell phone rang. It was Sergio, "Ciao, baby. Please you understand I at your casa but no can see. Man tell me no. You understand. I no want you go and think I not casa." I said I did and could not talk as I was boarding. Sergio was extremely sad. But, honestly, I did not feel like talking to anyone.

As I settled in my seat on the plane, the phone rang again. It was Vito, "Missy, please, honey. Have a safe trip. I love you. I am sorry for last night. I did overstep my boundaries. I was only thinking of you and knew just how upset you were. I was afraid this Sergio would only add fuel to the fire. Honest! I did not mean to interfere. Please call me when you get home! Okay?" I just hung up and turned off the phone.

Over my eight-hour trip home, I mapped out a plan for my life, both of them. I knew I had to make definite life-changing moves now if I was to survive another day. Isabella was a perfect person for the bookkeeping work. After all, it consisted of using only logic and rationality—something all men overlooked. However, I still would keep the total system to myself until I died.

I made notes to telephone Pietro, go with my gut in revealing the current problems, and leave out my empty heart. I would give Dommy one chance to do that, explaining on his own of Frankie and Mike's accident. Most importantly, I decided to open the box from Luigi and see what advantage the information would also give me. I would make it a point to add the notes and names I constructed on the plane to my paperwork against the families for my own safety. Gina would have to get a bigger safe!

To help relax, I watched a few adult cartoons and listened to music. I had thought Davido would be meeting me at the airport. As it happened, the plane was one hour earlier than expected. I rushed outside the airport where I was supposed to meet him. I had made many calls to Maria, who was afraid to tell me Roberto would be there instead of Davido. After two hours of waiting, in the cold, I could no longer feel my toes. I called Maria one last time. She advised me that Roberto was there. Great. Just what I needed now. Why I just didn't throw myself in front of one of those big buses and get the pain over with surprised me.

Roberto was waiting inside and I was outside. Big mess all the way around. I was so angry when Roberto finally thought to call Maria. See what I mean about men never using logic? Of course Roberto was all apologies, but I wanted to go for his jugular vein and ask questions later. I went directly to Maria's to see the baby. At last, Niccolo would make me smile.

I hated the thought of going home with Roberto. Why would I do that to hurt him again? I did not want anything to happen to Roberto. I saw a huge change in him, and for the better. He was a good man in these past years. Somehow I would have to make this all up to him. I just wanted to go to Gina's or stay with Maria, anything but that! Of course Roberto was bossing me as he usually does with the disguise of what was best for me!

"Elisabetta, you are exhausted and need to be home, in your

own bed. That is just the way it is going to be!"

The marionette just did as my strings were pulled. What happened to that bitch I left in Sicily who wasn't afraid to speak her mind? Where did I put those notes I made on the plane?

As tired as I was, I hadn't realized that Roberto's lawyer advised if I returned home, the divorce would go back to the two years waiting period. I wasn't going through with the divorce anyway. It was a big misunderstanding on my lawyer's part. Roberto was also lecturing me on the way from Maria's on how I was to stop the support hearing in two weeks, first thing the next morning. He wanted us to work out the money problems ourselves. I thought, The hell with the notes I made on the plane, where are my pharmaceuticals?

Roberto agreed to sleep on the couch! I never unpacked my suitcases! From Italy, I had made an appointment to see Gracie's eye specialist the next morning. If my spirit was right about Mike, God knows what will be found now about my eyes. One problem at a time—yeah, right! I locked my bedroom door and fell asleep.

Chapter Thirty-Seven

Early the next morning, I telephoned Gina and Gypsie. I had planned to see Gina after the eye doctor appointment to add the papers to her safe and collect Luigi's box. I stopped at the bank for the key in my safe deposit box and proceeded to the doctor's. Gracie was there waiting for me, and I felt safe for the first time in many weeks. My dear friend always had that effect on me.

As I was waiting my turn, Gracie and I talked about the key and Luigi's box. I asked her if she would be with me for the unveiling of this Pandora's box of crap. Gracie replied, "You know I will. Nevertheless, first things first. You need to clear your mind of that damn spook's premonition about your eyes. I need it to clear my own mind. I have been worried about you!" Before long, it was my turn for the doctor.

Each test conducted was excellent. I had 20/20 vision at my age and only needed slight magnifying glasses for close reading. The cataracts and glaucoma tests were negative. The last test, the doctor dilated my eyes again to check the pressure of the optic nerve. That is when he seemed concerned, "Elisabetta, I have never seen anything like this before. I need to take a picture of behind your eyes. I'll be right back!"

As he left the room, I said to Gracie, "What the hell is that all about? Everything seemed normal until just now."

Gracie smiled and said, "Nothing ever has been normal about you. Relax. He'll be back and I'll ask questions!"

The doctor returned, took close x-ray photos of my eyes, and asked that we remain until he made sure they developed without a problem. He returned five minutes later and closed the door. Gracie spoke up instantly, "Doctor, both you and I know how much I have been through with my eyes and aneurism. What did you see? I am sure I could understand and maybe explain to Elisabetta?"

The doctor looked at me and said, "I see two big holes, and I am concerned!"

As usual, I tried to joke, "I just don't see how. I wore pants today!"

The doctor laughed and turned to Gracie, "Your friend here has a great sense of humor. However, what I saw behind the eyes is very high hypertension pressure. It is so unusual to see a pressure that high in someone who is not losing their eyesight and does not have cataracts or other eye disease. In addition, I noticed that the hole that surrounds the nerves and blood vessels into the optic nerve is extremely large on both sides. I took a baseline measurement and want to see Elisabetta in six weeks." He then turned to me and said, "We will keep a close watch on this hypertension; however, it is the most unusual case I have seen in a long time. You have no other symptoms of a possible problem with your sight. Therefore, I plan to contact your doctor as well."

I looked at Gracie for some kind of hint as to what exactly was wrong with my eyes. She just smiled, patted my hand, and said, "It will be fine, don't worry. We will return in six weeks and check. Now, you can tell everyone you have four big holes!" The doctor arose laughing as he left the room.

Gracie and I left to go to Gina's and retrieve the box. I told Gracie again about the visit from my spirit friend. "Does this mean an operation, Gracie? I saw blood coming from his eyes when he visited me. That was the whole reason to see the doctor when I returned."

Gracie assured me she felt there was no need to worry. "You have enough now. Let's not worry unless we have to, you hear me?" Gracie demanded.

When we pulled into Gina's driveway, both Gypsie and Gina came running outside. My friends, I thank God for my friends. Of course, out came the champagne, martinis, and snacks. After a little catching up, I pulled Gina aside to ask if I could open the safe, add some papers, and take the box from Luigi.

When I returned to my friends, I felt awkward. I knew Gina and Gypsie were wishing I would open the box in front of them. I needed to explain, "You know all about my life. You all have lived it with me. But I feel I need to do this alone. Okay?" I had my mind made up that at least Gracie secretly would be there with me. I needed someone else to trust with this information, whatever it was. My friends understood completely.

As I held the box, I started to cry, "What control over my destiny does this box hold?"

Gina answered quickly, "Whatever it holds, you will handle it. Remember your character is your destiny. This is only a box!" The four of us spent the next few hours laughing and catching up on family gossip. After too many martinis, Gracie decided to drive us home. I had to put off opening the box for another day. I was not ready for it yet!

The next morning, between the jet lag, the sleepless night, and the alcohol at Gina's, my brain was fried. I was depressed and had a headache and diarrhea. Focusing on anything would be a challenge today. I immediately called Mark in California to let him know what was happening.

"Hey, sweetie, where are you?" he asked.

"Unfortunately, I am back here in the States. Roberto has contested the divorce and everything is horse crap as usual." I told Mark about the box again and that I was planning to open it.

As always, Mark was my strong rock, "Listen, Elisabetta,

make sure someone you trust is with you. Do not do this alone. Do you want me to fly there? I can catch a flight tomorrow." I told Mark it was not necessary. Unconsciously, I had already changed my mind to do just that, open it alone. I did not want anyone else hurt or involved in whatever might be exposed about my life.

I sat quietly for a few minutes. I needed a plan. I could not be disturbed when I tackled this box. I needed everyone to back off me so I could fully understand whatever it held. I telephoned Gracie and told her what I was going to do. "Elisabetta, you know I will be there if you need me. Better yet, you can come here to my condominium and I will leave you alone. Your family cannot bother you here. What do you think?" asked Gracie. There was my plan! I thanked her and said I would be there within the hour.

I packed up the beautiful box, the velvet satchel with the key, and my sanity (I hoped), and left for Gracie's. I could feel the adrenalin pumping and it was that exact feeling of 'flight or fight.' I was scared! However, I knew I needed to do this now. I was thinking of what happened to Mike in Rome, and maybe there would be something in Luigi's box to help me understand or protect me.

Gracie greeted me at the door with a hug and said, "I am leaving for the shopping center. I cleared off the table so you could spread out and left pencils and paper! You call me on my cell when you are through or if you need me! I can be back here in ten minutes. Okay?" I could only nod that I would do just that and Gracie left her house.

Chapter Thirty-Eight

I took a deep breath and closed my eyes for a second. I then turned off my cell phone and poured myself ice water. As I sat at Gracie's dining room table, I could hear buzzing sounds in my head. I sat the box on the table, got my glasses out of my pocketbook, lay the velvet pouch in front of me, and examined the outside of the box completely. It was a beautiful box with large hinges and lock. I thought, *This has to be older than Luigi.* I had never tried the key in the velvet pouch. What if this key belonged to something else? Aloud I said, "Well, here you go Missy, ready or not!"

I took the key from the pouch and realized just how old it was. "Please fit!" I said as I rubbed my hands gently over the top where the large angel and doves were. I inserted the key and turned it twice. When I heard a clicking sound, I knew it was opened. I wanted to stand and run. I was perspiring profusely and my head was now throbbing. I slowly lifted the lid afraid there was something in it that would hurt me not only mentally but physically as well.

There lying on top was a very old, hard-backed journal with

my name, Elisabetta Ameno, and a message: "Please read this first." The aged book was sitting on top of another antique-looking box. I said aloud, "Okay, Luigi, is this a joke? Each box will contain another until I have lost my mind completely!" I lifted the old book from the box and examined it closely before opening. I fanned through the book and realized it had to have been composed over many long years; and, I instantly knew it was Luigi's handwriting. I opened the book to the first page, held it against my heart for a second, took a deep breath, and started to read.

Caro Elisabetta,

If you are reading this now, I apparently am gone. If the Don is still alive, I apologize for scaring you with him! However, the Don is an honorable man. Don't be afraid of him. He surely will not hurt you in any way. I realize he is old but I have always trusted him. Believe in your heart that every one of us old men love you.

If Don Lazzaro is dead, see Isabella. Trust her! Teach Isabella everything she needs to know, but not everything you know! But, unfortunately, it is now over. Everything you and I have ever been taught is gone. My constant worry now is what is going to happen when all that love and loyalty we have for each other is gone with the old familgia. The new familgia is coming up quickly now.

Missy, honey, don't feel anger or bitterness towards anyone who brought you into this mess we all called a life but make your own choices now. Do It! Believe that all the men love you completely. But, now more than ever, make your own happiness.

One thing you never knew about me is I am an old-fashioned romantic. In Sicily, men I knew made fun when they saw me reading poetry. It didn't bother me. I always told them they were jealous none of them could read. Nevertheless, I loved flowers, beauty, and I often pretend-

ed that the world was run on love. Missy, I was wrong, dead wrong! That is, until you came back into my life. Even though this quiet part of my soul kept me going all my life, I found family again, a reason, a purpose, with you.

Missy, it has taken many years to write this letter to you and longer for me to find all the contents of this box. I sat one day after reading a Ralph Waldo Emerson poem and decided he was talking about you...! What lies behind us and what lies before us are tiny matters compared to what lies within us.

Missy, I believe in you and know in my heart and soul that you were always the strength of our family. I am the last person to give you rules, especially now, but please take this to your heart. That is what they are meant for. To help you before you see any papers I kept for you all these years. A lot of it might be what you learned from Moe. I cannot be sure. Unfortunately, a lot you never knew. Mostly, after all is said, I want you to be safe and happy.

Honey, my rules are simple ones. Know your enemies. In the life that was mine, in today's world, there is no respect for families, trust, love, nothing. Learn not to take things so to heart, shake off problems, and move on. Live your life not someone else's description of what your life should be!

Mostly, hold tight to what is important. Hold on to faith; it is the source of believing all things are possible. It is the fiber and strength of your confident soul.

Hold on to hope; even if it is hard to do. It gets rid of doubt and helps attitudes to be positive and cheerful.

Hold on to trust; it is the core of fruitful relationships that are secure and content.

Hold on to the best, love; it is life's greatest gift of all. It shares, cares, and gives meaning to your life.

*Hold on to **your** family, YOUR FAMILY; they are the*

roots and the beginnings you grew from; they are the vine that grew through time to nourish you, helped you on your way, and always remained close by.

Hold on to friends; they are the most important people in your life, and they make the world a better place.

Hold on to yourself; all that you are and all that you have learned, for these things are what makes you unique. Don't ignore what you feel or what you believe is right and important; I know what you were taught, the rules from Moe, but your heart has a way of speaking louder than your mind! Some of the old rules are just that...OLD!

Hold on to dreams; achieve them diligently and honestly. Never take the easy way or surrender to deceit.

Hold on! You have constantly made room for others! Just keep remembering others on your way, continue to take time to care for their needs. Enjoy the beauty around you. Have courage to see things differently and clearly.

Hold on and contribute; make the world a better place one day at a time and don't let go of the important things that have given you meaning to your life!

Missy, inside this box are many new things you will have to deal with. I hope the fact we are related does not change your love of family. It increased mine with just the birth of Moe's sons.

Elisabetta, believe in miracles, but don't depend on them. Don't mistake kindness for weakness. Don't be ashamed of honest tears, they help to cleanse the soul.

Now, honey, take out the old antique box. This box was your grandfather's. I have kept it safe all these years. Since Moe died so young, he knew nothing of the entire contents. Look at the front of this box. On the right side, turn the leg counterclockwise and a key will be there tucked inside the leg. Use that key to open this box.

I have layered the paperwork according to my

descriptions in this journal. Take your time, as most of these papers are extremely old and fragile. This first page, Elisabetta, is information on Pops!"

I lifted out the antique box and placed it on Gracie's table. The workmanship was magnificent and I wondered how something so beautiful could possibly hold anything evil. I found the key, opened this very old box, and found a white paper with a black hand printed on it! I stared at it for quite a while as the palms of my hands tingled to the point of hurting. I knew what that meant and quickly remembered Dad mentioning the 'black hand' of the mafia. I looked back at Luigi's journal.

Pops was instrumental in creating this 'black hand' in Sicily. However, I heard he had to escape arrest in Sicily and came to America in the very late 1890s or early 1900s. This did not stop Pops from continuing to help the people who were loyal to him, even from the States. He was indeed older than one hundred years when he died in the early sixties.

I sat and put my palm directly over this huge handprint and was amazed at the size of it. I remember Pops older always. At his young age, Pops had to be a very large, strong man. I looked back at the journal.

Missy, read up on the original reason for the black hand. They were not angels but originally had the right idea. They wanted Sicily to be independent. Just trust me and believe they were good men! And that is where your grandfather comes into the picture.
Your grandfather was Pop's right hand man, mentor, and the go-between for Sicily and America. They were like brothers. Your grandfather could come and go and kept Pops' legacy alive. That is until the opposition got wind of what he was doing. He also had to flee to

America or be killed. That part, I am sure, you know by now. So, these next envelopes under rubber bands, explains Pops' name, your grandfather's name, birth certificates, and deeds for land in Sicily.

As I slowly looked over the paperwork, I could only shake my head in disbelief. I found old passage papers for the boat to America, old pictures of my grandfather when he was young, with Pops at his side. There also were many announcements of deaths of people I never had heard of before. I saw a picture of a beautiful Sicilian woman holding a plump baby. I looked back at the book.

Missy, your grandfather was a very well-revered man by many people. He was a free lancer of sorts, and both Pops and he were resented and feared at the same time by the cafonis who craved power and money. Therefore, when your grandfather was forced to leave, there were men who thought him such a threat that everyone who was in contact with him, known amici, were murdered. This will explain the next piece of paper, my birth certificate!

I gently picked up this very big piece of paper, as large as a college diploma, and the only name I recognized was Luigi.

As you can see, your grandfather, my and Moe's father, was a busy man. He had two families...one here in Sicily with my mother and one in the States with your grandmother. I was born the same year as Moe. Missy, I am your uncle in more ways than one, but I will explain that as you go through all these papers. Let me explain the name differences on my birth certificate. When I was born, my mother knew she had to stay in Italy as all her family was here. I had to use my mother's maiden name so the men looking for your grandfather would not know and kill me or use me for bartering. My mother did this to protect me with the help of your grandfather [my father], Don Lazzaro, and Pops. However, I was saddened that my mother had to live her life carrying the marks of an unholy puttana rather than reveal the truth.

I sat quietly for a few minutes, trying to comprehend all this information. I was afraid to continue, and afraid not to! I looked back at the familiar writing.

Missy, the next pile of pictures has names, marriages, and birth and death dates, of family members here in Sicily. Some will be a shock, but it is way past the time for you to know. Use any information very wisely, or not at all!

I pulled out all the photos and papers on the next layer. I saw Luigi's family, his mother, aunts, uncles, cousins, Don Lazzaro and his family, so many people, so many faces, familiar but strange at the same time.

Now, look at the last picture. There you will see a beautiful woman that I have my arms around. She is holding the most beautiful little girl, a true angel. Look closely and then continue to read."

I looked at every detail, my old rules rising to the surface again. This woman was truly beautiful with a young Luigi's arm around her. She seemed sad to me even through the smile. I wondered if it was Luigi's wife although I knew she was older. I had never known he was married. So, I continued to read.

Missy, this was my mother, Margarita, holding my sister. My sister's name was Priscilla. Because of the reputation my mother had due to my birth, my mother had an unexpected visitor to our home one night when she was alone. The intruder was the only child of the Don's sister. Don Lazzaro's nephew! This stupido beat and raped my mother, which lead to the birth of my wonderful sister. Your grandfather contacted Pops, who talked to Don Lazzaro, and this nephew was handled. Missy, you will get to know this lesson... there are no small secrets if it involves the familgia!

I had to stop and catch my breath. I took a sip of water and tried to ignore the horrible feeling in the pit of my stomach. Why was I so afraid now to continue reading? Why didn't Dad tell me of his half-brother? Was he ashamed of my grandfather? I shook my head to get rid of that notion. I knew Dad and Mom better. I was very afraid to look at another piece even though I knew I had to finish this.

Missy, I know you had to carry many secrets over your life. This is one time I truly wish I could be right there with you to handle what I am about to say.

My mother raised Priscilla and me with the same love. She was a wonderful woman even though the town thought her lower than a 'puttana' at this point in time. After all, she had two children out of wedlock.

Don Lazzaro handled the problem even though it was his familgia. The Don's sister never forgave him for the killing of her only child and son. Now you will see an article announcing the horrible death of Rodolfo. He was found naked, castrated, with several objects found in his rectum. Missy, I am sorry to be so detailed but you need to know your roots, your legacy.

Now, I was getting sick to my stomach. My roots were with Mom, Dad, Junior, and Claudio! What freaking roots was Luigi talking about? What legacy? I forged ahead.

Priscilla was a good girl, sweet, kind, and gentle.

Unfortunately, in her very early teens, she fell in love with an older man. That man was Pietro and she became pregnant. Priscilla and my mother knew there would be consequences; so, rather then tell Pietro the truth, my mother and I sent Priscilla to the States where she lived with Moe, my half-brother and Elisabetta, his wonderful wife.

That move became the saddest day of my life and turned my mother into a recluse, mentally never the same. We never saw my sister again as Priscilla died during childbirth. Fearing that Pietro and Don Lazzaro would retaliate if they knew we had hidden a child from them, we had to make decisions, for the good of everyone and this beautiful baby girl. Moe, Elisabetta, and Pops wanted to keep this precious baby and raise her as the family she indeed was.

Your brother Junior was over six years old already and your mom and dad had problems having another child. Therefore, it was decided that you would be raised as their daughter. To this day, Missy, Pietro does not know you are his daughter! Absolutely no one knows!

Chapter Thirty-Nine

The tears were streaming down my face as I sobbed! My head was pounding, my heart broken! Who was I? What was I? Everything I believed all these years were lies? I felt betrayed, alone, weak, and void of all feelings. I needed Gracie with me before I could go any further. I felt as if I could die. I picked up the phone and called Gracie to return home.

One look at my face and Gracie knew it was not good news. "Oh God, Elisabetta, tell me what's the matter?"

Through my tears I answered, "Gracie, I don't know who the hell I am anymore. I just cannot believe anything or anybody now. Please, look at this letter from Luigi before I completely lose my mind!"

Gracie put her arms around my shoulder and said, "Elisabetta, lie down on the couch. Let me catch up to where you are now in this mess. Honey, there isn't anything we cannot handle. I know who you are! You are my dearest friend, the sister I never had, and a wonderful person. You always have been! Just lie down, please." I did as she asked and Gracie moved to the table and the pile of papers.

It seemed to take Gracie forever and occasionally I heard her whisper, 'Oh, God!" Finally, Gracie walked over to the couch and sat down. "Elisabetta, let's you and I start at the beginning and sort this out slowly. But first, we both need a drink!" As she walked to her kitchen, she said, "You stay over tonight. We will pick this up tomorrow. You have had enough for your old brain tonight. This is gonna take some time!" All I could do was close my eyes tightly as I sat upright. I thought, Just maybe all this is a bad dream.

The rest of the night, Gracie and I talked and napped off and on. She knew exactly what I needed, to talk about my parents, my brothers, and sort it all out. I could not understand how they were not my biological family. Claudio and I even had the exact blood...well, maybe because of Grandfather. I did not know what to feel or think. By four o'clock the next morning, Gracie and I were ready to tackle this complete history from the beginning.

Gracie poured coffee for the two of us and calmly said, "Honey, this is how I see it. I made notes last night as I was going over all this intertwined mess. Luigi and your 'dad Moe' had the same father. That made Luigi your true uncle and your dad your half-step-uncle. A nephew in the Lazzaro family fathered Luigi's sister. This makes Don Lazzaro your great-Uncle, once removed. Luigi's sister, Priscilla, became pregnant by Pietro, which makes them your biological parents. Rodolfo and Margarita are your maternal grandparents. Oh, Blessed Mother! This is so damn confusing!" With that, I started to cry again. Gracie continued, "Honey, I am sorry! But before we can go on with the rest of this box, we need to make these notes, okay?" I nodded.

"Elisabetta, you are the only child to Priscilla and Pietro, a great-niece to Don Lazzaro, and only living blood relative to both him and Pietro. Your grandmother's name was Margarita, your one no-good grandfather was Rodolfo; your mom, dad, Junior, and Claudio, were adopted family of yours, legally anyway! Well, except for your dad who was a half-uncle." Gracie shook her head as tears ran down her face. I was like a mummy, drained of blood and wrapped with this tight rope made of paper. Gracie grabbed my shoulders tightly and said, "The one and only thing to remember is you had wonderful parents, adopted or otherwise. They loved you, that I know as a fact!"

I was not so sure and asked, "Then why didn't I know? Why didn't Dad tell me, especially with preparing me for this life-changing job? How could Claudio and my blood be identical if I was not their biological daughter? I remember Claudio being born, for God's sake!"

Gracie answered as she also had tears streaming down her face, "Do you feel any differently now that you know? I am sure you do not! You had a loving family, and as your Dad told you many years ago, there is never enough time to do and say the things that need to be. Your mom was always sick. How and why would they tell you? You were their daughter as far as they were concerned. Then your Dad died so young too! The problems with Claudio and Junior were always overwhelming! When would have been a good time, honey?"

I knew Gracie was right. However, telling my heart that was another story! I hugged her and said, "I don't know if I can go on with the rest of this box! What other surprises are waiting to choke me?"

Gracie patted my hand and said, "This you need to finish! We will work it out; but isn't it better to know everything there is to know? What did Luigi say in that letter, 'you need to know your roots, your legacy'? There might just be that one piece of paper that will end this nightmare for you once and for all and give you freedom from this life! Ever think of that? Just look at this box! Was your life ever compiled this neatly? Lord, I know who my parents were and never had the family tree spelled out for me like this before. You owe it to yourself and your family. So, let's get back to it. What do you say?"

I closed my eyes and took a deep breath. Gracie was right. Luigi, uncle or not, loved me, as did Mom and Dad. I needed to work this out. Maybe there was a light at the end of this dark tunnel after all. "Okay! Let's get a drink first! Even rubbing alcohol at this point would be just fine!" I tried to smile. It hurt to do so!

Gracie poured wine and we sat down at the table again. I caught myself reading the past few paragraphs, repeatedly hoping it would change with the next reading. I sighed then and continued the next pile of papers. I looked to Gracie for strength as I handed her my birth certificate which read only 'baby girl Ameno' but had Priscilla's name as mother with Pietro as father written by the famous neighborhood doctor. Their last names were not Ameno. My dad again? Who knows! Gracie was busy making notes.

Next was a copy of another birth certificate showing my name with Mom and Dad as my parents. I then, for the first time, looked at the date; the same date Claudio was born. I guessed it was then that Mom and Dad realized I needed a birth certificate showing them as my parents, signed by the neighborhood doctor. Good old home delivery doctor that he was, I wondered if I could sue a person after his death.

The next paper was the death certificate of Priscilla, within three hours of when I was born. Attached to this paper were the pictures. I saw Priscilla, when pregnant, with Mom and Dad, holding Junior, at different family functions. The reality was hitting hard. This was true! Priscilla was a beautiful, extremely young woman, and I could see why Pietro would have loved her. I even saw my resemblance to this fair-haired woman with the huge eyes.

My hands now were shaking badly as I lifted out a few envelopes tied with a ribbon. These were letters from Pietro to Priscilla, addressed to her in Italy and apparently opened by Luigi's mother, Margarita. Priscilla never received these as she was in the States. I looked at Gracie and, after she realized who they were from, she said, "Elisabetta, they were your parents. Go ahead, read them. It might settle your mind a little."

I laughed, "Gracie, I'm not so positive of that; but I will read one anyway." I untied the ribbon and opened the first one. A quick glance revealed a desperate Pietro pleading that Priscilla return to Italy and to him. He wanted to "get married properly, an enorme {enormous} wedding and eventually raise a large family together." Pietro did not know of the pregnancy.

I put the rest aside for another time and picked up Luigi's journal. After finding where I left off, I read to Gracie:

> *Now, my sweetheart, I guess you want to kill the messenger. Unfortunately, I didn't even give you that option! You were raised to believe we were family, always had been, one way or another. The blood part I know was a shock and for that, I am sorry. But, you now know how protected you will be. Of course, that has to be your decision, when to let everyone else know. You use your instincts and it will turn out the way it should.*
>
> *Another piece of information, from before your accident Vittore found this little known fact of your connection to his father, the Don, and to Pietro. Vittore hated you for that family connection. You were a threat to him in many ways. I had to do what I did to protect you from this until it was indeed time for you to know. God forgive me, Vittore's death was a blessing in more ways than one.*
>
> *My mom always read the bible to me and, even today, I read it when I needed strength from God. Read it; and then read it again, and again, until etched forever into your mind and soul. Please do this for another lost soul...for me, Missy, please. The passage is from Matthew 16:26: 'What benefit does it have, if a man gains the whole world but loses his soul? What can man give in exchange of his soul?'*
>
> *Make sure you know if you want to disclose any of this! Do not let it change who you are!*

At this point, I had to stop. There was more in this box to comprehend, so much more to read in this journal of pain. I put my head on the table as Gracie rubbed my back. I sadly said,

"Gracie, this is so hard for me. It looks like Luigi's ledger has survived a hell of a lot. I just hope I am as strong! This minute it even hurts to talk or breathe. I am so confused of who I am and even where I belong!"

Gracie pulled me to a sitting position and softly said, "Everyone loves you, Elisabetta. You have gotten through horrible times, and you will again. Think of the kids and your grandchildren."

I could not help myself and answered, "Loves me? Love feels like an invitation for more pain to me! And, as far as my children and grandchildren, do I even tell them they are not who they think they are?"

Gracie then suggested I stay another night as she mocked my usual comeback, "Tomorrow's another day, Scarlet!

Chapter Forty

The next morning, surprisingly enough, I felt less stressed. Gracie and I decided to go out for breakfast. Gracie insisted we give our minds a break and maybe take the day off from this box of snakes as she put it!

"But, Gracie, I need to finish it before my trip in a few months. I need to know everything before I tackle this meeting with Pietro. If that is what I decide to do; right now I am not sure."

Gracie got my coat and answered, "We will. Do not worry. However, God, it has been so much to take in two days time! We both need a break. I have an aneurism, remember? You want to kill me? This has to be the topper of all cake toppers since I have known you. I might even take up seriously drinking soon!"

I called Roberto and explained a little of what I was doing with the contents of the box. Another surprise, he more than understood and only replied he'd be available if I needed anything. Thank the Lord! He was being compassionate. Did I die and go to heaven? I thought.

Gracie and I started out, and it was refreshing to see the sun and daylight. Both of us felt beaten as if the last two days ran into weeks. Gracie had secretly called Gina and Gypsie to have breakfast with us, and I was surprised when I saw them waiting at the restaurant. At least now I'd have some laughs.

Gina was her goofy self as usual and started with the server immediately, "We will start with Bloody Martin's. The hell with the Bloody Mary shit, we want the real thing…any man's blood will do!" She sent the server scurrying off.

I looked at Gypsie, "I thought you said you can keep her under control?"

Gypsie laughed, "Strong sleeping medicine, directly into the vein, is the only thing that can handle this bitch!"

Gina's comeback, "I passed bitch thirty years ago. You all should know I cannot be controlled by now!"

I thought to myself, Exactly my answer when in Sicily.

Gracie then informed them we were not to talk about the box, its contents, or my state of mind. Gina's reply, "What mind?" She then took the napkin, tied it around her head like in Italy a few years before, grabbed the knife and fork, and said, "Let them bring it on! Let's all go back to Italy now and show them what American women are capable of…whadda say?" I immediately pretended to move to the next booth. Gina yelled, "Don't make me come after you!" She scared all the people in the restaurant. I could see the servers trying to bribe each other to take our table. Damn, it was good being back with these nut cases. I could deal with them, at least.

The breakfast was fun and I felt more relaxed as our conversations flowed. They were indeed nut cases, and my mind never wandered back to the box. When we finished, Gina suggested we all play hooky and slip away to the casino. "It's only an hour's ride, let's go! Even if we only walk the boardwalk and watch the ocean."

Before I could answer, the decision was made it would be best for me to not only get away from the box but also go to the next state. "The farther the better," laughed Gina. Gina and Gypsy followed us back to drop off Gracie's car and we were off, in many ways!

My first hint that Gina and Gypsie already had this planned was when Gina stopped at a convenience store, pulled out a cooler from the trunk, and entered the store to fill it with ice. She then dumped the cooler in the back seat along with two large bags filled with olives, cheese, pepperoni, bread, nuts, and glasses, four bottles of wine, plates, and napkins. I looked at Gracie and smiled, "I could live right out of this back seat from now on....whadda you say, you up to it? We never have to go back to your house and face that box of snakes!"

Gracie then replied, "We are not going to think or talk about that box, remember. The rule for the day is only fun, conversation and maybe, some winnings."

The ride was a hell of a lot of fun! I then asked my friends if they wanted me to call Dominic. Maybe we could have a room just for the day. Just in case we lost early, got tired, or, I joked, if someone got lucky. It was fortunate that Isabella answered the phone. I put the cell on speaker and everyone talked to her for more than a half an hour. Isabella was so sad she could not be with us at that exact moment. However, Isabella did offer their condominium on the boardwalk, which I gladly accepted. After getting the name and phone of the person who had keys, we were on our way to Dominic's house before the casino. This trip was turning out very well.

As I approached the parking area of Dominic's condominium, there was a very distinguished white-haired man positioned in Dom's parking spot. Gina had to start, "Should I just run him over, duck down, what?"

I told her to let me out of the car and wait until I spoke to him. As I approached, it was someone I had never met before and I became uneasy. Being very coy, and remembering those damn rules, I simply asked, "I am sorry. Is this space private? I am to visit my friend's condominium in this building. My name is Elisabetta," as I extended my hand.

What relief when he kissed my hand and said, "Mrs. D said you would be here. My name is Tommaso and it is with much pleasure I finally meet you. Let me help your friends with bags and pull right into this spot." He waived for Gina to pull in as he moved to the side and gently took my elbow.

It took the four of us some time to clear the mess in the car from eating and drinking all the way. If a cop had pulled us over, we would be in jail. Tommaso just looked in amazement and asked for our bags. Of course we did not have any suitcases. He just grinned and said, "I see you travel light!"

We followed behind Tommaso as he carried the cooler. I whispered to Gina to behave herself and added a please. Of course, I had been at Dom and Isabella's condominium before, but none of my friends had ever seen it. It was beautiful, and Gina immediately went to touch and admire everything. Tommaso put everything into the kitchen. He then turned and I introduced him to the girls. He seemed particularly interested in my Gracie and was about the same age. "Mr. D has mentioned Gracie to me over the many years. If there is anything you need, I will leave my cell phone. Please call for anything!" However, he never took his eyes off Gracie. I could not have been happier as I watched her blush.

Tommaso handed me the keys, walked to the door, and turned, "Please remember, call me for anything. And, by the way, if you would like to have dinner, I can take you to a wonderful Italian private restaurant close by." He left still looking at Gracie.

Still blushing, Gracie looked at me and said, "Was he hitting on me? I have not had anyone hit on me in many years! Was he hitting on me, really?"

I smiled broadly, "I believe so there, cutie! Why not go to dinner with him tonight? He seemed to want to. Who knows, you two might just hit it off. Gracie, you are always alone or dealing with my life and crap. Come on, let's do it! I will call Isabella and get the low-down on him."

Gina then replied, "If he is a 'beat' we will have him 'whacked'." I had to laugh at her. I never heard that said except in the movies. Just then, my cell phone rang. It took me by surprise when I heard Sergio on the other end. He was obviously upset, and I went into the bedroom to speak to him.

"Are you okay? You sound terrible. What's wrong?" I asked.

Sergio hesitated and said, "I am in Austria and I got call from ospedale {hospital} that mio padre {my father} had fall from bed at home. How can he fall when cannot move at all? Giovina is at ospedale adesso. I no understand?"

I could not comprehend what he was saying. Dear Lord, this was the third accident when Sergio was away from home. Am I the only person on this earth who realizes there were three separate accidents over the years when she was alone with family members? It gave me a shiver up my spine as I said, "Sergio, are you sure it was an accident, another accident? I am sorry, but I think she is evil. I cannot shake that feeling. What are you going to do?"

Sergio was quiet for a short time. "I am going home now. Mio padre no move in bed when I leave home. He had no strength and was on feeding tubes. How?" Sergio was fighting with himself. He did not want to believe it very well could have been on purpose.

All I could say was, "Please, Sergio, my prayers are with you; but I cannot be here for you any longer. I am so sorry. I wish I could say something to make this right. Just check into the accident, okay?" Sergio, sounding heartbroken, promised as he hung up the phone. I could not let on that mine was broken too!

When I exited the bedroom, Gypsie was making drinks. I went over to her and explained the call. Gypsie adamantly said, "Believe me. That was not an accident. Giovina has been hoping for way too long for the old man to die. No one could make me believe it was not on purpose. I just talked to the family last week. The old man could not move at all. He was paralyzed and in a semi-coma."

"That's enough bullshit," Gina yelled. "We are here to have fun. You did warn Sergio over the years that Giovina was evil.

Let him deal with her black cat, bat wing, blood of frog, caldron-turning ass." I had to laugh. Gina was right; I could do nothing to help.

As we left the condominium for the casino, I turned to Gypsie and said, "I hope the hell Giovina doesn't have any of my hair or fingernails. She is one scary bitch!"

At the casino, we went directly to the private club. As we sat around the bar, I asked Gracie if she thought about meeting Tommaso. I knew I would have to persuade her. Therefore, I called Isabella. "Wow," said Isabella. "I get two calls on the same day and no one has died!"

I could not resist and said, "Not yet anyway," referring to Sergio's father. I told Isabella the story and she too was convinced we should use Giovina as a partner to Mano. I then asked about Tommaso. Isabella informed me that he was a "pussy-cat" and definitely a gentleman. She thought it a great idea to get Gracie together with him. That was all I needed.

I turned to Gracie and said, "It's set! I am going to call Tommaso and you two go to dinner somewhere. It will be fine! You don't need to worry!" Gracie reluctantly agreed as Gina and Gypsie jumped up and down at the bar. After the call, Gracie decided she would meet Tommaso at Dominic's condominium in about five hours. That way I could warn Tommaso of what we three would do if he touched Gracie in any way.

Now came the fun part as the four of us hit the casino floor. We decided to pool our money and go for the big jackpot. We walked around for a while until we came upon a dollar slot machine with a scene from Gone with the Wind. Gracie said to me, "There you go, Scarlet. It is perfect. It is actually calling your name!"

I had to laugh, "With my luck, I don't plan to touch it! Someone else has to pull it. I'll watch."

Immediately Gina spun around and asked, "Pull what? I am good at pulling things!" Don't tell me I will have to sedate her before this day is over, I thought.

Since Gracie was the best soul out of all of us, we decided

she should touch the machine. We had about $400 between us and started with the three coins at a time...nothing, nothing, nothing, and then BAM! Gina stated screaming, Gypsie was clapping, and Gracie and I looked at each other as if to say, What the hell is this! Gracie and I had no idea we had just hit for $10,000. When Gina screamed, "It's the jackpot...Wahoo!" Gypsie and I had to sit down, Gracie was speechless, and Gina took off dancing up the aisle singing..."We won, we won, oh yes, we won!"

Chapter Forty-One

We left the casino even happier than when we arrived. I just kept hugging Gracie. "Wow, $2,500 a piece is not chump-change. Thanks, honey. Only you could win with your pure soul! The rest of us are black clouds. Now we get you ready for the dinner!"

Gracie held her head and said, "I feel ridiculous at my age. I am nervous. I don't even have anything else to wear. What if it is an expensive place?"

I laughed, "It had better be; besides, just wash the armpits, and essentials and you are ready to go. Gina, give Gracie your cell phone in case she needs to call me, okay?"

I then raided Isabella's closet as I had done in Sicily many times. Isabella had a beautiful black sweater coat, a bright red v-neck sweater, and a perfect white scarf with sequins to go along with Gracie's black pants. We traded Gina's earrings, Gypsie's pocketbook, and my heels and we redressed Gracie for her big date. She looked wonderful and happy up until Tommaso knocked on the door. "Damn!" Gracie whispered.

"Listen, Gracie," I said as I put my arm around her shoulder, "believe it or not there is a sense of honor among these men. Tommaso will be a perfect gentleman or have to deal with Dominic. They know not to break the trust. It shows disrespect. I want you to go and have a great time." Gracie left with Tommaso, the look on her face was priceless. You might think we were sending her to the wolves. I told Tommaso, "Bring her back after dinner. Don't make me send Gina after you." I smiled but meant every word!

After the door closed, Gypsie seemed a little concerned, "Elisabetta, will Gracie be okay?"

Jokingly I replied, "Listen, I have learned over the many years to not have any romantic feelings about the familgia. Besides, a killer is usually someone you are close to, not a stranger. Gracie will be fine." I could see the fear on Gypsie's face and quickly said, "I am only joking!"

The three of us walked to the boardwalk for fresh air. It was a beautiful day and we did not want to return to the casino and lose our winnings. We talked about our lives, our children, our friendship. Gina was the one who asked first, "Elisabetta, what are you going to do with Roberto?"

I thought for a second and surprisingly answered, "I am going to stay and work on the marriage. Try to forget what happened over all these years. All my intuition is telling me to do exactly that! Everything happens for a reason…my meeting Sergio, my new grandson, maybe all leading me to this direction. I have enough to deal with and at my age, I am getting very tired of it all. What did you say earlier, Gina? We can always have Roberto whacked!"

We were laughing as we walked when I noticed a few men near a bench about half a block from us. I could tell by the size one was Vito. As we got closer, I warned Gypsie; to my surprise, she smiled. As we approached, Vito had his back to me and I put my finger on my lips to tell the other men to be quiet. I then put my hands over Vito's eyes. He merely put both hands over mine and said surprised, "My Missy!" He took my palms, kissed them both, and turned around. "Come here, honey. Give me a hug!

Gina, how are you? And, Gypsie, it does my heart good to see you again." He then kissed them both, introduced us to his friends, and insisted we go with them to eat. Yes, this had turned out to be a perfect day!

Vito immediately asked if we were alone. I told Vito that Gracie was with us and had gone out to dinner with a man named Tommaso. Gypsie again was the mother hen as she asked, "Vito, this Tommaso is okay, right? Gracie will be safe."

Vito put his arm around Gypsie and said, "Of course, that is a promise. God, Gypsie, I really have missed you. To think it was all over that crap in Rome! Come on, my favorite girls, andiamo!"

So as we walked, slowly I might add, with about fifteen hundred pounds around us, even the birds stayed clear! Gypsie and I were on either side of Vito; Gina was bringing up the rear with a man on each side. When I turned around, she looked lost between these two giants. There was one man walking in front of us and one man walking alone in the very back. Escorts, yeah, I knew better! I had to flap those lips "Vito, why so many 'friends' hanging close? Problems I should be aware of coming my way?"

Vito smiled, "It would have to get by me first. No, Missy, no problems. I am just handling some business here. Tell me, did you open that box?" Vito could tell by the look on my face, "That bad, honey? Whatever it is, we will handle. Listen, you know you can tell me if you need or want to, okay? Call me in a day or so. I want to know the dates you are returning for the meeting. Right now, it is a beautiful day, and we are going to take advantage and show off these gorgeous women on our arms.

As we approached where they parked the limos, Vito asked that we take two cars. He looked back at Gina and said, "Okay with you, Gina?"

"Only if I ride shotgun!" she laughed.

Gypsie looked at me and said, "It is way past the time to medicate her today!"

We seemed to drive only ten minutes to this not so impressive little restaurant a few miles from the boardwalk. However, the restaurant had a locked gate with a guard. The man approached the limos, scanned who was there, talked Italian to Vito, and unlocked the gate. Okay, what was that rule? Sit with your back against a wall to see who might enter. Ha, after that journal of Luigi's I can handle anything.

To my surprise, the atmosphere in the restaurant was as if we stepped into Italy by just opening the door. I loved this place and was surprised to see Tommaso and Gracie sitting at a table. Immediately Tommaso walked over to Vito and kissed him. However, when Vito asked them to join us, I could tell Tommaso wanted to be alone with Gracie. I whispered to Vito, "Let's leave them alone." We moved to a very large table in the back.

There were two men with Vito whom I had never met. One was Carmine and the other they called Pockets. I did not want the explanation of that name! However, they were gentlemen and probably a little older than Vito. They apparently lived near Atlantic City all their lives.

As we all sat around laughing and exchanging stories, Carmine said he used to be the rider on the diving horse on the boardwalk. Looking at the size of him now, it would have to be two Clydesdales connected at the hind-end and a much bigger pool of water! Carmine told us of an incident during one dive. "We had to ride the horse bare-backed and hanging on was a feat in itself. The drop, I believe, was about forty feet. Back at that time, money was hard to come by so I decided this was for me. I did maybe four shows a day. But, in the beginning, getting the damn horse to take the dive was almost impossible. If you really want the truth, the horse was smarter than me. I remember my first dive, the horse was backing away, and I was pushing it to go forward. He reared up on his hind legs, I almost slid off, was hanging onto its tail, as both of us went in the water. The problem was the horse crapped all the way down. It was blowing all over the front of me and I could not let go." It was the funniest story we had heard in a while, and Vito then went on to tell of Lorenzo and the dogs.

Dinner was finally over and I stopped at Gracie's table to see if she wanted to leave with us. Tommaso seemed sad to see Gracie go; but, she promised to keep in touch. Pockets drove us back to Dommy's condo. Vito mentioned he would again be in Italy the same time as me. It was a good day!

After Gracie changed her clothes, we gathered our cooler, filled it with more ice, and helped ourselves to a few bottles of wine. We were off for the trip home! We joked with Gracie constantly about Tommaso but she genuinely seemed interested in seeing him again. I was thrilled, however, I made a mental note to check into him a lot more, especially after Gracie confided Tommaso openly talked to her about Dominic and Mano. This was against any rule I had ever learned. Tommaso had to be stupid.

Gracie said, "Tommaso said Dominic was a narcissist, a legend in his own mind, always thinking the world revolved around him." I was shocked! I agreed with Tommaso, Dommy did not take criticism or rejection well either, but it was not Tommaso's place to say it.

Gracie continued, "You know me, Elisabetta, I just smiled and listened. Tommaso must have felt comfortable with me because he then went on about Mano. He said Mano was the biggest sociopath he ever met. He said Mano had no workings inside him for either moral or emotional feelings; therefore, Mano never felt guilt or empathy for anyone and was suited only for crime and enforcing the family code."

Now I was really getting angry. Just who did this Tommaso think he was and what was his standing in the family to feel comfortable speaking of either of these men in that way. I asked Gracie, "Who else did he drive into the ground?"

Gracie hesitated with this last analogy, fearing it would really fire me up! "Honey, he then went on to Vito. He said Vito was always paranoid. To Vito, the rest of the world has a problem. He felt people conspired against him or his loved ones. He was always protecting someone or another because of his fear."

I sat quietly thinking for a few seconds, and replied, "I think

I need to make a call to a few people and find out more about this character. However, Gracie, be sure, I will never mention your name. Something stinks with this nutcase. Just stay away from him until I check this out."

Chapter Forty-Two

The next day was very busy with airline reservations, family, phone calls to Isabella, Gracie, and Vito, and for just that day, the box never entered my mind. By bedtime, however, I knew I needed to finish it. I was feeling very uneasy after those open remarks from Tammaso to Gracie and felt I needed to continue reading the contents of the journal. Therefore, around midnight, I left for Gracie's house.

After four hours sleep, we tackled the box again. It took several minutes to find where we had left off and I began reading:

"Okay, Gracie, let's see…the passage from Matthew… then …here it is:

Make sure you know if you want to disclose any of this! Do not let it change who you are!

I continued to read Luigi's journal:

Lou, change your way of work if you are still keeping notes. They were okay with us, but not today. Please, use

only your memory. Today, notes are death papers. Keep
everything in your head and a copy of everything safely
tucked away. However, believe me again when I say your
bloodline will now keep you safer than ever.

Your padre, oh, I am sorry, Pietro, is a good man. I
believe he is much like Moe. Give him a chance to be in
your life at your discretions. Priscilla would be happy
for this. Of course, I know you are now saying...he has
brass ones...after all we have knowing kept from you;
but, at your age now, you understand so much more of the
reasons why.

The next pile of papers tells of my mother, Margarita,
and her family line. They too were no angels. My grand-
father on mama's side was the worst of the worst in Italy.
He was one of the biggest reasons Priscilla's pregnancy
was hidden. There was only cruelty in his heart and soul.
However, he was one of the richest men in his time. This
leads to the deeds and locations of the family homes in
Sicily that now belong to you."

I stood up and paced as Gracie looked on. "I am afraid to
even look at these, Gracie! All I want is to go back to about a
month ago and start over. It looks to me as if none of the men
wanted to deal with anything complicated or painful. Any inter-
nal conflicts were just dumped into this damn box for me to handle. Vito was right when he asked me at Luigi's funeral if I
thought I was ready for this. I should have doused this box with
holy water before even attempting to open it."

Gracie the friend that she is, only listened to me, patted the
chair for me to sit down, and shook her head. I sighed and did
just that as I continued:

Honey, there is an instruction sheet, a lawyer to con-
tact, and all the information you need to do whatever you
wish with the properties. However, there are also a lot of
my Mama's jewelry, her father and mothers belongings,

and Priscilla's baby items, which the lawyer has for you.
I sincerely hope you pass this on to your grandchildren,
of course, only if you decide to tell them your story!

I methodically opened all the deeds and other papers attached and tried to comprehend the worth of all this. After a lifetime of struggling, this was neatly tucked away in this box! There also were many Italian bankbooks showing astronomical amounts. Okay, was this yet another test for me; moreover, if I accepted this wealth, what or whose blood would be on my hands as well? Luigi did say his grandfather on his mother's side was cruel. There is just too much else to pay attention to at this point in my life.

"Gracie, what the hell will I do with all this property and how do I know if this lawyer is corrupt or not? Do I entrust Vito to handle all this for me?" I was in shock.

Gracie jokingly replied, as she rubbed my back, "We could always put Gina there somewhere and save a lot of money on in-hospital shock treatments." That certainly took the tension level down immensely and I had to laugh! I looked back at the journal:

Well, honey, most of the surprises is now finished at least on my end. Now Pietro might have a few. Just stick to your guns (poor choice of words here) and go with your instincts. I cannot stress that enough.

There is one thought I always had in regard to your spirit friend. I wanted to tell you on many occasions. Is it possible that he is your grandfather on my sister's side? I am talking about Rodolfo, the nephew of Don Lazzaro who raped my mother, which lead to Priscilla's birth and then you? He might have felt responsible or it is his penance here on earth before he can even enter into Hell! When I think of that hypnosis session many years ago when he told you he was your father. It was his fault Priscilla was born, and maybe his penance is to protect you since Priscilla died in childbirth. Who knows? Maybe just an old man rambling on...but anything is possible. I learned this in my long lifetime.

Remember, my Elisabetta, there is no one exactly like you. I often asked myself what I had done in my life to deserve you. You have kept your family together by your strong personality and independence. Do as you wish with all this information; but, I am truly hoping you do not keep these secrets from the people you love.

Listen to your heart, honey, what is it telling you? I know you. It is telling you to not choose. You have to in this instance. Choose for you. Sometimes the hardest person to save is you.

So, my beautiful niece, my wish is for you to be as happy as you have made so many, to get as much love as you have given, and to have every wonderful blessing for many more years!

There were so many moments when you understood too much and asked for too little...the understanding woman in you logged too many miles in other people's shoes.

Think kindly of me even after all this I have dropped on you. I have loved you always, amore mia.

Ti Amo, Zio Luigi

As I gently closed the journal and returned all the papers to the two boxes, I sighed, "Gracie, these men, their lifestyles, it is so hard for me to believe that compassion and cruelty can live side by side in one heart. All I know for sure, I need another suitcase just to take this stuff back to Italy. I need to face Pietro and take it from there. However, I will tell Vito. I trust him completely. And, thank you for being here for me!"

The last thing I placed in the box was Luigi's journal, the remainder of which consisted of poems written by Luigi to me. I wanted to read these, and the letters from Pietro to Priscilla, at a more quiet and personal time. Today, I had enough!

Chapter Forty-Three

When I arrived home, I telephoned Vito. He was excited over having dinner with us the other day but more excited over seeing Gypsie. "*Come va*, Missy! Are you going through that freakin' box? *Dimme*, what can I do?"

I immediately explained the conversations between Gracie and Tommaso and asked, "Vito, who is this guy to say things like that to her? He deliberately put down family to a stranger. Isabella thought Tommaso was a gentle man and no one should be worried. Was she wrong?"

Vito cleared his throat and said, "We have had problems with Tommaso for quite a while. Just likes to blow off his mouth. I will handle it; don't worry. Tell Gracie to stay away from him. She is entirely too classy. Now tell me your plans for Italy. Anything you need to talk to me about with that box?"

I had to laugh, "How many years do you have? Yes, if you can! I would love to meet you before the trip. Give yourself plenty of time though and bring your medications. On second thought, bring some for me too!"

We agreed to meet the next day, and I made many notes for

Vito. I wanted it to be easier for him to understand, even though I still did not! Maybe Vito could help me as to just how I was going to approach Pietro with the fact he was my father! I needed to think that my father was Moe, biological or not!

As usual, Vito was at my home on time and immediately I felt safe. "Buon giorno, Missy," smiled Vito, "Why the sadness in those beautiful eyes?" When I did not smile, Vito's concern shown on his face, "Come on, honey, what the hell was in that box that makes you look this upset?"

I hugged him hard and replied, "You better sit down with this one! It is a mind-blower!"

After pouring coffee, I sat the large box on the table. "Vito, I am not sure if you knew any of this but I am going to give you the short version of its contents. Have you taken your medications today, because, here goes! I have proof that Pietro is my father and that my mother was Luigi's sister, Priscilla."

Vito put his hand up to his mouth and gasped. The look in his eyes was pure shock and terror. I held my breath waiting for his response. Vito kept shaking his head as if what he heard was unclear. When he removed his hand from his mouth, Vito's voice was hoarse. He was at a loss for words. "But...wait a minute...what the hell...are you sure, honey? Is this a trick by somebody, a damn sick one at that...ah shit, come on...say that again!" I merely pushed the box closer to Vito and opened the lid. Vito looked at it warily and then at me. "Missy, I have known you all your life. I knew your mom and dad. What is this shit, and who else knows this? Are you sure it is true? Is this the stuff directly from Luigi?"

I just shook my head and Vito knew! If this was in the box from Luigi it was all very true and Vito looked as scared as I did. "Okay!" Vito finally said. "Coffee is not going to get me through this. Where's the booze?" I left the table and returned with a shot glass as Vito quickly poured two shots and drank both down quickly.

I was the first to speak up as Vito choked slightly on the second shot. "Vito, what the hell am I going to do with all this? I'm still in shock!" I went on to explain everything in the box hoping Vito would come up with a magic trick to turn back time. Vito sat still shaking his head.

"Missy, does Dominic know any of this? You know he is going to need a straitjacket when this hits the fan. My God, Missy, we are talking about Pietro being your father. Do you honestly think Dominic is going to be able to handle any of this? Dom will go ballistic!" Vito pushed himself away from the table and started to pace and continued ranting, "Honey, do you have any idea what this means for you, your family, or your life?

The tears started to fall as I begged Vito, "Please help me with this. What is in store for me? What do you think is going to be Pietro's reaction? I am worried more about him than Dommy."

Vito rubbed his hands together, took a huge sigh, and again asked, "Who else knows about this?"

"Gracie was with me through it all. She is the only one," I assured Vito. "I am extremely realistic after all these years. Please, Vito, don't sugarcoat anything. Where do I go from here?"

It was Vito pleading at that point, "Missy, give me a little while longer to understand this. It sounds as if you already have decided to tell Pietro. Am I right? Do you plan to confront him on our next trip? If so, I will definitely be there. Just give me a little while longer, please!"

Vito then sat back down at the table and proceeded to look quickly through the contents. I kept very quiet as I listened to Vito curse in Italian at each pack of papers or page of Luigi's journal.

When Vito finally spoke, I was in a daze and I jumped. "Honey, listen. What do you feel about confronting Pietro with this? Tell me and, you know, sweetheart, all this stays just between us. I think Pietro needs to know before Dominic. I have my reasons for that, so just trust me. I know we are in agreement that Dom won't handle this very well. Missy, you are the only one who can make this decision. You have the most at stake here, however, also the most to gain. Think about that before we make that trip. Also think about staying as long as it takes and settle this with Pietro."

Vito then came around the table and put his arms around my chair. "I know Gracie had to give you the best advice. She's a woman and always had your best interest at heart. She will understand what you are going through much better than I do. Don't blame yourself for any of this. For some reason, most women blame themselves for everything. Men will blame anything but. I will call you tomorrow and let you know the details of our trip. If I may make a suggestion, honey, if you decide to speak to Pietro do it after the meeting. You can do it! I know Pietro. There is no reason to be afraid. I will have your back and be right there with you." Vito kissed me on the forehead and left.

Before I had a chance to work anything out in my mind, the trip was upon me. Vito had booked the trip for six weeks. I had no idea how to get through the next day, let alone six weeks in Italy with Pietro! However, I had prepared myself for any scenario. I spent the time before the trip to copy every sheet of paper, deed, as well as Luigi's ledger. I was not going to take any original papers with me. They needed to be safe and I said a silent prayer, "Please, Lord, no more dreams."

I sat down the night before my trip and tried to explain the situation to Roberto but, only enough to keep him safe. He knew I needed to make this trip and was fearful for me.

"Elisabetta," Roberto asked gently, "Do you want me to go along with you? Maybe there will be trouble. Are you sure it is safe?" I knew nothing would happen to me physically...now, mentally, that was another story. However, I assured him I could handle anything; at least that is what I had been taught.

I carefully packed the copies of the contents of Luigi's box and kept it close to me. Vito had booked our flight and I was surprised it was first class. His reply to my questioning the first class treatment, "I need the room for my big ass. You need to make room in that big heart before talking to Pietro!" I ordered a drink as soon as the plane taxied down the runway.

Vito and I talked as we studied the copy of Luigi's journal. I touched Vito's hand and whispered, "It's almost surreal! In addition, the fact you knew nothing of this amazes me. Vito, you are slipping," I tried to joke. Vito was lost in the journal and seemed not to have heard me. I closed my eyes and tried to think of what I was going to say to Pietro.

Almost an hour went by and Vito awaken me by rubbing my hand, "Missy, this is hard for me reading all this. I watched you sleep and thought how innocent you looked and how you were going to handle this last sucker punch!"

I stretched and sat up straight as I lay my head on Vito's shoulder. "Unfortunately, Vito, I am no longer innocent. I have choices to make of what is true or not, to clear the dense mist always in my mind. I don't expect to comprehend this in one day. Hell, it took all my life of building this mental confusion to where it is today. I still cannot understand why no one ever told me I was adopted."

"Missy," Vito replied quietly, "what if Pietro rejects the whole idea of you being his daughter even with all this proof? Are you ready to handle that?"

This was one time I was speechless. I wasn't sure if I'd be happy or sad over that rejection!

I smiled up at Vito, "Tomorrow is another day, my Rhett Butler!"

Chapter Forty-Four

In the Rome airport, I made the decision to go directly to Sicily and not stop at my *casa*. Vito was surprised! I merely replied, "I need to handle this straight on. No side trips to change my mind. I am afraid I might just chicken out." I thought, *Go with you gut on this one...thanks, Pops.*

As usual, good old Lorenzo was waiting with his cheery smile. "Ciao, bella! Elisabetta, it always seems you get more beautiful."

I laughed as I hugged Lorenzo, "Only because I am standing next to Vito. He makes me look good!" However, when I entered the limo I was shocked to see Mano sitting in the front. "Mano, where did you come from? Were you on the plane?" I became very nervous.

Mano leaned back, took my hand, kissed it, and replied, "Missy, no, honey. I arrived a few days ago. Hope you don't mind I hitched a ride to greet you?" I looked directly at Vito and he knew I was not a happy camper. Noticing this, Mano added, "Sorry, V, I should have told you before the trip."

Vito was quick, "What the hell is going on, Mano? Did

Dominic put you up to this? Dimme, now!" Vito's reaction only made me feel more insecure. Mano continued to reassure Vito that he was only in Italy to protect me. Just in case! I thought, Okay, if I run fast enough I could board again and return home.

Even though no one in Italy, except Vito, knew of the box's contents or that I had planned to talk to Pietro, I was scared, "Protect me from whom? Is there already a problem with this meeting? I've only been in Italy for half hour!"

No one had answers and it seemed we traveled hours before Vito finally spoke. "Lorenzo, stop soon for mangia. We all need to talk before Pietro's!" When we reached a restaurant and bar, I did not know if I wanted to be in on this conversation or not. I had to go with my intuition this time. I knew I'd be better off not knowing anything before this meeting. Whatever was going on, if anything, I had no control. I had to focus on the meeting and my talk with Pietro.

As we settled at a back table, I immediately asked Vito, "Do I have to be included in this little talk? I'd rather not, if that is okay with you. I want nothing more on my mind when we have the meeting with the families." Vito knew what was planned with Pietro and agreed whole-heartedly that it was for the best. Therefore, after the men ate, I returned to the limo to wait. About forty-five minutes went by before they all returned and we were on our way.

After the short plane hop to Sicily, I was becoming more anxious as we approached Pietro's villa. I breathed a sigh of relief when Vito squeezed my hand and winked. Whatever the problem, I was putting myself completely in his hands. I had bigger fish to fry!

Pietro was waiting with open arms as we exited the limo. "Elisabetta, you look wonderful!" He hugged me and kissed both cheeks. I could not look at Pietro the same way. I felt uncomfortable for the very first time, and I believed Pietro sensed it! "Don't tell me Dommy's giving you problems again? You will be happy to hear that he hasn't arrived yet—although I had my gardeners check every hole!" I had to laugh at Pietro's sense of humor.

I quietly replied, "Oh, I don't miss Dommy at all. I am looking forward to seeing Isabella. Thank you, Pietro, I feel wonderful. Thank you again for your gracious hospitality!"

Pietro looked at me strangely, "Elisabetta, why so formal all of a sudden? Are you sure, you are okay? Do you need more time or something before the meeting? Whatever, I will fix it."

I thought, as I hugged him, If only this could be fixed that easily.

I smiled and left for my usual bedroom suite. I felt as if it was home after all these visits. I unpacked as I anxiously waited for Isabella to arrive. So, when Vito knocked at the door, I ran to it excitedly. "Oh, it's you, Vito!"

Vito shook his head, "Grazie, amore mia. You make me feel so welcomed," as he entered my room. I felt terrible for hurting Vito. It was not intentional but I knew Vito was aware of the turmoil in my head. "Listen, Missy, dinner will be at eight. I expect Dommy and Isabella will be here soon. The meeting will be after breakfast tomorrow with the families. When or how are you going to ask Pietro for a private one-on-one? And more importantly, how are you going to explain the meeting to Dom?"

"I am taking a minute at a time since I arrived. Vito, I have no idea. Maybe I can ask Isabella to keep Dom busy while I meet with Pietro. What do you think?" I asked.

Vito scratched his head and said, "I will find a reason to get both Dom and Mano out of the house for a few hours. Would that help? Let's keep Isabella out of this. We don't know how Pietro is going to react."

I agreed, and as I opened the door, Isabella was just about to knock. As Isabella and I hugged each other and cried, Vito said, "Isabella, good to see you. Tell me you left Dominic home. That would make both Elisabetta and I happy!"

When Vito closed the door, Isabella dropped her handbag on the bed and said, "Problems already, honey? Something going on I should know? You look stressed! Well, more than usual before one of these 'meeting with the mindless'! Should we find a hiding place and drink?"

I laughed, "Let's just hide in my room for a while. Where's the drink cart that seems to follow you everywhere? I want to stay away from the mindless ones as long as I can. The meeting will be tomorrow after breakfast…that is soon enough!" Isabella was already calling for room service as I spoke.

I had little time to catch Isabella up on all that was happening in my life. We talked about the upcoming wedding of Claudio and Nicole, how grown my grandsons had become, and my honest efforts to make life easier for myself; however, I was not going to tell her about Pietro. That was one secret of my soul I had to keep to myself. Before we knew it, it was time to dress for the dinner party. My heart was not in it at all, but I was so happy Isabella would be there by my side.

I had packed my dress from Maria's wedding, and I felt happy just remembering that moment. When Isabella was ready, it surprised me that Dominic was not with her. I asked, "Was there a meeting this afternoon, or is Dommy MIA?"

Isabella assured me. "Unfortunately, Dom is not MIA and there was a meeting, but I have no idea why. Let's go get drunk. By the way, honey, you look gorgeous in that dress."

I smiled, "I feel great in it too. Reminds me of the wedding. And, my dear, you are no slouch yourself. Let's go dazzle them a little, the pain in the asses."

When we exited my room, there were no escorts. Isabella and I looked at each other. "Isabella, this is very strange. I guess they think we are finally old enough to find the ballroom. This might be our chance to disappear. You game?" Isabella just locked arms with me and smiled.

As we approached the ballroom, my heart finally settled to a steady place but my mouth was like desert sand. I hesitated and took a deep breath. Isabella seemed puzzled, "Come on, honey, you have done these a hundred years. You looked frightened. No one in there will harm you. You should know that by now! You had better talk to me later. I know there has to be something going on! Look! I see a waiter with a tray that has our names on it!"

Isabella and I instantly grabbed a glass of champagne and walked toward Dominic and Pietro. Of course Dommy had to make a fuss, but I was too busy staring at Pietro. Dom knew immediately there was something troubling me. "Hey, Missy, you okay? You feel okay? By the way, you both look beautiful." As Dom stepped aside to kiss Isabella, Pietro approached me.

"Dom is right, for a change" Pietro smiled, "you are Perfetto {Pcrfect}! Dimme {tell me} what can I do to erase whatever is bothering you?"

This was my chance as Dom and Isabella had walked to the bar. "Pietro, please, is it possible to speak to you alone before I leave your casa. But I would like to wait until after the meeting, if that is okay with you?" I sounded like a little girl begging her dad to go to the dance!

Pietro hugged me and replied, "You just tell me when. I have wanted to speak to you since you arrived. Honey, nothing is a problem when it concerns you!"

I smiled as I took his arm and walked to the bar. My mind was spinning as I thought, We will see if nothing is a problem when I tell you, dear Papa!

The cocktail party went as usual and I met Carmine and Pockets again. Apparently they take care of business in New Jersey. If I had known that before the trip to the casino, I would have begged out of dining with them. So, when Vito approached me, I just quietly pinched him on the arm. "Hey, what was that for?" asked Vito. I ignored him, for now.

Chapter Forty-Five

The next morning I was exhausted from tossing all night. Isabella called early to have breakfast. I told her I rather have it delivered. I did not want to deal with anyone before the meeting. Isabella was just as happy and said, "No problem here. I'll call down and be right over."

As soon as Isabella was in the room, I hugged her and hung on for dear life. "Okay, girlfriend, we better talk! Please, what is wrong with you this trip?" Just then, our breakfast of sweets, coffee, celery, and Bloody Mary's arrived.

Isabella and I settled on the balcony and I started to open up. "Isabella, most people in this world only want to be happy. I believe I was born to be happy and to be loved unconditionally. I have always tried my best to be the best. I never asked for anything in return from anyone. I only wanted the same kind of love and trust; however, I always recognized that I had this character flaw of never really trusting too many people. It is because of the way my life had always been, those damn rules. It was not the true me, the me I remember as a child." Isabella tried to speak but I needed to go on. "Recently I made my mind up to change. I need to let go of all the past and only look forward. But, at my age, it is damn scary."

Isabella put her hand on my shoulder, "Elisabetta, I know who you are deep inside. As does all your friends. The trust thing has to be earned and, God knows, there were many things that stopped it from happening. My husband was a good example. You have been hurt in ways that would make most people shutter. However, the one thing you have down pat is your patience and understanding of people around you. You have a beautiful soul. Don't let anyone make you feel differently."

After breakfast, Isabella told me she was going somewhere with Dommy, Vito, and Mano after the meeting but would be back before dinner. I knew then that Vito had come through with his promise of getting everyone out of the way. I was relieved Pietro and I would not be interrupted.

As I entered the meeting room, all the men stood up. A flush of embarrassment reddened my face. I had to joke, "Wow! All this for me? Please." I motioned for them to sit. Pietro pulled out the chair next to him and beside Vito. Instantly Vito patted my back and I felt safer.

Pietro started the meeting with a prayer for Don Lazzaro. "May the Don's soul be at peace. He will be missed by all of us. But I am sure he is running everything 'by the book' as we speak! I also want to thank everyone for the smooth transition as I take my much-honored place at the head of these families. You all know I am fair and my door is open to any problems any might have. I only pray that we all work together as one family. That is the way it always has been. And, as someone dear to me once said…don't mess with what works!" With that remark, Pietro winked at me.

"I will be handling the meetings a little differently than before. I would ask that Elisabetta give the reports from Lou at the beginning. She need not be here to listen to our other businesses. I am sure this will please Elisabetta and give her more time to relax and enjoy my villa. Is that acceptable, Elisabetta?"

I was thrilled, "Absolutely, and thank you, Don Pietro." I

knew when I said it Pietro was surprised. However, it seemed very strange to me also to address him that way. But, hell, it was better than addressing him as Padre. I then went on with all the reports. I felt like a robot, as if I was having an out-of-body experience. I only seemed to enter back into myself when Pietro congratulated me, and Lou, on a perfect job. When Vito patted my back, I knew I could ask to be excused. "Don Pietro, if I am finished, may I leave now?"

Pietro came to pull out my chair and kissed me on both cheeks. "Yes, Elisabetta. However, I would like to see you for a few minutes this afternoon." I agreed and could see the look on Dommy's face. He was not thrilled.

Isabella was sitting outside in the garden when I approached her. "Great! That was fast, honey, any problems?"

I assured her it was efficient as usual. "Elisabetta, let's take off for an hour or so. It will give you a chance to see Joey Thumbs and we can grab lunch somewhere else. What do you say? The meeting will go on at least a few hours."

I smiled, "Sounds wonderful to me, but it might upset Dom, Vito, and God knows who else!"

Isabella sneered, "I thought we just had that talk about changing your life and not living in the past. Trust me; no one will even know we were gone!" Before I could rethink this, Joey arrived and we were off to lunch. Something was telling me it was wrong, but for once, I ignored the rules.

It was a hazy afternoon as Isabella and I entered the restaurant on the beach. I took a deep breath. I loved the smell of the water. Isabella and I sat at a table away from everyone and Joey sat very close by. "I feel badly," I said to Isabella. "Shouldn't we ask Joey to join us?"

Isabella just laughed at me. "Okay, Dear Abby, you are in Sicily now. Joey would be punished if he ate with us. I think you need to learn a few more rules, especially here in Italy. But, first, we need to drink and talk. And, in that order." I took note that the cameriere {waiter} cautiously approached our table. Isabella ordered and he backed away as he bowed.

I had to ask, "You are kidding me, right? Isabella, is this hidden camera or something, huh? Did you set this up? The waiter looked scared to death!"

Isabella patted my hand and merely replied, "I am known in these parts! This is one of my many hideaway. And besides, Joey would have been on anyone like Mano is to meat if he came too close. Sweetie, you are not in Kansas anymore. You are going to have to get use to it! Here's to our pulling one over on the mindless wonders." She raised her glass. "Elisabetta, you have to admit this is fun. We are not taking orders from anyone right now! It certainly makes me smile."

I quietly replied, "That is not only a fact I will admit to, but would like to do it more often. I feel like I am playing hooky from school. You know we might be punished for this! Actually, we need to leave in an hour. The meeting will be over soon!"

We finished our lunch and Joey returned us safely. We were walking into the foyer as the meeting doors opened. Isabella just looked at me and whispered, "I have them timed down to the second." Pietro then asked if I would see him in twenty minutes. I thought I would be sick to my stomach. I started to perspire but assured him twenty minutes would be perfect. Dommy motioned for Isabella, and I watched as they left with Vito and Mano closely behind.

I returned to my room to gather all the copies I had made of Luigi's box. It seemed like an hour went by instead of twenty minutes when Pietro telephoned my room. "Elisabetta, join me in my library when you are ready." I started to shake uncontrollably and could do nothing but hang up the phone.

Chapter Forty-Six

I tapped lightly on the library door, half-hoping Pietro would not hear me. "Elisabetta, please come in," Pietro said as he opened the door. "Honey, can I get you coffee, tea, anything?" he politely asked.

I merely clutched the file and replied in a hoarse voice, "Yes, thank you, I could use aqua please." While Pietro was ringing Carla, I was conscious of the perspiration dripping from my hands. The file was getting limp. I brushed it off with the sleeve of my shirt and took a seat in front of his massive desk. Memories of my meetings with Don Lazzaro flashed before me, and I knew that they were just a piece of cake compared to this meeting. Carla appeared in a minute with water and ice. I smiled at her but could feel my lips quiver.

Pictro broke the silence, "Elisabetta, I wanted to talk to you privately to make sure things are running smoothly with our arrangement with Dominic. I want you happy. I want to discuss telling the other families about Lou and to assure them you are working with all the families. If any of them have half a brain, they already surmised it anyway. I wanted to get your feel on this before and to assure you again, there will be no problems. You friend Sergio has been working out perfectly for the family. He is a hard worker. But Sergio knows it is over between the two of you."

My thoughts immediately went to Sergio, and I realized it had been a long time since I talked with him. Thank God, Sergio decided to do what I asked and make money in Italy. Good, that was one less problem for me to worry about.

Pietro continued, "I am true to my word in that you, your family, friend, and any loved ones are protected always. Are you and I okay with this?"

I looked down at my folder and said, "Pietro, I wanted to see you about something completely different. I hope you will bear with me, as it is very difficult. This could change your plans in so many ways. Have patience with me."

Pietro looked very concerned and quietly answered, "Elisabetta, whatever it is will be okay. I do not want you upset over anything. You need to talk with me. Honest, go ahead; tell me, what can I do?"

I sat back against the chair and tried to relax. Every fiber in my body was hurting, but it needed to be said. "Pietro, I finally opened the box from Luigi. There were so many things that I cannot understand. I confided in only two people about the contents. However, I feel you also need to know. I have been shocked and scared over this Pandora's box. It has unleashed a lot of questions and sorrow for me."

Pietro leaned forward and took my hand, "Listen, there isn't much I haven't seen in my lifetime or a problem that could not be worked out. Just tell me and we can figure it out together."

It was time! But, how and where would I start? "Pietro, I had a young life and parents only some people wish for, but since opening Luigi's box, I feel as if I am still a child who never knew complete freedom. The box has made me realize I do not need to prove anything any longer. I don't have to keep promises that were filled many years ago. You know my mom was right when she told me that hell was here on earth and what you do with your life determines when you are reunited with God. But you see, I did not have the opportunities to determine my own life. There were always those damn rules. It was decided for me."

Pietro looked puzzled and worried. "Honey, make your point. Tell me about the box. What does it have to do with me?"

I covered my mouth with both hands, as if that would stop what I was about to say. I opened the file on my lap and rubbed by hands on Priscilla's death certificate. "Pietro, this is going to be just as big a shock to you as it was to me." I gasped, swallowed back the tears, and I handed it to him.

Pietro's head dropped and he covered his eyes to hide the tears. "My God, Elisabetta, where did you get this? I tried to never think that my Priscilla rejected me or our love. I have surrounded myself with things, like music and pictures from when we were together. I had hoped she met someone who loved her the way I did. All these many years, I had to believe in the way I live my life in order to control the overwhelming frustration of losing my only love, having no control, and never seeing Priscilla again. You mean Luigi knew Priscilla was dead and all these years never told me?"

Tears were running down my face as well, but I had to go on. "I am afraid so, but there is so much more. I know your pain, believe me. Do you want a break from this and to resume later?" I had hoped Pietro would agree. I felt so much heartache for him.

"No, this is my pain to handle, Elisabetta. You go on with what else is there," Pietro painfully replied as he wiped away his tears.

"Well, Pietro, unfortunately, it is also mine." I handed Pietro my original birth certificate with the picture of a pregnant Priscilla with my Mom, Dad, and Junior. "This is going to be even harder, I am afraid."

Pietro looked at me with sorrowful eyes and took the certificate. He grabbed at his heart, and I was afraid the shock would kill him. Pietro was crying openly now, "Elisabetta, I find out my love is dead and a best friend kept it from me. That is hard enough to live with, and now you tell me there was a child because of our love. Wait! Priscilla was living with your parents in the States. Priscilla used Moe's last name! But it says here I am the father. What happened to the baby?"

Pietro was just staring at the certificate and I watched as he put the tiny footprint on the certificate to his lips and kissed it. At that point, I completely lost it. I sobbed as to what was going to happen when Pietro finally was thinking clearly. I wanted him to realize, without my saying, that I was his daughter.

Pietro was in shock as he started to pace the floor. "I am sorry, Elisabetta, for you to hear this, but the families take an oath that no man touches another family member. But if I had my hands on Luigi or the Don right now, I would have killed them myself. I know Don Lazzaro had something to do with this too. Just who were they all protecting I can't..." Just then, Pietro spun around and almost tipped over as he grabbed his desk. "Dio mio, Dio mio, Elisabetta, it is you! You are my child. Tell me, please!"

I put my head in my hands and the tears were uncontrollable. Pietro walked to his sofa and slumped down. I was afraid to look at him but could hear his sobs. Finally he spoke, "Honey, how long...how long did you know this? Dio mio, blessed Mother, what you must be going through!" Pietro arose from the sofa and knelt down on the floor beside me. He took his hand and raised my chin to look at my face. "You are my daughter! I always saw a resemblance, especially recently, but tossed away those thoughts as only wishful thinking. You look like Priscilla and my madre." As he said those words, his legs gave way and he dropped to the floor.

I immediately went to him. All this information could kill him, I thought.

The caretaker was alive and kicking as I cradled his head to mine. "I am so sorry. I just recently found out when I opened the box." Pietro got up on his knees and pulled himself up by the desk. He was weak as he helped me from the floor. We walked to the sofa, he cradled me in his arms, kissed my forehead, and we both cried again.

"My beautiful child, you came as an act of true love between Priscilla and I. Please don't ever believe that is not true. I am so heartbroken that we were kept from each other. And by the people I trusted the most."

As I wiped away my tears, I said, "Pietro, there is so much more we need to go through in that box. I also never knew the truth. I loved my parents; I had the best childhood ever. How do I, at my age, accept all this. I loved my dad. I need to accept myself before I can accept any other father." Just saying that statement hurt and I felt I was being disrespectful to my dad.

Suddenly Pietro closed his eyes; "You are now the most important person in my life. You have a place in my family and in my heart. My life has always been empty as Priscilla left a hole where my heart should be. Please, Elisabetta, give me a chance to know you better, to work some things out for the both of us. You are a part of me. This means your life will be different!"

As Pietro said that, I never expected the guilt and the fear that suddenly took up residence in my head. I had such fear because of my children and grandchildren in this kind of life. And, I had the guilt because I, through no fault of my own, might not have enough time to know Pietro the man...not the Don. I rearranged my life always for everyone else, did I have the strength to do it just one more time for Pietro? Did I even want to? I became frightened and those lips of my starting flapping again, without thinking, "Pietro, the way I see it, I have a lot of things to make up and a lot of focus on my family...my family...not a father who came into my life this late. I know none of this was your fault; just the same, it must have been what God wanted. I need time. You have to understand that, please!"

Pietro took my hands and kissed them, "Honey, this all eventually will come out. I want the world to know you are my daughter! I knew Priscilla, and she was only mine. Her madre sent her away! Priscilla did not go willingly. I know that in my heart. I want to give you everything I can, share my life with you, and enjoy the family I never had."

I could not hear another thing, my head hurt, "Please, Pietro, I need to take a break. I need to lie down and get myself under control. Can we continue this later?" Pietro remained quiet for quite a while. I handed him the original letters he had written to Priscilla and asked, "Look through these. I will leave the rest of the file also. As you can see, they are copies. I have the rest of the original documents in a safe place. Maybe you can answer some things. Is it possible for you and me to have dinner alone tonight?"

Pietro arose, hugged me almost to hurting, and smiled, "I cannot think of anyone else in the world I'd rather have as company. Thank you, Elisabetta."

Chapter Forty-Seven

As soon as I entered my room, I collapsed on the bed. The muscles in my neck and shoulders felt like rubber bands. *Well, I thought, the worst might be over. I have to trust Pietro at this point.* I arose to go to the bathroom to get a wet cloth for my head and ran water over my wrists. I wished my 'brother' was there and the thoughts of 'Dio' brought on more tears. The overwhelming stress and weakness that comes with crying your heart out took its toll and I fell asleep. I had no idea how much time had past when I awoke to knocking on my door. I don't know what came over me as I yelled, **"Go away,"** sounding like a spoiled child.

"I will not," replied Vito. "Open the door, Missy, please!" I arose reluctantly, unlocked the door, and returned to bed. As I was covering my head with the blankets, I could feel Vito take a seat on the bed. "Come on, honey, talk to me. How did it go so far? I have been worried sick over leaving you alone for this crap!" I uncovered my head, sat up, and hugged Vito. However, when I tried to speak, nothing would come out of my mouth. Vito hugged me as my tears started again, "Listen, Missy, I will protect you from anything. You know that! Do you realize just how powerful you are right now?"

It was as if the demon from hell took over my voice as I went berserk, "What! Vito... how can I be so powerful and so helpless at the same time! Dammit! Dammit! I screamed as I paced the floor. Why me? Haven't I paid enough in this lifetime?"

Vito's only concern at that point was getting me to calm down as he grabbed my shoulders, "Missy, you listen to me! You have always done a beautiful job with this work, your parents, your brothers, your family, and putting up with all of us. This...you also will handle! I don't have to ask Pietro's reaction because I know! Any man would be happy to call you his daughter. Am I right? Pietro needs as much time as you do. This won't all fall immediately into place. Honey that is not the way life is...you of all people know that rule by heart. Come on wash that beautiful face. I'll call downstairs for a snack."

As I did what I was told, I thought, That seems to be the answer to all their problems, let's eat and everything will be right with the world again!

When I came out of the bathroom, I realized Vito was talking to Pietro on the phone. Pietro had called my room, worried that I might need something. Being a smart ass, I yelled, "Yes, Vito, tell Pietro I need a lot of time. Can he promise me I'll get it?"

I stood still and listened to Vito's conversation, "Yes, Don Pietro. I will stay with Missy for a while. She will be okay. Yes. We will meet with you later. Yes. Only recently did Elisabetta confide in me. I did not know any of this from Luigi. On my honor, Don, and I am sorry. But my Missy needed to confide in someone who would understand she needed to handle this herself. Yes, I understand..." and Vito hung up the phone.

As Vito turned, I could tell that he was angry with me for the first time in my life. "Missy, stop! This is a shock to everyone. Do not take it out on Pietro. He is the victim here too. Where's that rule of not going with the heart. Get yourself under control. You are to see Pietro in an hour for dinner."

The marionette that I am did as the strings directed me. Vito waited for me to dress, lecturing me all the time on thinking before I spoke. "Don't get like Dommy, for God's sake. I know you are in shock honey but take a few minutes at a time. I am going to walk you to Pietro's private dining room, and maybe the two of you can come to some kind of mutual ground. I truly wish I could make this go away for you. Missy, you have to handle this alone. But, I will be close by. Okay?"

I was numb as Vito escorted me to lion's den! Vito kissed my cheek and whispered, "Missy, you are the one always telling everybody else that 'everything happens for a reason.' Right? Remember that and behave." I squeezed Vito's hand as he walked me to Pietro.

"Buona sera, Elisabetta, thank you so much for agreeing to join me for dinner. Please what can I get for you to drink?" Pietro asked as he pulled out my chair. I tried to request champagne but felt as if I swallowed a hair ball and went into a coughing fit. Pietro was nervously watching me.

After a drink of water, I tried to ease the tension by saying, "Excuse me, Pietro. I think my throat just closed. Maybe Carla could bring champagne intravenously for me." Pietro snapped his fingers as Carla approached. "Buona sera, Carla, and grazie," I smiled. I caught myself fidgeting with my clothes, my napkin, and my hair. Pietro took my hands to stop me.

"Elisabetta, please relax. I know this is hard. I don't know where to start either. I have faith that between the two of us, we will get through it. Thank you for the letters you gave me this afternoon. Such wonderful, loving memories that I wished my Priscilla had a chance to read them. Tell me, did you read any?" Pietro asked sadly.

"I only read one, Pietro. I hoped I might be able to read them all if it is okay with you. They might help me understand you as a man, as a person, before all this..." as I pointed around the room. However, right this moment, I find it hard to understand anything." I looked at Pietro and boldly asked, "Are you as angry, lost, hurt, and confused as I have been?"

Tears came to Pietro's eyes as he softly answered, "Elisabetta, I have felt all those feelings and more, all my life. I have some answers now and find it a little more comforting, especially where my Priscilla is concerned. Let me help you. I want to tell you of this angel of a girl, as I remember her! Priscilla had special warmth, a gentleness, and light around her. I knew the minute I saw her I would love her forever. Sounds pazzo, si? But it is true. I think it is the reason you draw so many people to you. You have that same warmth, along with that beautiful smile of yours. We were so young! Priscilla didn't have a chance to live, to see how she made me happy, and see our beautiful daughter." Just then Carla brought our antipasto. Pietro merely said, "Buon appetite," and wiped away a tear.

We sat eating in silence until Pietro asked, "Elisabetta, please do me that favor. You asked if you could read the letters. I hope you do! Priscilla never had that chance. I am not all evil; I never was! I think it will help you understand my love for your madre."

With that statement, I cringed. I was still fighting it. Priscilla was not my madre, Elisabetta was!

Pietro saw my reaction and apologized. "I know," he said. "We all need time!"

We continued through each entrée in almost silence. Pietro was very attentive and, at times, seemed to be trying too hard. I tried to relax the both of us by asking, "Pietro, it is hard for be to believe you are Sicilian. You have lighter complexion and finer features than Dominic."

Pietro dabbed his mouth with his napkin and replied, "Per favore, don't compare me to that matto {lunatic}. You are right, though, Elisabetta, I was born in Liguria in Savona. It is on the Golfo di Genova {Gulf of Genoa}. When I was a baby, my parents moved to Sardegna {Sardinia}. We moved again when I was maybe ten years old to Sicily. My madre and padre both worked for Don Lazzaro; then, eventually, me. Priscilla, God rest her pure soul, was born in Sicily. Her father was very powerful; I believed even Don Lazzaro feared him. That had to be why her madre shipped Priscilla to America, and I would guess her padre never knew of the baby. He would have killed Priscilla. He never spoke to Priscilla's madre after Luigi was born."

I could not help myself, "Pietro, your talk this afternoon suggesting I should face my heritage, my roots, and take the place of honor as your daughter. I then have to ask you, would you have chosen this life deliberately for your child of Priscilla's? Are you so willing to throw me, your daughter, into this male-dominated jungle you call a family?"

Pietro gasped a deep breath and softly replied, "Elisabetta, it is who you are. If you were born here, there would have been no misunderstanding about your heritage. But, now that you know who you are, I want you protected. You have to understand your role and position now in Sicily. You are my daughter. Listen! From what Dominic and Luigi told me over the years, you were a wonderful daughter to Moe. You are asking me to demand less. This is who you are...my daughter. Moe and Elisabetta had to be the greatest parents. I see how you have grown and that love for them shows honor and respect. How can you not want me to protect you and my family?"

The fact that Pietro made that last sentence in claiming my family as his own scared me to death. I did not know what was facing me in the future let alone allowing Pietro's involvement with my family. The mother in me came out fierce and unrelenting, "Pietro, as I see it, I didn't need your protection all these years and I don't need it now, especially with my implication with the family meetings. I now can have my own back. As far as any authorities are concerned, I can say I attended these visits in Italy, especially Sicily, because you are my father. Nevertheless, this does not give you claim to my children or my grandchildren as your family. Nothing has to change in the handling of my business. I will continue as before. However, I will not take demands right now from anyone."

As I arose to leave the table (without asking to be excused), Pietro grabbed my hand and arose. "Elisabetta, we have become

very good friends over the many years. To me, that is the foun-
dation of a future for us. We do have mutual respect; it seems a
good place to begin. Please, allow me to walk you to your room,
and that is not a demand."

Chapter Forty-Eight

When I arrived at my bedroom door, Pietro kissed my hands, "Elisabetta, *buona notte*" {good night}. However, as he walked away, Pietro stopped and asked, "Elisabetta, do you believe in ghosts?"

I had to smile, "Spirits. Pietro, I believe there is definitely energy out there. In fact, one has been with me a long time. Nevertheless, if you want to label it a ghost, then it is a ghost. I personally don't like to call it that; but I believe there is certain energy out there, absolutely! Why?"

Pietro just touched my cheek with his hand and sighed. "Rest, please. I will see you tomorrow!"

As I closed the door and turned, there sat Vito on my sofa. "Damn, you scared me, Vito. For a second I thought my friend was back. Don't do that! What's the problem? Am I going to be punished for sneaking in late?" I tried to joke.

While Vito was trying to get up from the couch, I removed my jewelry and shoes. I had to smile, "Want me to call a front-end loader?"

"Dom is right, smart ass! I just happen to be running interference. Dom is anxious to speak to you about meeting with Pietro. He is very suspicious. I told him you were asleep. Tell me, how was it tonight?"

I walked over to Vito, who was almost out of the couch, and pushed him back down. "Don't strain yourself!" I laughed. "I just don't like the fact Pietro is already talking of his family. I cannot accept this myself yet. Vito, you know me, I am waiting for the other shoe to fall, or whatever trick might be up Pietro's sleeve, or what kind of game he is playing. It is hard to trust completely. I have seen too much."

Vito rubbed my hands and replied, "Are you serious? Missy, you know the name of the game. The name of the game is survival, a game you know how to play very well. If I may say, you seem to be handling it well tonight. I wish I could say the same thing about Dominic. Isabella told me he is pacing like a caged animal. When are you going to drop this pile of crap on him?"

I arose, "Vito, Claudio and Nicole's wedding is soon. I want to focus on dealing with that right now. It is a wonderful event and I want to savor it. I need to understand everything first with Pietro and find my own way before telling anyone he is my father, especially Dominic. I would appreciate it if you could continue to run interference between Dommy and I, just until I figure this out, okay? Will this get you in trouble, Vito? I love you too much for that!"

Vito just smiled, as he held out his hand to help him get off the couch, "I love you too! So, we might be in big trouble." As Vito stretched to untie the kinks in his back, he continued, "Have a good night sleep, Missy. I can handle any trouble, especially from Dom. What's the little bastard say, 'done and done'?"

After Vito left, I showered and was just about to crawl into bed, when there was a light tapping on my door. I almost wanted to pretend I was asleep but knew whoever probably could see my light on. I took a deep sigh and opened the door. "Dommy!" I was shocked. "Is Isabella okay? What is the matter this late? I was just going back to bed!" Luckily, I remembered Vito had told Dom I was asleep. I moved aside and Dom entered my room.

"Missy, what is going on? Are you having problems with Pietro? Has he made a move on you?" Dom ranted on without a breath. He would not give me a chance to say a thing, but that statement made me laugh, uncontrollably.

"Are you serious, Dommy? Where the hell is your head half the time? Of course, Pietro did not make a move on me. There is something wrong with you! Isabella is right; we should put you to sleep. Is there a veterinarian near by? Go back to your room, nutso." I laughed as I kissed him on the forehead.

Dommy just shook his head and replied, "I want to talk with you tonight. Something is going on and I don't like it. I have no idea where you are or what you are doing, and I worry! Especially here at Pietro's with his circus freaks. I want to know if you have decided to join his circus here. Have you?"

I slammed my door. Dom had no idea that this was the worst possible time to push me in any way, but I said, "Listen to me! I have had enough with people asking something of me lately, and I do not like it! Pietro has been a gracious host. By the way, talk about circus freaks! Who helped to keep me in this circus all my life! I had my own private circus going on in my life, always; however, did anyone but Vito ever take notice? No! So, here I go again, in the center ring of my own private three-ring circus. This time I will have to really impress, do my usual juggling with flame-throwers act while riding a tricycle, with a monkey on my head. That should be a real crowd pleaser! Dommy, I am tired of trying to keep you sane while everyone around you goes Insane! Get the hell out of my room!" I screamed.

Dom just gave me an evil stare and left. I felt wonderful to get that out of me. I needed to scream at someone and he was the perfect one to attack. I realized I wanted to do that for a long time. It had been quite a while since Dom and I had it out! Now I could go to sleep with my head a little clearer...yeah, right! There was another knock. I flew to the door as if my ass was on fire. "What!" I screamed as I opened my door.

"Hey." Vito yelled back at me. "Isabella called and said you and Dom were going at it! Dom told her you asked him to leave."

"I didn't ask him!" I replied. "I told Dominic to leave! He can be such an asshole when he wants to be!" It was my time to rant some more. "Talking about circuses, whose side I was on. I'll give him a circus, the hairy bastard!"

Vito gently took his hand, put it over my mouth, and said, "Calm down! May I come in? You are losing it. You know that, don't you." It was not until then that I finally realized the truth— I was being a total lunatic.

"You are right, Vito. I am sorry. It has been a long, long day! It feels like it was a weeklong! Dominic always knows how to reel me in and I was stupid enough to take the bait, again.

"Missy, get some sleep. No one else will bother you tonight. That's a promise!"

Chapter Forty-Nine

I heard talking outside my room, and I looked at the clock on the nightstand. It was three o'clock. I was ready to kill someone as I got out of bed, opened my door, and saw Mano sitting in the hallway. "Mano," I asked, "what are you doing here in the middle of the night?"

Mano looked at me innocently and replied, "Missy, it is three in the afternoon. You slept almost all day. Vito told me not to let anyone bother you, especially Dommy. You okay, honey? Can I call downstairs for some food?" I was in shock.

Being the smart ass, I replied, "I had to pass on last night to the other side...I did not hear a thing for over twelve hours. Mano, please take my pulse!"

Mano could see the look on my face. "Missy, I'll call for food. You take your time. I'll let Vito know you are awake. Take a shower; you still look tired. Let me get Isabella, okay?" I just nodded to Mano and closed the door.

As I exited the shower, Isabella entered my room pushing a large food cart. "Hell, girlfriend, I thought you died. I tried to get past Mano several times this morning. They even took the phone off the hook last night…". Isabella placed the phone back on the cradle and continued, "I had this in my room for the past three hours. Do you know how hard it is for me not to finish all the Bloody Marys? Come on, get your ass out here, and sit with me. No one is around. We can hide away until dinner tonight!"

I hugged Isabella and said, "Buon giorno to you too, girl-friend. Are you still talking to me after pissing off Dominic last night?"

"Elisabetta, I love it! It brings me glee when Dom is pissed and I am not the one directly involved!"

I had to smile. "Glee—what the hell is glee? Where did you find that word here?"

Isabella went on excitedly, ignoring me, "We get the full works today. Massage, hair, nails, the entire treatment, all complements of Pietro. Now, that is what I call hospitality. Come on, honey, tell me, all kidding aside, you okay? Is there something I can do to help?"

I just waved Isabella away as I sat down, "Now, that would be a miracle to talk about. Could you make my life simple for a while?"

Isabella had to have the last word as she poured our breakfast. "Listen, I remember my mother telling me…wait…something about Einstein…and miracles. Let me think…Yes, listen, I am not just a pretty face. Einstein said about miracles. There are two ways to live your life; one is as though nothing is a miracle, and the other is as though everything is a miracle…so there! Damn I'm smart!" Isabella laughed.

I jokingly patted Isabella's hand as she handed me the Bloody Mary and replied, "Your knowledge is astounding to me. Better than your singing anyway!"

The weather was just perfect today. Of course, the sun would be going down instead of rising, but I loved it just the same. Isabella did not push me and I was grateful. We discussed Claudio and Nicole's wedding, the children, grandchildren, and enjoyed each other's company. No stress, just peace and quiet until Vito approached the balcony.

"Missy, you feeling better today" asked Vito as he rubbed my shoulders. "Isabella, it is so good to see you. It is your turn now to run interference. I was told to deliver a message that you two are due for your pampering, whatever the hell that is!"

As I arose and hugged Vito, Isabella said, "And we deserve every bit of that pampering too! Retrieve us in about a week!" Vito just hugged me back and said nothing. Isabella and I were on our way.

"I am looking forward to this today." I smiled at Isabella. "My whole body is in knots." As we approached the spa area, we could see women scurrying around. I thought the Queen of Sheba was arriving. As two very strong-looking women lead us in different directions, I joked to Isabella, "Maybe we should be afraid!"

The women lead me to a very large room they called the "rain room." Here I was to enjoy the healing powers of this special water. I felt very conscious of my nakedness with these women watching. There was a nine-jetted rain bar, first very gentle and misty, but then with vigorous jets of healing waters in combination with a power massage by an object that looked similar to a fire hose. It whipped me around like a tornado with nothing to hold on to...not even my dignity. As I screamed for help, the one woman, I now secretly called Brutus, told me that it was best for my circulation, anxiety, detoxification, and relaxation.

I then exited and Brutus caught my limp body with large towels. "Now, you are one," she sneered. I drug my beat-up, bruised body to the next step. My newfound friend Brutus and her accomplice wrapped me in a heated flotation sanctuary, similar to the ones in the movie Cocoon and sent me afloat. I felt like Moses. I was afraid I would be beamed up at the end and wondered if Isabella was surviving all this! My being afraid of the water did not help me to relax in the least.

The next pampering for me was being kneaded like dough by not only Brutus but also her accomplice, I now named Demon-a. In perfect synchronization, these two strong women stoned every inch of my body with hot and cold stones. I almost felt one slip into a spot where no stone should every go…and it had to be a damn hot stone at that. I rolled off the table onto the floor as Brutus made a good catch.

I again drug my stoned body to the next step. The one good thing…I met up with Isabella. We headed for yet another exciting step of a floral foot soak and warm calf wrap. This, at last, was wonderful as they offered us what I believed to be green tea. As I relaxed and sipped, the sake burned my tongue and my nose ran. Isabella drank it down as if it was spring water.

Our last pampered step was the healing and energy room were Isabella and I sat on fluffy floor pillows, served more sake and rice cakes, which clung to the roof of my mouth like cement. Almost the same as when the dentist takes an impression of your bite…you cannot open your mouth unless they use a crowbar.

As Isabella and I crept back to our suites, she turned and asked, "Did we have fun yet?"

I had to laugh, "I always felt my ending would be by stoning. I was right!" Overall, we did feel great about one hour later— no doubt the sake helped!

Chapter Fifty

As I dressed for dinner with Pietro, I took mental notes of things I wanted to say. Each conversation with him was becoming easier. So, when I entered the private dining room to greet Pietro, I felt very relaxed.

"Buona sera, Pietro," I said as I kissed him on both cheeks.

"Elisabetta, you are beautiful as ever," Pietro replied as he kissed my hand.

I smiled, "We have got to stop meeting like this. Dommy is furious and thinks you are up to no good!"

As Pietro pulled out my chair, he said, "Dom might not wait as long as we would like to get to the reason we are meeting privately. Elisabetta, we might need to speak with him soon."

I took a deep sigh and smiled, "Yeah, it's scary. Nevertheless, it is time. I do feel badly keeping him in the dark. Besides, we both know Dom could do something crazy if we wait too long."

As Carla served dinner, Pietro announced, "Buon appetite." After only a short time Pietro continued, "Elisabetta, tell me what are you thinking."

I looked up and had no idea where to start. I was in deep thought but decided to trudge ahead, "Pietro, I worry because there is no double standard. Sicilians only believe in one way of power…a man."

"Elisabetta, let's get something straight, you are my daughter. Your life is richer than you think and that is a big thing," Pietro responded.

I looked in his eyes, 'Pietro, that's just it. It is hard to explain why sometimes it is the small things that last in my mind. My parents returned once from their usual Christmas Florida trip and Mom brought me a wooden salt and pepper set. It was a little Dutch boy and girl and I thought it was the most wonderful gift. Mom told me it was for my 'hope chest' for when I marry. I have them still today. Now you offer me the world. But, is it coming from your heart?"

Pietro tried to interrupt, "Why are you crying?"

I tried to smile, "Don't mind me, I cry at parades. Please let me finish. Before I knew you were my father, I had accepted the fact I was alone as far as my immediate family is concerned. I am not afraid of it. I find sanity of mind in solitude. However, deep down inside I think to myself…I cannot lose another person I love. It is way too hard. I am afraid to get close again. They are the only parents I have ever known. I always said that a person could only lose one mother and father because your heart cannot take on that pain again. You will never have enough time in your life to completely heal. Going through all my tough times in life can be a good thing but I only wanted to do it once. How many lessons are there?"

I forged ahead, still watching his eyes, "Listening and watching my grandsons is magic. I have to smile and thank God every day. No matter what age, we are all still children…does that make sense to you?"

Pietro poured champagne in my glass and replied, "Yes! I am not without a heart. I too, at my age, think often of my madre and padre. They were hardworking, loving parents to me. Elisabetta, there is one thing I will ask you to do. You did it voluntarily for Moe, Guido, and Luigi. Why not me?"

"Pietro, what is it you want from me?" I asked sadly.

"Ascoltare mi {listen to me}, from your heart. You will see I am an honest man...well, with you I am. I promised I would give you the time you need. Just do not wait too long. I am old. Please give me the pleasure of knowing my only child, my beautiful daughter, listen to me, and love me if only for a short time."

"Pietro, I have always felt a connection with you from the very first time at Guido's funeral. There have been people I instantly disliked...you were different. My fear, honestly, is that my children and grandchildren will be affected in a very negative way. To wake up one morning and realize everything I ever told them was not true. Not intentionally, but not true just the same. I thought a lot lately, what if my life was all over tomorrow, what would I personally regret. I realized I'd regret not opening the walls around my life and let you in if only for a short time."

Pietro replied, with tears in his eyes, "I am so happy to hear you say that to me. Believe me, Elisabetta, I don't only worry about my...sorry...your grandchildren...but, as we spoke earlier, one of us has to speak with Dominic. You know my history with Dom and his constant arrogance. However, I will suggest you, or we, have Vito there. And, it would be better done before you leave my casa. I will be with you if you desire. Any way you want to handle it, okay?"

"Just what I look forward to doing...throw a couple of opposites together and make them argue. It doesn't take a psychic to predict that things are going to get tense at dinner. However, I agree. But, with everything Dommy and I have been through, I have known him forever. Dommy respected my dad and, in his own way, has always loved me. Pietro, a lot of people, especially men that come across as arrogant are protecting themselves. This will be a shock to say the least. I will do it before I leave here. Will you call and invite Isabella and Dom for dinner?" I asked.

Pietro quickly responded, "Domani {tomorrow}. We will do

this domani. You'll see it will all work out!"

I kissed Pietro on the cheeks, "Yeah, right, I tell myself that, too!" As I started to leave, I remembered a question Pietro had asked at one time. "Pietro, why did you ask me if I believe in ghosts?"

Pietro cleared his throat and seemed to feel uneasy, "I have heard stories over the years of your connection to this male ghost. I do understand, from many, that it is real...at least to you. I have to ask, Elisabetta, do you think it is Priscilla's padre, the nephew of Don Lazzaro?"

It surprised me that Pietro felt what others had told me. "Pietro, I don't know. I am not afraid any longer, which is a good thing. Other people have surmised the same and it could very well be; but, why me. Someday my ghost might find a voice; and, if so, I'll let you know," I laughed.

Pietro hugged me tightly. "You go rest, Elisabetta, I will make the call. Buona notte {good night}."

As I entered my bedroom, I somehow felt more at ease. Had I unconsciously decided to take the next step? I put that thought aside when Dommy came to mind. How was he going to take this news. I was sure it would not be lying down. The connection between Pietro and I would be a hard pill to swallow. I knew when Dominic was threatened he could be dangerous. After all, I was his "Ace" in that Dommy felt he had some control over me against the 'other' family here in Sicily. I hoped Isabella would be with Dom tomorrow at dinner.

I decided I would call Gracie and fill her in on the talk with Pietro. I felt lonely all of a sudden and needed to talk to a close friend. Gracie answered quickly, "Honey, I have been worried sick. Are you in Sicily? Have you talked to Pietro? I have been on the edge of my seat since you left. I have so many candles lit here the fire company has called. On top of that, Gypsie and Gina have been asking all kinds of questions. I keep putting them off."

I sighed, "I am sorry, Gracie. It has tough to say the least. Pietro is taking the news wonderfully it is Dominic I am concerned about. I plan to tell him tomorrow at dinner. I do not care about the fire company; get in another hundred candles or so! And, do me the favor of getting together with Gina and Gypsie and bring them up to date. It is okay to tell them everything. I would not want them to hear it from someone else."

My dear friend replied, "Just so you are okay. I don't give a rat's behind of the others there. Only you. I will call Gina and Gypsie now and set up something for dinner tomorrow. Hell, it looks like the horse crap will hit the fan in two countries tomorrow. You get some sleep. Call me when you get back to your casa."

Gracie was my best medicine, and to my surprise, sleep came quickly. There were no dreams or visits from my friend. Had I found peace, or had my spirit?

Chapter Fifty-One

I awoke to a slight breeze coming in off the water and wished I could stay in bed. My first thought was of Sergio. I had no idea why; but I felt he was in trouble. I sat up and called my messages. There were fourteen and I was shocked, everyone in the States knew I would be busy. I surmised it had to be calls from Italy. Almost afraid to hear them I dialed my pin number and listened to one after the other. Eleven of the messages where from Sergio. He sounded sad, desperate, and pleading for me to return his calls. I felt torn between my worry for Sergio and facing Dominic that evening. I could not handle another thing. However, my heart got in the way again and I dialed Sergio's number.

I heard Sergio's voice crack when I said, "Ciao, are you okay?" It took a while before he could utter a word. I thought we had disconnected.

"Why have you decided we are no more?" Sergio asked almost sounding like a young boy. "I called all numbers for you but you no answer. Dove vai Tu {Where are you going)? Are you in Italia?"

I could immediately sense there was more wrong. "Sergio,

what's the matter? Are you sick? I am in Sicily right now. Are you in trouble? You know the rules now that you are working with Pietro," I reminded him.

Sergio sadly replied, "My padre die this week. I want see you but you no answer. I have resolution now for you and me. Now I will have my life. I have told Giovina we will divorce now."

Well, that hit me like a ton of bricks. Sergio's father had died and he was already planning on a 'me and him' scenario. Yep, I definitely can not handle this right now, I thought. However, I said, "Sergio, I am so sorry. But, your padre was sick for such a long time. He is in a much better place now. But, a divorce, now! Take time for you to make a life for yourself and maybe with your family. Do not make me the reason for you to leave your family. There is so much happening in my life now I cannot deal with this. A lot has changed in my situation at home and with my family. I cannot explain now, but I will before I leave Italy, I promise."

Sergio was silent for a few seconds, "I love you. This is what I have been waiting for. Why you not happy for you and me? Please, I see you after Sicily?"

I made a promise to Sergio before I hung up the phone; however, it was with both fingers crossed, because I was not sure I actually could follow through with it. I still had tonight and Dominic to deal with. That was a much more dangerous situation. I regretted getting those damn messages. I should have left well enough alone.

I was just about to jump in the shower when my phone rang. It was Isabella. "Hey, girlfriend, Dominic and I just got invited to Pietro's for a private dinner tonight. Should I be afraid? You have been very tight lipped since you arrived." Isabella laughed.

I did not know how to answer, "Isabella, good morning. Afraid of what? Is Dommy acting up again?" I tried to cover up my having to tell a white lie to Isabella. It went against my grain.

Isabella said, "You know Dommy, immediately he envisioned a SWAT team waiting for him. He is gearing up to be ready for anything. This is the very first time Pietro has invited us to a private dinner. Should I have my strapless dress fitted with a bullet-proof bra?"

I smiled at Isabella's humor, "I didn't know they made vests that big! Isabella, I would never put you in a situation that I would not be willing to put myself in! With our secret agreement for the work you will be doing, there will be times like this. Listen, tell Dominic to calm down or I will send someone to take him away. I am looking so forward to seeing you tonight. Now, Dommy is another story."

As I began to dress, my stomach was in such knots. I said aloud, "You probably have the biggest ulcer building up in this old body from all the stress." Just then, there was a knock on the door. I grabbed my robe and opened it to find Pietro. "Buon giorno, Elisabetta. Did you sleep well?"

I immediately apologized for my appearance and added, "Yes, thank you. I slept very well. Have you had colazione {Breakfast}?"

Pietro smiled and stepped aside as the waiters rolled three tables into my room. "I had hoped we could relax on the veranda and eat together. Do you mind?" Pietro asked.

I thought it was a great idea and smiled, "I would love it. Thank you for being so thoughtful. I am fame {Hungry}."

The tables were set up on my veranda as Pietro and I sat down overlooking the beautiful water. I spoke first, "Pietro, Isabella called this morning. Dommy definitely feels there is something on the menu tonight besides food. I assured Isabella everyone would be fine. I am correct, right?"

Pietro assured me, "Elisabetta, we all know this is going to be difficult. The two of us will be able to work this out with Dominic. Isabella also has a strong influence on Dominic, whether he wants to admit it or not. Elisabetta, it needs to be done! There will be no problems we cannot handle."

When we finished, Pietro suggested I relax at the spa before dinner. It was then I asked if I could possibly go shopping also.

His reply was quick, "No, Elisabetta, I feel it better for you to stay on the grounds for today. Humor this old man and let me be a little protective!"

I smiled but was very annoyed. I felt as if a father was telling his little girl to stay in the yard. I decided I needed my 'music therapy' as I continued to dress. It is right what people say, music can tame the savage beast. Talking about savage beasts, I decided to hit the spa this afternoon as Pietro suggested. I hoped Brutus and Demon-a were on vacation.

I poured myself another cup of coffee and walked to the veranda. My mind was spinning. I knew Pietro and I definitely had walls put up between us and obstacles we needed to overcome. I also realized we had to work on it together. There were thoughts flying in and out of my mind. I did not even understand who I was. Right at that moment, I was like a jigsaw puzzle. Bits and pieces of me here and there.

As I returned to my room to ready for the spa, I realized I had not seen Vito in a few days. I was worried he might not be at the dinner, or at least close by. I picked up my phone to call. "Vito, where are you? Please tell me you are still in Sicily. Pietro called for a private dinner tonight with Dominic and Isabella. I think we might need to call in the green berets."

Vito was happy to hear from me, "Not to worry, Missy. I am here, staying at Pietro's with you. I have just been hiding out."

I had to laugh, "You are kidding me. There are no places big enough for you to hide! Will you be near the dining room tonight before the explosion of Dommy's head?"

"Missy, please. I will be so close you will smell me. Just relax." Vito calmly answered.

I missed Isabella by my side as I made my way to the spa. Unfortunately, Brutus met me with a sinister grin. "Bella, it is good to see you again. What is your pleasure for today?" she asked.

"A naked, breathing Dean Martin, singing Italian love songs to me, a glass of Asti Spumate, a few pieces of dark chocolate, and the energy to enjoy every one of them." I smiled.

Brutus smiled a toothy grin and said, "When I get finished with you, you will have the energy to do just that...take them all on, honey. Well, maybe not the Dean Martin...damn shame too; he was maybe the only man I could have gone after myself...knowing all too well, I'd hurt him."

I had to smile as I grunted and groaned to get on the table. "Please, only a facial, light massage, and music today. I am still healing from the last session." I requested. To my delight, Brutus turned the music to a medley of Dean Martin love songs. I thanked her and realized that I really did like her, all three hundred pounds of her.

After the treatments, I felt absolutely invigorated and relaxed at the same time. Tonight would be tough, but the treatments made me feel as if I could take on the world. When I entered my room, I saw a beautiful dress lying on my bed. There were fresh flowers on every table. Folded next to a vase was a small note. "Caro Elisabetta, figlia unica. Dal profondo del cuore, Ti Amo, Pietro {Dear Elisabetta, my only daughter, from the bottom of my heart, I love you, Pietro}. The tears blinded me as I held the note to my heart.

I walked to the bed and realized the dress was the same Robert Cavalli I had worn at the dinner party when Don Lazzaro was alive. Pietro had remembered how much I loved it and had it delivered for me. I was taken back by all this attention but could not forget what I would be facing at dinner. Aloud I said, "Well, old girl, you'll look like a million dollars if Dominic chokes you to death."

When I exited the shower, my phone rang it was Vito. "Missy, the dinner party will only be the four of you. I want you to know that Dommy and Isabella just arrived. Listen, honey, I will be right on the other side of the door. Remember, everyone there loves you; it is better to get this pile of crap over and done with. Things will turn out for the best, you'll see."

I thanked Vito. His call relaxed me more than he could ever imagine. I gave myself one last look in the mirror and said aloud, "Okay, here you go. Remember the rules. Look Dommy in the eyes, try not to go with the heart, and find a two by four…." Remembering Pops advice, I had to smile.

As I closed my door, Isabella was coming down the hall. "My God, girlfriend, you look stunning. Is that the dress by Cavalli? How did you manage that and tell me how I can do it too!"

I rushed to hug her, "Boy, am I happy to have you escort me. Look at you, too. The lady in red! I think there is a song about you. All kidding aside, how is Dommy?"

Isabella answered almost in a whisper, "He is losing it. Dom has been yelling, pacing, cursing, and being an all around pain in the ass since the invitation. After all these years, Elisabetta, I am use to that but it is the unknowing that has made Dom more paranoid. Should I be worried?"

I locked arms with Isabella and white lied again, "I hope not. Let's go!"

Chapter Fifty-Two

When we entered the private dining room, I anticipated seeing Pietro and Dom sitting, glaring at each other from across the room; however, to my surprise they were actually sharing a drink and smiling. I whispered to Isabella, "This isn't good! They are actually being civil!" I immediately went to Dommy and hugged him. I could feel how tightly he was hanging on and it worried me. I stood back, still holding onto Dommy's shoulders and looked him in the eyes. Dommy looked away. From all my training, I knew this was not going to be a good night.

Dinner was sociable and we even laughed at some of the funny parties over the years. Nevertheless, I could feel my body tense as if unconsciously I knew the outcome. Isabella stayed close to my side as we entered the library for after dinner drinks. I, of course, had to make a joke. "Well, this is what it looks like after a dinner meeting. Isabella and I were never invited before tonight. I almost expected dancing girls in here! Does this mean we all have to smoke cigars?"

As Pietro offered Dommy a drink, he held his glass high, and said, "Here's to family; to all of us. Dominic this is a new regime, new rules, a new beginning. Cin cin." However, Dominic put his on the piano. I thought to myself. Here it comes!

Dominic spoke, "Okay, Pietro, enough of the bullshit. What is this dinner really all about?" Afraid, Isabella put her hand on my shoulder. Dominic continued, "Is this about your feelings for

Elisabetta? Well, forget it. This is one young girl you cannot have; over my dead body!"

I had to interfere, "Dommy, I appreciate the 'young girl' comment, but you have it all wrong here. There is nothing like that between Pietro and me. You have to trust me on that! Besides, I take offense to you even thinking that of me. Come on, let us sit down and discuss this like adults. Do you remember what an adult is Dommy?"

Isabella left my side; put her arm in Dommy's as we all walked to the couches. As soon as we were seated, Dommy started his lips again. "Don't think for a moment you can separate Elisabetta and me after all these years. It would be like giving up my Isabella or my own daughter. I will protect both of them with my life…or yours, if necessary."

Pietro tried to reason, "Listen, Dom, it will not have to come to that. If you would only listen to what we need to say, it will be okay."

Pietro looked at me and I knew I needed to be the one. "Dommy, you know I love you even through all the things in our lifetime. This is going to be hard for you to understand. Just promise me you will let me talk without interrupting. You have been in my life almost forever, good and bad. Take a deep breath and relax."

I then tried to break the tension. "Pietro, please, we need something stronger than these after dinner drinks. Dom will have a Jack on the rocks, I will have Southern Comfort, rocks, and Isabella will have vodka, rocks, and ask for a stiff one for you. Then, we get down to business."

The drinks were immediately put in front of us. I looked around the room and was relieved to see neither Mano nor Vito. I then softly said, "Dommy, you remember that box Luigi left for me. It had many papers and information that I still cannot understand. Maybe you can help me to figure this out, okay? Please just listen. It took me a while to open the box and sometimes I wish I had left it alone; however, I cannot go back now. Dommy, I have proof that Pietro and Priscilla were my parents, and…."

Dommy screamed before I could finish my sentence. "You have to be shitting me. That is impossible. This is some kind of ploy for Pietro to take control of you. Elisabetta, you cannot actually believe that!" Dom was now standing, waving his arms and screaming. Isabella sat with her hands over her mouth staring at me in disbelief. I arose to try to talk some sense into him.

Pietro sat forward and tried to calm Dommy down. An impossible task, Dommy was punching the piano, throwing things on the floor, and cursing like a drunken sailor. However, Pietro forged ahead, "Dom, this is true. I knew nothing of this either. All the paperwork is in the box from Luigi." Before Pietro could continue, Dominic rushed Pietro knocking the couch backwards.

I screamed and Isabella sobbed as Vito entered the room from one end and Mano appeared from the opposite. I stood perfectly still with my hands out from my side to keep both of them calm. "Vito....Mano...come on, let's not get nuts here. I don't want anyone hurt." I looked right at Mano and quickly asked, "Mano, whose side you on?"

Mano replied, "I am always on your side, Missy."

I looked at Vito, pleadingly, "Please, break this up," as Pietro and Dommy continued their fight. However, when pulled off Pietro, Dominic arose holding a small gun against the back of Pietro's head. Isabella cried harder as she tried to walk to Dominic.

Vito put out his hand and said, "Isabella, stay where you are! You too, Missy, do not move! Dommy, listen to me; do not make me do something I will regret. Put down that piece now."

Dommy continued to rant, held the gun tighter against Pietro, and screamed in Pietro's ear, "I won't let you do this. Elisabetta was the daughter of Moe and Elisabetta. Is this some kind of sick way to take control of everything? Is this a way to get back at me because you thought I killed your brother? You will take something I love too. Missy, you listen to me, and you listen hard. If there is any justice in this life, this all has to be a fucking mistake. Anyone is better than this shit stain here as a father

254

for you. Come on; tell me you don't believe it is true…please!"

I answered, crying, "Dommy, it is true. Please, Pietro is my father. Dommy, I know it is a shock…please, honey…think."

Mano was in shock, and when he spoke, I could tell it in his voice, "Yo, Dom, you are screwing up big time here. I don't know what the hell is going on, but I will not stand by and have you make this stupid mistake."

Vito added, "Dom, you know I have always protected Elisabetta. Both Mano and I will from you too. Come on, look at Isabella and Elisabetta. They are your life. Talk to them. It will all be worked out."

There was silence and then Dom said to me, "Missy, listen you don't know what you are getting into here. We protect you. Your birth father, if that is what he really is, is a worthless bastard, a criminal, a killer!"

I smiled and tried to get Dommy to let go, with his dignity in tack, "And I suppose you are the second coming of Christ?" I walked toward Dom with my hands out "Dommy, it will be okay. You know I love you! This will not change who I am here." I patted my heart. I tried to smile as I said, "You pain in the ass…knock it off!"

Dom lowered his gun as Vito was quickly on him and walked him to the couch. Mano was helping Pietro and ran for towels as both men were bleeding.

Dom drank down the Jack, put his head in his hands, and said, "My better half is supposed to mean your wife…Isabella knows how much I love her, but Missy was the one. She brought the best out in me in that she made me want to be a better person."

I knew Isabella did not take offense as she hugged my shoulder.

Pietro said, "Dom, we will sit down with you. Look at everything in that box. We need to work as a family in many ways now. You are Elisabetta's family, and I will respect that—even though you bring a gun into my home and make this dinner a freak show! Just the same, I still ask that you respect that I am also a big part of Elisabetta's family now. I am blood family. Do we have a truce here?"

Pietro arose and extended his hand to Dominic; however, Dom, the stubborn jackass, just said, "Give me a minute to process this shit. I need some air. I will be right back." Dommy left the room with Vito closely following.

Part of me was angry with both men; I turned to Pietro and said, "I am going to negotiate here. If you want me to work towards a relationship with you as my father, you have to respect all members of my family, my children, grandchildren, friends, everyone. You will not have control over any of them, Dommy included. Is that a truce you can live with?"

I stormed from the room to find Dommy. Vito was just standing outside on the patio, watching. "You okay, Missy? Well, it is over for now. Will you be okay with him?" He pointed to Dominic sitting on the steps.

I kissed Vito, "I will be fine. You go ahead inside. We will be in shortly." I walked to Dommy and sat down beside him on the steps. He had the entire bottle of Jack Daniels, which he was drinking off and on. I took the bottle from him and took a swig, "How did you think you could get away with that tonight? What kind of a guest are you? Guess who's coming to dinner tonight to assassinate the host's ass—and in Pietro's own home." I took another swig of Jack and handed the bottle back to him. "You need this more!" I lay my head on his shoulder and we sat silent for another ten minutes. "Come on, Dommy, let's go in. Isabella is a wreck. We will work this all out; I will need your help to do it, after we get you on pharmaceuticals, of course!"

Dommy put down the bottle, looked me in the eyes, and said, "Missy, I have been through everything with you. Pietro being your father is just a little too much bad luck for one person."

I grabbed Dommy's hand and softly said, "Dom, I do not see it that way, and I have had a lot of time to work this through in my head. It is my way now to get out from under all this, help my children and myself. My whole life has been set for just this exact moment. You do not, believe, for one second, that dad trained me and did not honestly knew that the truth would come out some day. Dad probably thought he had a lot of time to tell me. Please, what happened tonight was crazy even for you! Promise me you will let me handle the problems now between Italy and home. This is a good thing; I believe that with all my heart."

Inside the library, after the apologies, handshakes, hugs, and kisses, Dommy and Isabella left the memorable dinner party. Pietro asked if he could walk me to my room, and I declined. "At least," Pietro added, "Dommy seems more at ease."

I only thought to myself, Nothing lasts forever.

Chapter Fifty-Three

It was a cool night as I walked my balcony. I felt calm as the moon shown brightly on the water. This home of Pietro's was magnificent, and I oddly felt quite at ease and safe. I closed my eyes trying desperately to settle the thousand thoughts going in and out of my mind. Strangely enough, I remembered something Mom always told me: "Be careful what you wish for...". I thought about my life, marriages, parents, and how lucky I was to have my beautiful children and grandsons.

The thoughts of Sergio's divorce, what he might expect or hope from it, and me, scared me to death. There was a time I could have walked away in a second. Everything in my life had changed now! I shook my head and wondered if anyone else wished his or her life could be lived in reverse. I did not want God to think I was not giving thanks for my blessings; however, sometimes I did not take the time to remember them all.

I felt responsibility for the problems between Pietro and Dommy. Why, I did not know. However, in my heart, I knew that situation was definitely a powder keg, one I would have to sit on until my butt calloused. Again, I was stuck in the middle.

At that exact second, I knew I would remain doing their dirty work until they took the pencil from my dried-up dead body.

I did decide to talk with my children and tell them of this life…the grandfather they now had. I hoped they would understand, but I was very afraid they would not. I was having an identity crisis of my own. Did I really think it could not effect them? I knew this talk to them would have to happen before Pietro showed up at my door. In the end, it would be beneficial to them financially. Something I always worried about for my family. I would secure their future one way or another.

Roberto had been trying hard to keep his promises and I knew, at my age, I didn't want to start a new life with another man. Talk about coming into a relationship with baggage! Moreover, sometimes my baggage was carrying guns. That and the body slowing falling into my feet would send any man screaming into the night. Both these men enjoyed their freedom; Sergio always had! Why would he want to get into another marriage or relationship? I would have to deal with that later. Sergio had my heart, but it would be like going from the fat into the olive oil.

As far as Sergio, I knew I would leave Italy without talking with him. Sergio needed time to think out his life as well. Just like the rest of the people I loved, I would give up anything or anybody to keep all of them safe. I knew Sergio was in love with me but how could I give of myself now. I had very little pieces left to divide. Sergio's decisions needed to be without talking or seeing me. They needed to be for him…not for me. When I returned to Italy, I, Scarlet, would handle it then. Did I have enough strength in this beat up heart to let go of another person I loved?

My thoughts then turned to the evenings events. Pietro and Dominic would have to put up with each other. I needed a referee shirt to wear when those two were together! I knew the only way that could happen is if I remained doing the job I was raised to do. I would continue to prime Isabella for the work, giving her only a small portion and nothing more. I would continue to hold the reins; then I would be sure of Pietro and Dominic behaving. How much more could I do? I was getting so tired of the secrets, the double life, and the tarnished soul!

I would continue my relationship with Pietro and attempt to understand. I meant what I said to him tonight, I had no real regrets to this point. I would not want him to die not knowing all the truth. I wanted to know more about Priscilla, without feeling disrespectful to my parents, Moe and Elisabetta. I would try to blend all these wondering souls into a family I would be proud to be part of.

I sat on my bed and it came to me like a light bulb above my head, I was still being the caretaker, enabler, mob confidant from so many, many years ago. I had not changed! So many people around had, but I never did. It was like brainwashing. I could go from one disaster after another with apparently little affect. Over the years, I have said I would do so many things different- ly. But did I even have a choice of where to go from here? How else was I able to keep a soul, any soul?

As I lay back in bed, I finally, after all these many, many months, felt my spirit's presence. "Where you been, old friend?" I quietly uttered. I pulled the covers up, and said, aloud, "Here lies a true lost soul, born to a legacy of lost souls, her good heart never known to herself."